# Barbara's Desert Cafe

## Kevin T. Jones

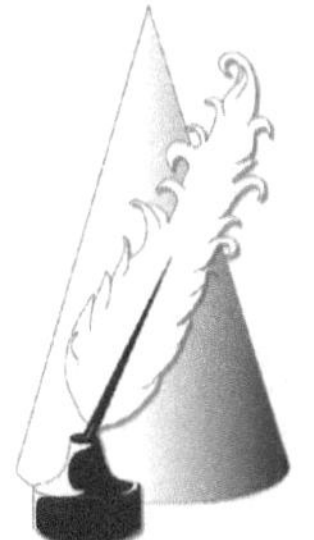

Foolscap & Quill

ISBN 978-1-938143-57-1


Foolscap & Quill
P.O. Box 1018
Morrison, CO 80465
http://www.foolscap-quill.com

# Table of Contents


1. Piñon Pie    1
2. Lost Valley    7
3. Tickup's Cave    17
4. Ralph's Bird Feeder    21
5. The Storm    27
6. Dill Pickle Cole Slaw    33
7. Pronghorn Guide    37
8. Beef Jerky    43
9. Triangle Dancing    51
10. Porter Rockwell    57
11. Trout Napoleon    63
12. Old Ephraim    69
13. Ancient Ones    73
14. Doggie Treats    77
15. The Guardian of the Canyon    85
16. Election by Stochastic Process    91
17. The Lighthouse Canyon Watcher    97
18. Rapture    105
19. Healing    111
20. Dutch Oven Beer Bacon Chicken    113
21. Pictures of Pictures of Pictures    121
22. Rex Jex and Clive Smythe    125
23. The Cast Iron Miracle    131
24. Lost Valley Clangers    135
25. Helga of the Meadows    143
26. Church Meeting    147
27. High Wind Warning    153
28. Clive's Cavern    159
29. Eleanora Poultice    165
30. Blessing    169
31. Poet Laureate    175
32. Indian Fort    181
33. LGBT Sandwiches    187
34. Rowe's Studio    193

35. Search Warrant 197
36. Zucchini Casserole 203
37. The Statue 207
38. Aspen Camp 211
39. Huevos Pendejos 221
40. Mole Negro 225
41. Head Hunter 231
42. Ancient Treasures 237
43. Bacon Jam 241
44. Voodoo 247
45. Salvation Lake Museum 249
46. The Cove 257
47. Repatriation 263
48. Chiranhas 269
49. A Girl's Best Friend 275
Acknowledgments 279
About the Author 281

# Recipes


| | |
|---|---|
| Piñon Pie | 6 |
| Piñon Gravy | 15 |
| Dill Pickle Coleslaw | 36 |
| Ralph's Beef Jerky | 49 |
| Ralph's Camping Beans | 49 |
| Maggie's Triangle Dance Cookies | 55 |
| Stewed Chicken and Corn | 62 |
| Trout Napoleon | 67 |
| Doggie Treats | 84 |
| Brigham Tea | 89 |
| Lost Valley Barbecued Turkey | 95 |
| Vesta's Healing Broth | 109 |
| Dutch Oven Beer Bacon Chicken | 119 |
| Dutch Oven Blueberry Seven-Up Cake | 120 |
| Cast Iron Miracle Skillet Cornbread | 134 |
| Lost Valley Clangers | 141 |
| Gooseberry Chile Jam | 142 |
| Saltines with Velveeta and Vienna Sausages | 180 |
| Myrlene Webb's Garlic Bean Spread | 180 |
| LGBT Sandwiches | 191 |
| Zucchini Casserole | 206 |
| Evelyn's Iced Tea Punch | 209 |
| Deer Liver and Onions | 219 |
| Huevos Pendejos | 224 |
| Mole Negro | 230 |
| Bacon Jam | 246 |
| Jalapeño Cheese Spread | 262 |

# Illustrations

by Carel Brest van Kempen


"I am Tickup. I am Uinta and Uncompahgre Ute."     12

"Some of the first settlers in the valley thought the rock art had special powers."     46

Rockwell dismounted, and pulled open his long duster coat to reveal his gun belt.     58

"Of course they have names."     78

"I felt good. I felt as if I was going to heaven."     108

"God forgive me," she mouthed, to nobody in particular.     128

Ralph led the parade, dressed in a ballerina's outfit.     136

"It was red, bright red, and it had forked horns, like antelope horns."     154

Betsy came forward and lit the sage bundle, using a burning brand from the small fire she had kindled.     170

"It's the Gooseberry upside-down man."     194

Taking his time, he measured his breaths, chose his shot, and took it.     216

Finally, he turned and faced Kenny. "May I put them on?"     254

# Chapter One

# Piñon Pie

Present Day

The mud-spattered, dust-covered Toyota 4Runner lurched to a gravel-spitting stop at the wide spot in the road at the entrance to Ralph's driveway. Ralph looked up from the envelopes and fliers he had just pulled from the mailbox, pulled back the throttle on his Sears 12.5 horsepower lawn and garden tractor, killed the engine, and sat waiting as the SUV's front door swung open. Out leapt a young man, clad in cargo shorts, a t-shirt, and river sandals. As quickly as he had exited the vehicle, he stopped, sandals skidding on the gravel as had his tires seconds before. He slowly walked to the front of the truck and stopped short, some 20 feet from Ralph.

Perhaps he had never seen a man wearing a pink leotard and knee-high green rubber irrigating boots. Maybe he thought it odd that the lawn tractor had a mannequin head wearing a gas mask as a hood ornament. Maybe the toy action figures glued all over the tractor's body had caught his eye. Perhaps the leather and iron helmet with antelope horns protruding from it seemed a bit odd, or the armored bodice topped by a necklace of two three-pronged fork-like ornaments.

At any rate, he flinched when Ralph stood, his frizzy graying blonde hair standing nearly on end in the swirling breeze where it protruded out from under his helmet and its pronged, black horns. Rising to his full 6'7", Ralph stood on the running boards of his tractor and waved a rusty pair of long-bladed old-fashioned sheep shearing clippers in the young man's direction.

"You here to see about the manure spreader?" he asked.

The young man blinked his eyes and looked around.

"Um wha... manure spreader? No, no. I'm here to see Mr. Carter. Er, um Ralph Carter," he stammered.

"Well," Ralph said, swinging his leg over the seat of his tractor. "That's me, I guess. What can I do for you?"

"I'm here to tell you about some Indian rock art that's been stolen. It's the falling man pictograph up on Skull Creek," the visitor said. "It's gone. Somebody sawed it off."

"Crap," Ralph muttered.

He stroked his chin.

"That's terrible news. Just like the other one. Good grief."

He sat back on the saddle of his tractor and shook his head.

"My name's Kenny, Kenny Clements," the young man said, stepping forward and extending his hand. "I'm the Curator at the State Park museum. We met at the water quality meeting. You looked, well, different then."

"I remember now, Kenny. Sorry to startle you. This is worrisome news. I want to hear all about it. I was just heading over to Barbara's for some coffee. Why don't you join me?"

≈ ≈ ≈

At the café, Ralph led Kenny, who was kind of short and stocky with a shaved head, back to a booth near the rear. They sat and Ralph waved to the waitress.

"So you're the guy who wrote the book. The rock art book?" Kenny asked.

Iris, the waitress, arrived, and waited patiently as the conversation continued.

"I am," Ralph replied, "That was quite a few years ago, and it is kind of dated, but yeah, I wrote it. Still sell a few every year. I've been planning to update it, but I just haven't gotten around to it."

"Afternoon Ralph, Kenny," Iris said, her order pad and pen ready, "What would you like?"

"Afternoon to you, too, Mayor. Piñon pie for me, and coffee," said

Ralph.

"Same for me," said Kenny.

"Coffee? Are you sure you want more coffee?" Iris asked

"Um, yeah," said Kenny. "Maybe make it decaf."

"What's it matter to you, Iris? Are you on coffee patrol?" Ralph asked.

"Just looking out after my customers," Iris replied. "Kenny was drinking coffee here all morning. He just left to find you about five minutes ago."

"Oh, so you already know each other," Ralph said.

"Extremely well," Iris said, raising her eyebrow smirkingly toward Kenny. "I brought him coffee and he asked if I knew where to find you. I forgot that you were having a practice for the parade."

"Practice is over, thank goodness," Ralph replied. "I won't have to listen to the marching band again until Saturday. Or wear that antelope hat. Makes me feel like a Raiders fan!"

"So that's why you're dressed that way, and have those things all over your mower—you're going to be in the parade?" asked Kenny.

"I don't usually dress this way. Well, sometimes I do," Ralph chuckled. "But my mower is always decked out. It's my way of assuring that nobody will steal it. Yeah, this Saturday is the big Lost Valley Days Parade and Pageant. I'm the Clive Smythe character. Kind of the Grand Marshall and Drum Major of the whole wingding. Lots of fun, really, you ought to come."

"Sure. I'll probably be there," Kenny replied, although the look on his face seemed to Ralph to indicate that his level of interest in the Lost Valley Days Parade and Pageant would be right up there with, say, a trip to Lawrence Welk Village.

"Did he tell you?" Iris asked. "About the Falling Man?"

"Yes," Ralph nodded. "Yes he did. Well, just that it was sawed off. If I may ask, Kenny, how did you discover it? Had you been out there before?"

"Um, yeah, I'd been out there once before, about a year ago with a Rock Art Society tour. But I was out there yesterday with a group from State Parks doing a damage assessment after the wildfire. You probably heard about it—there was a lightning caused fire just below the site about two weeks ago. Part of the burned area is on state land, and I was out helping see what needed to be done, you know, to re-seed the vegetation without wrecking historic sites and riparian areas, that kind of stuff."

"Do you have any pictures?" Ralph asked.

Barbara Haywood, the owner of the café, came over to the booth and joined them.

"Iris told me about the falling man panel. That makes two, doesn't it?" she asked.

Ralph nodded.

Iris left to get their order, and Ralph, Barbara, and Kenny looked at the photos he had taken of the damage. A slab of the rock had been cut away, leaving a two inch deep, four foot by two foot depression in the cliff face, right where the Falling Man pictograph had once been.

"Crap," Ralph said. "It is just like the other one. Same thief probably."

"What do you mean?" Kenny asked. "This is happening in other places?"

"The upside-down anthropomorph pictograph over in Gooseberry Canyon was sawed off sometime last summer. Looks just like this one. Whoever did this knows what they're doing. I know of a lot of places where people have tried to cut rock art out and steal it, but they usually fail and the rock breaks apart. This looks like they are making deep cuts, making sort of a trench around the figure, and cutting in behind it somehow. Pretty sophisticated."

"So two upside down man pieces of rock art have been stolen," Kenny said. "Are there any more?"

"I only know of three," Ralph said. "The ones in Gooseberry and in Skull Creek that were stolen, plus one in Lighthouse Canyon."

"Do you think somebody might be going after all the falling men?" Kenny said.

"Maybe," Ralph said. "Kinda looks like it."

"Can we do anything?" Kenny asked. "Like post guards or something?"

"I worry about the one in Lighthouse Canyon," Ralph mused. "We should probably check on it, make sure it's still there. I'm assuming the state people know about the theft, right?"

Kenny nodded.

"The State Parks rangers know about it, and we should probably report it to the Bureau of Land Management, too, since whoever took it had to cross their land. I'll report it to the sheriff, too, but I'd guess the rangers already have. We should tell the tribal police, too, or maybe the Tribal Cultural Preservation Office. They may want to tell their spiritual leaders. Some of them might be pretty upset by this."

"That's good, Kenny," Ralph said. "We need to have all the eyes we can get looking out for the thief. That rock art is nearly a thousand years old. It's irreplaceable. Unbelievable that someone would steal something that is so incredibly important and meaningful."

He paused for a moment.

"You know, it's kind of funny, or weird even, Kenny, that you discovered the theft when you were there after a wildfire. Funny, because I discovered that the Gooseberry Creek falling man had been stolen when I went out with the county people after that big flash flood in Gooseberry last summer. You remember it, the one that killed poor Mrs. Norris and her two dogs. Tragic. And strange. A weird coincidence, I guess."

Iris returned with the pie and coffee, and Ralph and the Kenny ate silently as they pondered the possible reasons someone might saw rock art panels off of cliff faces and steal them. And they wondered what kind of person might do that kind of thing.

## Piñon Pie

1 cup piñon nuts, toasted*
3 eggs
2 tablespoon butter, melted
2 tablespoon flour
½ teaspoon vanilla extract
pinch of salt
½ cup sugar
1 ½ cup dark corn syrup
1 unbaked pie crust

Toast piñon nuts in a dry frying pan over medium heat, stirring constantly, until they become lightly browned. Be careful not to burn them.

Beat eggs. Blend in melted butter, flour, vanilla, salt, sugar, and syrup. Sprinkle nuts in pie pan. Gently pour mixture over the nuts. Bake in 425°F oven for 10 minutes.

Reduce heat to 325°F and continue baking another 40 minutes. Allow to cool before slicing.

* Preferably from the Piñon Pine tree native to the Great Basin and Colorado Plateau, *Pinus edulis* or *Pinus monophylla*. Imported pine nuts from Europe or Asia will do, but are not nearly as fragrant and meaty.

# Chapter Two

# Lost Valley

Pioneer Times—circa 1855 – 1865

Maggie and Bill Baggs, their teenaged daughter Lily, and two younger sons, Cletis and Floyd, along with five other families, including Billy Buck and Mollie Tittsworth, were assigned by Brigham Young to accompany Bishop Mahonri Jensen and his family to settle the Pachoose Valley, some distance southeast of Salt Lake City. Their task was to build a fort, pacify the Indians, and create a rich and verdant agricultural colony for future migrants, all to increase the reach and influence of the church.

Maggie and Bill had come across the plains with a wagon train of converts, most of them from New York and Pennsylvania, looking for freedom from religious persecution, and to establish farms and families. They had arrived in the Salt Lake Valley in July, and were rather quickly given their assignment. The small group set out in early August, loaded down with their belongings, some firearms, tools for building the fort and homes, and a small ration of supplies. Following a few days behind would be freight wagons laden with food and other necessities, and cowboys with livestock to supply the needs of the settlers until they could become self-sufficient.

The journey south was a pleasant one, as the group made their way through the Salt Lake and Utah Valleys, following relatively good roads, and enjoying the kindness and generosity of Saints along the way. Their journey became more difficult when they veered to the east, into the mountains. They followed a steep and narrow valley up and away from the Great Basin, into the rugged Wasatch Range. Bishop Jensen had ridden the trail with scouts the summer before, and was familiar with the lay of the land. No matter how rugged the going became, he and his wife Cleora remained cheerful.

"O, the lush beauty of our home is so great that it brought tears to the Prophet when he spoke of our calling. And I have seen with my own eyes the grass, as high as the belly of a horse, the streams clear and blessed with an abundance of trout. Herds of deer and elk roam the meadows. It will be a glorious home, and Heavenly Father has willed it to us and our children," Bishop Jensen assured the weary travelers. "Have faith, our home awaits us."

The days stretched into weeks, and the travelers crossed the Wasatch Plateau, and wandered through rugged country of spectacular uplifts and deep canyons. The steep mountains were flanked by the deep orange-red colors of the changing oaks and maples, and higher up the quaking aspens displayed their dazzlingly bright yellow final display of the fall. At the foot of a majestic set of cliffs, Jensen announced that their new home was just over the crest of the uplift ahead of them. He said that they needed to go another ten, or at the most, twenty miles over the mountain to reach the Pachoose Valley. The narrow canyon they followed into the mountains gradually dwindled, until there was no trail at all, yet Bishop Jensen remained positive.

"Just beyond blocky cliffs, the valley opens up, you will see."

And when they passed beyond the blocky cliffs, he was just as certain that the valley lay beyond the forested slope. And beyond that, just over the next rise. And so on.

The first snow came the last week of August. Not enough to impede their travel, or cause great suffering, but enough to remind the travelers that fall was approaching. While they had plenty of water, the feed for the horses and oxen was sparse, and all were weary from the difficulty they had in ascending the steep canyon. Each day the men went ahead with picks, shovels, and axes, and created a road where none existed. The rocky canyon provided little room between the rushing water and the ascending cliffs, and the going was treacherous as well as difficult. The travelers all knew that they were lost, and that they were heading higher and higher into the mountains just as the cold weather was coming. Bishop Jensen remained optimistic, and told them daily about how he recognized this landmark or that, and how they were nearly to their destination.

Riders sent to scout ahead assured the weary group that the head of the canyon would eventually open up into a wide valley, and despite Bishop Jensen's enthusiastic descriptions of what lay ahead, those who had seen it reported no more than a mostly sage-covered flat, which, to the bone-tired settlers, was nevertheless appealing. The travelers were no strangers to hardship, as they all had crossed the continent to reach Deseret, and they were hardened by their journeys. They were, however, troubled by the coming winter weather, as they all knew well that cold and snow had killed many of their fellow pioneers along the trail west.

When the small group finally crested the narrow canyon and saw before them the open, intermontane valley, they felt great relief. They could see a substantial open area, with cottonwood trees meandering through the valley bottom, signifying a creek or river, and several other verdant spots which likely marked springs.

"The beautiful Pachoose Valley, just as I remember it," exclaimed Bishop Jensen. "Our blessed home."

The other travelers shook their heads, as they knew that Bishop Jensen was either lying to them or lying to himself, as nobody had been up that canyon, which they named Nettle Canyon, for all the stinging thistles along its banks, for a long, long time. Maggie Baggs, in particular, shot her husband Bill an incredulous look, as she had from the beginning doubted Bishop Jensen's competence and honesty.

The group made their way toward the trees in the distance, and sent riders to scout the surroundings. The valley was not the agricultural paradise Bishop Jensen had made it out to be, although it was not a bad place to homestead, and the surrounding mountains were incredibly beautiful. A wide meadow just above the small river that ran through the valley contained the standing and fallen trunks of hundreds of cottonwood trees killed in a fire some years before. The level ground and the ready source of construction material and firewood made the choice of a place to start building an easy one.

Winter came early and hard. Snow quickly covered the pass through which they had entered the valley, choking off the only route they knew through which they could have sent riders to seek help or inform others of their situation. Everyone in the party, even the smallest children, became engaged in preparing for the coming winter. All able workers pitched in as they cut and shaped logs, raised and fitted them, and gradually their homes took shape. They chinked the gaps with adobe mud and roofed them with layered bark, grass and reed thatching, and even layers of soil. Rough masonry fireplaces were constructed, and supplies of firewood were laid in close by. Simple corrals for the livestock were constructed, and plans were made for constructing dams and irrigation ditches for farm fields in the spring.

Construction was important, but even more pressing was the task of obtaining food. The limited supplies they had carried with them were dwindling, and despite Bishop Jensen's optimistic proclamations that the supply wagons would soon catch up with them, the settlers knew that they were on their own, and that their prospects were bleak. Each day one or two men set out on horseback looking for game, which they found regularly, but their needs were such that the deer or two, a handful of rabbits and an occasional duck or goose did not suffice to nourish all in the group.

One cold October day, when the chilling wind blew steadily in from the west, and occasional snowflakes swirled about, Billy Buck Tittsworth, who had been hunting, galloped into the settlement.

"Indians," he shouted. "There's an Indian camp in the trees over by the lake."

The announcement brought everyone to the corral where Billy Buck tethered his horse.

"How many," asked Bishop Jensen, posing the question all were pondering.

Would it be a war party, planning to kill them and take their children to sell as slaves?

"How many?"

"Two tents. Tipis, I guess, but they look pretty small," Billy Buck answered. "Only four horses. They saw me, but didn't come after me.

I just rode straight here."

"Well," said Bishop Jensen. "Maybe just a small party. One we could handle. Men, get your rifles."

"Now wait," said Bill Baggs, raising his voice a little. "Let's not go over there shooting like a bunch of idiots. It might just be some women and kids. They didn't chase after Billy Buck. Let's just go over and see if they might be friendly. You know, let's be neighborly."

"I'm not saying we should fire the first shot," Bishop Jensen answered. "But they are Indians, and we are at war with them. Most of them are just savage killers. We'll go over there, but if they show fight, we'll do our duty and send them all to hell!"

After some animated discussion, they decided to send four armed men under the leadership of Bishop Jensen to investigate the Indian camp. The rest were to stay at the settlement and keep careful watch in case of attack.

Wispy smoke rose from the Indians' camp and scattered quickly in the wind. The approaching party could see several people crouched by a fire between the two tents. One man walked toward them from the camp, and another, on horseback, holding a rifle, watched from just inside the cover of the trees.

"Show no fear, troops. Sit tall," Bishop Jensen instructed his men.

Billy Buck Tittsworth, Bill Baggs, and Melvin Jones rode just behind the Bishop, all holding rifles, but not looking or feeling much like troops.

"Stop here and cover me," Jensen instructed them as they approached the lone, and apparently unarmed, man.

"Me chief," the Bishop hollered to the Indian. "Me the Jefe." He looked back at his men. "Me have many guns. No want fight with Injuns. Injuns give guns to Jefe." The Bishop held out his hands and gestured to the Indian. "Give guns to Jefe,"

The Indian looked at Bishop Jensen, then at the other men. He held out his hands to show that he had no weapons. Then he spoke, not to Jensen, but to the other men.

"Is this man really your chief?" he asked. "Why do you let someone who can't even speak English represent you?

Tittsworth chucked. Bishop Jensen glared at him.

"I am Tickup. I am Uinta and Uncompangre Ute."

"Who is really in charge?" the Indian continued. "As you can see, I have no weapon."

He stepped around Bishop Jensen's horse to speak directly to the other men.

"Who are you? Are you Mormons? Are you lost? I have been watching you build your houses for many days. I wondered when you would finally see us, so I moved our camp into plain sight. We do not want trouble, but we will fight you if that is what you want. My men will surround you and kill you all if you attack."

Bishop Jensen was flabbergasted.

"Wwwwwwhat do you mean, talking to me like that. I have many men, and many more coming. Don't threaten me! Don't you dare threaten me."

"Hold on there, Bishop," said Bill Baggs, riding forward. "Hold on. Let's all just start over."

He dismounted from his horse, leaving his rifle in its scabbard attached to his saddle.

"I'm Bill Baggs," he said, walking up to the Indian and extending his hands. "I'm from Tennessee."

The Indian stepped forward and took Bill's hand in his.

"I am Tickup. I am Uinta and Uncompahgre. Ute. I've heard of Tennessee. I hear it is a beautiful place."

Tickup, well over six feet tall, towered over Bill, and the smile that took over his face seemed genuine and friendly, and Bill smiled as he replied, "Pleased to meet you Tickup, pleased to meet you."

"I'm the Chief here. The Jefe," Bishop Jensen called out, still sitting on his horse. "You come back here Baggs. I'll do the talking."

"Just calm down for a minute, Mahonri," Billy Buck said to the Bishop, moving his horse between the Bishop's and the two men. "Don't make things worse. Let Bill talk with him."

Bill and Tickup continued talking. Tickup invited him to come over by the fire where he introduced Bill to his wife Mincy. They squatted by the fire and warmed their hands and Bill felt completely at ease with this near giant of a man whose background was so different from his. Bill and Tickup forged in those few moments by the fire, while their armed associates watched from horseback, a friendship that would last the rest of their lives, and which, for the short term, probably saved the lives of all of the settlers.

Tickup and his family, along with his brother Wopsok and his family, were gathering piñon nuts, and had been set back by the early winter weather. They had some nuts stored, and there were still plenty of nuts on and under the trees, but the harsh weather was hampering their efforts. Bill had never tasted piñon nuts, and when offered some by Mincy, was surprised at how tasty they were—rich, and tasting a bit of resin.

Over the coming days and weeks, Tickup, Mincy, Wopsok, and his wife Chapoose showed the settlers how to collect, roast, hull, and prepare pine nuts. The settlers invited the Utes into their homes and helped them build cabins in the small settlement, as they knew that the Indians were stranded in the valley as they were, and the tents they lived in would be dreadfully cold and miserable, especially with the young children both families had. The settlers shared their beans, bacon, and flour with the Indians, and all worked hard to harvest and store the piñon nuts for the winter. They learned many ways to prepare the nuts, including how to make a gruel of the ground nuts that Tickup called piñon gravy, to mix them with meat and fat in small cakes, and to eat them plain by the handful. The settlers were all thankful that the Utes had shared their knowledge and their food with them, and they were all delighted when Tickup told them that there were plenty of big fish in the lake, but since it was frozen, there was no way to get them.

"I grew up ice fishing in the winter," said Billy Buck Tittsworth, "in upstate New York. I bet we can catch some of those fish."

And so he did. He chopped holes in the ice and lowered hooks and lines and was able to bring in a steady supply of large cutthroat trout. Between the supplies brought by the settlers, the piñon nuts, the trout, and a never again seen abundance of pronghorn antelope in the valley, the settlers and Tickup's band survived the winter and built a community of great strength, bonded through common struggle and victory over starvation, hostility, and death. The small initial settlement became the center of the town, which would later come to be known as Lost Valley, in the center of the valley of the same name. The lake that supplied the trout that fed the settlers became known as

Salvation Lake, and the creek that ran the length of the valley as Piñon Creek.

Bill Baggs's cabin, the largest and most well-built, and which later became the tack room for the Lost Valley Inn, remains to this day in the center of the Lost Valley City Park, with a brass plaque commemorating it as the first structure built in Lost Valley, and as a property listed on the American Registry of Historical Sites. Tickup, Mincy, Bill and Maggie Baggs are all depicted in bas-relief in the pioneer memorial in the park, and are all also portrayed each year by school kids in the Lost Valley Days Pageant.

### Piñon Gravy

Grind roasted piñon nuts with mano and metate, with a mortar and pestle, or by some other means such as in a food processor. Mix with water or broth to a gravy-like consistency. Season with salt and pepper to taste. Heat in a pan until warm. Delicious when used to make a braising liquid for a pot roast or other meat. Eat with meat or vegetables or with bread. This is a very rich and nutritious food.

# BARBARA'S DESERT CAFE

# Chapter Three

# Tickup's Cave

Pioneer Times—circa 1855 – 1865

Immediately after their first encounter with Tickup and the Utes, the settlers held a meeting in the open area of their camp by the creek, near the corrals they had built for their animals, and close to the center of the concentration of downed cottonwood trees with which they were building their cabins. They built up the fire in the central fire pit and gathered when the men returned.

"That Buck said he had more men who would kill us if we attacked them, but I don't believe him," said Mahonri Jensen, striding around the fire at the center of the gathered group. "I think he is just lying to us. Bluffing. I think we should go back over there and take them all prisoner. Shoot them if they fight. I don't trust him."

He stared intently at Bill Baggs, then at the rest of the group.

"Now just calm down Bishop," Bill Baggs said, stepping forward, and opening his arms. "Just calm down, please. His name is Tickup, not Buck."

He looked at Jensen.

"And what if he is not lying? What if there are a dozen men back in the trees ready to fight? What about that? And why, why would we even want to take them prisoner or shoot them? Why not just trust them? Why not be trustworthy ourselves?"

"I agree," chimed in Billy Buck Tittsworth.

"Me, too," added Melvin Jones. "We oughta listen to him. They know what they're doin' out here in these mountains, and we don't. He said he'd help us, and God knows, we need some help. We ain't gonna make it through the winter without something more to eat than what we brought. And other than them pine tree nuts, I don't know what that might be. And I thought them nuts were pretty tasty too."

"What do you mean? What are you thinking?" Jensen strode to the front of the group. "We've got wagons full of supplies right behind us. And herds of cattle. The Saints won't let us starve. We have supplies coming. We don't need to beg for help from these heathens. Look at them, they are filthy savages. We don't need that kind of help. No, not me. Not my family."

Bishop Jensen folded his arms in from of him and stomped his foot to emphasize his point.

"Dang it, Bishop, you know darn well that we are not in Pachoose Valley. We made a wrong turn somewhere. Those supplies are headed somewhere else. And even if they followed our trail, nobody's bringing a wagon over that pass we came through. Not until Spring anyway. There's three feet of snow up there." Bill Baggs looked upward toward the clouds. "And more on the way."

"Here's the way I see it, if you will let me speak," said Maggie Baggs, stepping forward to stand among the men.

Bishop Jensen's lip pulled back in the beginning of a snarl, and the other women looked around at one another with questioning eyes. Bill Baggs stared at Bishop Jensen, who remained silent.

"I think Heavenly Father sent us to this valley. We were headed for someplace else, and He had us turn and come here. We do face some challenges, some very serious ones, but I don't think Heavenly Father would place obstacles in our way that we cannot overcome. We have to work together, and be strong. And I think those Indians, I think Heavenly Father put them here not for us to fight or to fight us, but to see what kind of souls we really are. Heavenly Father is testing us—are we kind and generous? If so, then He will help us. The Indians will help us. Are we mean and full of hate? Then the Indians will fight us. And kill us. Or we will starve. That's what I think."

"Well, Mrs. Baggs, your opinions are out of place. And wrong. We were kind and trusting in Nauvoo, and look what it wrought. Think about that."

Jensen hitched up his pants and straightened his hat.

"This is a meeting of great importance, a meeting of leaders. Of men. Please go back to your wagon and tend to your children, while we men counsel and determine how to proceed."

Bishop Jensen pointed toward the Baggs's wagon and motioned with his finger for Mrs. Baggs to leave.

Maggie Baggs's eyes widened. She glanced at her husband and strode immediately toward Bishop Jensen, gathering speed and momentum with each step. Jensen's jaw dropped and he backed up, nearly stumbling. Bill Baggs leapt forward, caught his wife in his outstretched arms, and brushed Jensen, sending him tumbling. Maggie Baggs stopped, encircled by her husband's arms.

"Jensen, you are the reason we are in this mess. You led us up the wrong canyon. You've filled us full of your idiotic lies, and now you want to cause even more trouble. Don't tell me to go to my wagon. Don't you dare talk to me that way. Our lives are at stake. The lives of our children are at stake, and you are here saying we ought to go off shooting the only people who can help us. I can't believe you. I really can't."

"Now, now, everyone calm down," said Billy Buck Tittsworth. "Everybody calm down. We're in a tight spot, and we're all tense. Now Bishop, with all due respect, I tend to agree with Maggie. Let's act with good faith toward these Lamanites. They are God's children, too, and they may be able to help us. Let's act in peace, and I believe they will as well. Anyone else, what do you all think?"

Some of the others present nodded in agreement. Some looked at their feet.

"Like I say, them pine tree nuts are pretty tasty," Melvin Jones said, nodding his head. "Real tasty."

The next day, with gusting winds advancing ahead of the coming storm, Bill Baggs rode with the Ute Tickup through the piñon groves where the other Utes were gathering the nuts.

"See, we're knocking them down onto these blankets," Tickup said. "We spread the blankets under the tree and knock the cones down with these sticks."

He showed Bill a pole fashioned with a wooden hook on one end.

"You can hook this over the branch and shake it and make the cones drop. And ones that don't fall, you can just hook them like this and pull them down."

"I see some of the nuts are falling from the cones. How do you get the rest out?" Baggs asked.

"Well, since it is so late, and cold, we'll just take the cones over to the cave and pile them there. Then when it is too cold and there is too much snow to keep harvesting the cones, we can get the nuts out and roast them and hull them. It's better to do that in the cave where it is warm and dry, than out here in the snow."

Tickup loaded two large sacks of the harvested cones on the back of his horse, and put two more on Baggs's horse, and the two of them rode to the cave. On a hill overlooking the lake, the cave mouth was easily wide and high enough for the men to ride their horses inside and under the drip line. Once inside, Tickup dismounted, and motioned to Bill Baggs to do the same. They unloaded the sacks, took them to a corner of the cave, and emptied them onto a large heap of pine cones.

"This is a darn big cave," Bill Baggs remarked walking and looking around. "And it's pretty warm in here. A lot warmer than out there in the wind."

"We are going to make our camp in the cave," Tickup said. "This storm is going to bring snow and cold. Maybe just for a few days, since it is still not winter, but it looks like this storm is going to be strong."

Bill nodded in agreement. Both men looked to the western horizon, where the menacing, dark clouds amassed, moving their way.

"You are welcome to bring your camp here with us," Tickup said. "You are all welcome. There is room."

# Chapter Four

# Ralph's Bird Feeder

Present Day

"Whoa, I love maps, but this is unreal!" Kenny exclaimed, walking up to the map-covered wall in Ralph's upstairs workroom. The entire wall was covered with USGS quadrangle maps taped together to form a continuous map seven feet high by ten feet wide. "What are all the pins with numbers on them?"

"Oh, those are places I want to keep track of. Archaeological sites and rock art mostly, but other things like good camping spots, swimming holes, hot springs, pretty scenery, whatever place I think is worth remembering."

"So you have a file or something that matches the numbers on the pins?"

"Yep. It's kind of like my own pre-digital Geographic Information System. I also have the data digitized, and have started a big rock art database that takes pictures from anybody's camera, as long as they have geographic info attached, and links them to a geodatabase. It's just in the early stages, but growing fast. People love to share photos of places they've been, cool stuff they've found."

"Isn't this what you do? I mean for a living. Over at the college?" Kenny asked.

"Kind of. I teach math and statistics at the Community College. And some computer courses. But the rock art and archaeology, they're just my hobbies. Well, more like my passions, really."

"So, are the upside-down rock art figures on here?" Kenny asked, examining the wall-mounted maps.

"Yeah, they're the ones with the big red pins. I marked them when this trouble started so I could start figuring out if there were any patterns, or other places we should be looking."

"They kind of cluster right around Lost Valley," Kenny noticed. "Well, all three are right here near Lost Valley. Seems kind of odd."

"It wouldn't surprise me if there were more. We just haven't looked everywhere."

"So these two are the ones that were stolen—the ones with an X on the tag?"

"Yep. The one in Gooseberry, and the one you reported, over in Skull Creek Canyon. The only other one is the one in Lighthouse Canyon. Unfortunately, it's pretty well known, thanks in part to my own book, dang it, and it's not too hard to get to. I think we ought to keep an eye on it. Here, I'll show you some pictures."

Ralph pulled a file folder from a cabinet drawer and opened it on his drafting table. He also turned on a computer and pulled up some photos and maps on the monitor. Ralph and Kenny pored over the photos and descriptions of the Lighthouse Falling Man. It is a solitary painted figure on an isolated cliff face, about three feet high and a foot and a half wide. It depicts a male figure with two horn-like protrusions coming from his head or hat. And he is upside down.

"Well, we should go over and check it out. How about this weekend?" Kenny asked.

"Sounds good. I have a few things to do before I can go, but I think it'll be okay. I'll see if Tommy wants to go. He knows that country really well."

"When was the last time you saw the Lighthouse Falling Man?" Kenny asked.

"Well, I'm checking the dates on these photos. Looks like about five years ago. It's been a while."

"Hope it's still there," Kenny mused. "You know, some of the early settlers in the valley thought the rock art had special powers. I think they learned that from the Utes. Ephraim Jensen, he was the postmaster here—I think he's Bishop Jensen's grandfather—anyway, he had a bunch of artifacts and things that are now in the Museum. We have his journals, and he wrote about this Antelope Cult. That's what he called it, said there was Antelope Power in the rock art and artifacts. He collected all those unusual artifacts from Gooseberry, from right where the Falling Man was. He was pretty much in awe of the artifacts and especially the antelopes—the pronghorns. He said they had lots of power, power he claimed to have seen, and felt. He wrote in his journal that the first time they dug around in the cave at Gooseberry they thought the Antelope was trying to kill them."

"Kill? How?" Ralph asked.

"A storm. Lightning. Wind. They thought it came right for them after they dug around in the cave and took some artifacts. He said it was only the first of many things that convinced him of the power of the pronghorns. The falling man was like a Pronghorn Shaman or something. I don't know exactly. But he was changed for life. Frightened too, but somehow lifted up. His journals are fascinating. Things like that are why I love my job. I get to read crazy stuff like Old Ephraim Jensen's journals."

"Well, it seems like the Falling Men or the Antelope Gods or whoever might still be sending storms and weather after people," said Ralph. "That flood that killed Mrs. Norris around the time the Gooseberry Falling Man was stolen and the fire in Skull Creek. If I believed in that kind of crazy story I'd say those Pronghorn People or whoever they are were still flexing their muscles. I'm too much of a scientist to be carried away by any of that kind of talk. An Antelope God sending a storm after someone. Nope. Can't happen. No way."

Ralph stood. "Like a beer?" He opened a small refrigerator and took out two cold beers.

"Come on up to my observatory," he said, heading toward a tight spiraling set of stairs in the center of the next room.

"Holy shit, this is high up," Kenny exclaimed, as he emerged onto the small deck atop the second story of Ralph's mobile home. "Why do you live in a two story mobile home, anyway," Kenny asked. "I mean, other than because it is a cool as hell. Other than that."

"That's basically it," Ralph answered. "I was living in one of them, the downstairs one, and a friend just gave me another one when he moved to Paraguay. Well, one day I got to thinking and scheming about how great it would be to put one on top of the other. I talked to my friend Bill who works in heavy construction, and we figured out how to do it, and well, here we are. We built a pretty solid framework of steel to hold this top one in place, so it's not going anywhere. I mean, it is cool, but I wanted to get up high for one other reason, too."

"What's that," Kenny asked.

"So I could see my bird feeder."

"Huh?' Kenny puzzled.

"See, over there, just beyond the hill. You can't see it from the ground, only from up here."

"What is it?" Kenny asked. "Looks like a tree house or something."

"It is, kinda," Ralph explained. "It's a platform about ten feet up. It's back in the middle of the property so nobody bothers the birds. It's a bird feeder."

"I don't get it," Kenny said, looking at the structure through binoculars Ralph handed him. "I don't see any birds. Just some, some bones or something."

"Oh, birds like it. There's one now."

"Holy shit," Kenny exclaimed, "Some huge bird just landed on it. What is that? A buzzard? And another one is landing too. Man, they're big."

"Well, it's not an ordinary bird feeder," Ralph replied. "It's for vultures. And magpies and ravens and birds like that. Sometimes I get eagles there, too, but mostly vultures. That's who I made it for. Vultures. Turkey Vultures. I love Turkey Vultures."

"What do you feed them?" Kenny looked at Ralph with a kind of worried look on his face.

"Carrion. That's what they eat. I get carcasses from ranchers and farmers. I also pick up road kill when I can. I have an arrangement with the DOT and the Fish and Game. I can collect road kill in certain areas."

"So it's kind of like a Tibetan Sky Burial, just for road kill." Kenny pondered.

"Exactly," Ralph replied. "When I go, I want to have my body put up on the feeder. Let the birds take me away. I think it would be a perfect way to give your body back. Perfect."

# BARBARA'S DESERT CAFE

26

# Chapter Five

# The Storm

Pioneer Times—circa 1855 – 1865

Tickup's family had a small sleeping area set up in the rear of the cave when the first of the settlers arrived. They helped the new arrivals find level, protected areas to place their bedrolls and build fires. The large cave, over one-hundred feet from the entrance to the rear wall, and about half that in width, easily accommodated the two Ute families and the thirty or so settlers. Only Bishop Jensen and Orson Platte and their families stayed behind at the settlers' camp, Jensen insisting that he did not need the charity of savages to weather a storm.

The wind blew hard and cold, and when the snow started in earnest, the flakes were small and bounced when they hit the ground and they piled up rapidly in depressions and against obstacles, and the settlers could not see more than a few feet beyond the mouth of the cave. They put their livestock in a small sheltered cove near the cave with the Indians' horses, and built up their fires and laid down tarps and blankets on the dry cave floor. They ineffectually instructed the children to walk carefully so as to not stir up the choking dust. They started soup pots cooking over low fires, and Mincy, Tickup's wife, showed Maggie Baggs how to make tea from the leaves of the ephedra plant. The light from the fires and from several candles cast a warm glow on the sandstone walls. The wind swirled outside the cave's entrance, but the massive stone mountain that encased them kept the wind away, and the temperature was moderate, even comfortable, despite the treacherous conditions just beyond the protective drip line.

"I pray that the Jensens and Plattes are safe and warm in this tormenting storm," Bill Baggs said, looking out from the cave entrance.

"I am sure they are bundled up in the dugout, with a fire to warm them," Melvin Jones said. "They won't be as comfortable as we are, here in this cathedral," he said, looking overhead at the arching ceiling, lit by the flickering firelight. "I sure am glad this Tickup invited us to stay here in this cave. At first I agreed with Mahonri—I'm not taking my family into a cave. I had no idea it would be as nice, and warm, as this. Hell, I might think of making my home in a place like this."

"I feel good about the animals, too. They're probably better off than they would be over in the corrals. I hope the ones we left behind are safe," Bill said.

"Oh, they'll be all right," Melvin said. "They've got shelter, and can get down to the creek. They'll be fine. We'll all be fine. These Indians sure helped out a lot though. Really a lot."

When night fell, the settlers and their Ute hosts retired to their sleeping areas, and, bundled together as families, slept well and warm, despite the drifting snow and icy wind just outside their sanctuary.

In the morning, after some porridge and more ephedra tea, the men organized into several parties to check on the livestock, gather firewood, and to check on Jensen and Platte, and convince them to join the rest in the cave. Mincy and Chapoose, Wopsok's wife, began opening the pine cones to extract the nuts. They showed the other women how to roast the nuts on winnowing trays, and how to hull and winnow the nuts from the hulls. The immigrant women were anxious to learn, and they worked together and learned some critical skills from their new friends. They asked Mincy and Chapoose to help them make winnowing trays when the weather cleared, and laughed and teased each other when they awkwardly spilled the nuts when learning to winnow or got their fingers stuck together with pine pitch.

Firewood was plentiful in the area surrounding the cave, and despite the blizzard that raged sometimes with great ferocity, sometimes with a gentle but steady snowfall, the men were able to gather a great number of branches and downed logs, which they piled just inside the entrance to the cave. Melvin Jones and Billy Buck Tittsworth found Bishop Jensen's dugout covered nearly completely by drifting snow, and after describing the warm, dry comfort of the cave, convinced the families to return with them to the other settlers, although Bishop Jensen stubbornly insisted that it was only because of the wives' desire for comfort that they relented.

On the way back to the cave Melvin Jones shot a pronghorn antelope, and when he and Tittsworth carried it into the cave late that afternoon, a cheer went up. Soon the cave was filled with the smells of roasting and boiling antelope meat, and with all the settlers together in one place, a festive mood prevailed.

"This is the closest thing we've had to a building to gather in since we left Salt Lake City, and that seems like ages ago," said Maggie Baggs, smiling as she stood from tending her fire. "This cave is really like a big hall, or a church or something. And I appreciate it more, knowing that it is part of nature, and it is protecting us. Like it was made just for us."

"My family has come here for many generations," said Tickup. "And we feel the same way. This is a special place for us, and when we need it for protection, it is here for us to use. There are many places like this that the ancestors have handed down to us. We call this place Wanzi Cave, or Antelope Cave, because we come here in the fall and sing songs to Wanzi, the Antelope, and to collect pine nuts."

"Do you always camp in caves?" asked Bill Baggs.

"Only when the weather is bad, like this, or in the middle of winter. We would rather be outside. Caves are smoky and dusty. They are good when you need them, but they are not good to live in all the time."

"I saw the drawings on the wall—the sheep and the people and the spirals. Did you make them?" Bill asked Tickup.

"The big ones are from the Ancient Ones. The people who lived here before my people. They made those little houses up in the cliffs. My people make writings, too. Our healers and priests make them. They have power, good power, and sometimes bad. The drawings of the Ancient Ones, we don't know. Our healers don't know if they are good or bad. They might bring harm, hurt people. So our healers kill them. See that mark in the chest of that big one here?"

Tickup carried a burning stick to the side wall of the cave to illuminate one of the figures.

"See this mark here on his chest?"

He pointed, and Bill Baggs looked and nodded.

"That is where one of our healers killed this spirit. They strike it with a stone, one strike in the chest. It leaves a mark, see?"

He pointed to a small indentation in the stone.

"And see these sheep? All killed, see?"

"Why kill sheep?" Baggs asked.

"They may look like to sheep to us, but they could be something else," Tickup answered. "When our healers make pictures it could look like something, but really be something else. See this one—it looks like a snake?"

Baggs nodded.

"This was made by my people. By a healer. And it looks like a snake, but it could be for something else. Sometimes the word for something sounds like something else, or reminds people of something different. Sometimes a snake stands for a storm, and sometimes for a battle, which can be called a storm. Sometimes a sheep is a person, and sometimes it is a mother with her child. Sometimes a sheep is a ghost. And pictures that look like people, they might be *Siants*[1], or night lurkers. These pictures are not like your pictures in books. They *are* the thing they represent, and they are alive and can do things. We need to be careful around them. Very careful."

"Let me show you one more thing," Tickup said, reaching down and taking a new torch from the fire. He walked to the back of the cave, ducked beneath a low overhanging bulge in the roof, and turned. He blew on the burning brand until the flames erupted. He held it up in front of his face and lit the rear-facing part of the low cave roof. There, illuminated by his small torch was a tiny painted figure. The red paint was not easy to see against the orange sandstone of the cave.

"Come close and look," Tickup urged Bill.

The figure, about the size of Bill's hand, was a human-like shape surrounded by what appeared to be tiny birds. The figure in the center

1 *Siants* are witch-like tricksters in Ute mythology that trick people and steal or kill their children

depicted a male with what appeared to be pronged horns coming from his head. The figure was drawn upside-down, and in its position in the back of the cave, appeared to be swooping down from above, surrounded by tiny birds, about to fly down from its spot and out toward the front of the cave.

Bill studied the figure. He drew in a deep breath. For a few minutes he could find no appropriate words to speak. Finally he turned to Tickup.

"That is incredibly beautiful, he said "and mysterious. I found myself imagining him flying down from the rock and out the mouth of the cave. And are those birds? Tiny birds? This is, well, this is really something."

Tickup held the light in place until the flames started to dim, causing the figure to disappear before their eyes.

"This is the Wanzi—the Watcher. The Antelope Watcher. Some call him a guide. The Antelope Guide. This cave is his home. He has other homes, but this is his true house. The center of his land, the center of this valley. He watches over this place and helps the people and the creatures. We talk to him and sing to him. I will show you how to talk to him and how to sing to him. He will watch over you."

Tickup turned to walk back to join the rest of their group in the front of the cave, then stopped.

"Wanzi can bring harm, too. He must be treated well, treated with respect. If he stops watching after you, bad things can happen. He keeps the little devils and water babies and *Siants* away. If he stops watching after you, trouble may come. Storms will come, and wind and lightning, and battles. He can be a guide and a helper, but he can be an enemy, and no one wants Wanzi to be his enemy. No one."

"But I will teach you. You can talk and sing to him, and be his friend. You won't have to worry."

Tickup smiled, patted Bill on his shoulder, and headed toward the well-lighted part of the cave and the sounds of laughing children and spirited conversation.

The settlers and their Ute hosts ate pine nuts, beans, and pronghorn that night, and they built large fires and visited and laughed as the storm continued to rage just feet away. Tickup and Bill Baggs talked much of the night about the geography of the area, about their families, about Ute culture, and about their plans for the future, and they enjoyed each other's company greatly. And Baggs noticed that Tickup politely refused on several different occasions when offered the pronghorn meat.

# Chapter Six

# Dill Pickle Cole Slaw

Present Day

"Oh my goodness! Bishop Jensen, what a surprise," Iris exclaimed as she answered the door to the small house she shared with her friend Ruby. "What brings you to this neck of the woods?"

"Well, Mayor, I just wanted to check in on you and see how you're doing," the bishop said, his hands clasped in front of him.

"Golly Bishop, I'm doing just swell. Really flippin' swell," Iris said in a cheerful voice. "Are you here on city business, or is it something else?"

"No, it's not city business. I'm just here to see how you're doing. We sure do care a lot about you and your family, Iris. Maybe now is a good time to come back to church and be with your family and friends. And Heavenly Father."

"Gosh Bishop. It's mighty nice of you to keep pestering me like this all the time, but like I keep telling you, I'm just fine and have no reason to let you, or anyone else dig their claws in to me again," Iris said, hands on her hips, looking straight into the bishop's averted eyes.

"I really came to invite you to the singles ward mixer we're having this Saturday. All the young people are getting together. They do it all the time, you know," he said, and paused. "This Saturday there will be refreshments, really good ones. Sister Nash is making her lemon bars, and Brother Boomgarden will be the, um.., DJ, I think they said, or something like that. You might meet somebody special, you never know."

"Oh, you mean I could come to the singles ward mixer and maybe meet a nice boy," Iris asked.

"Yes, yes of course." Bishop Jensen lit up just a little. "Singles wards are great places to meet someone special. I met my wife Janell at a singles ward bowling party."

"I know plenty of boys, Bishop, but I'm not really interested in, um, you know, being with a boy. I like girls. I'm, well, I'll just say it. I'm a lesbian. Could I come to the ward dance and meet a nice girl to hook up with?"

"You're a… what? A lesbian? Iris, you've dated boys. Your mother thought you were going to marry Ronnie Rudd before he joined the army."

"Well, Bishop, I guess I've become enlightened. I don't need to keep pretending to be the way everybody tells me to be. I'm not about to marry Ronnie Rudd or anybody else."

"Well, is Ruby your um, girlfriend then? She's your roommate. Do you mean you and Ruby um, do, um, I mean, um, homosexual things?" The Bishop stammered.

"Well, I am a lesbian," Iris declared. "I do it with girls. I do things with girls that don't even have names in the Mormon language. But not Ruby. Yet. I keep trying to persuade her." Iris laughed.

"That's evil, Iris."

Bishop Jensen's eyes widened.

"The Stake President told us about how you people recruit others to your sinful ways. Poor Ruby. I hope she has the strength to resist."

"Oh, she's got plenty of strength, Bishop." Iris smiled. "She likes, um, boys and um, doing stuff with them, you know, about as much as anybody I know."

"That's good," Bishop Jensen said. "I mean, that she likes boys. Not so much that, well, um, whatever."

He fidgeted a bit and looked around and over his shoulder.

"You know, Iris," said the Bishop, regaining some of his composure. "Heavenly Father still loves you. He loves homosexuals, and all sinners. Yes he does. As long as they don't act on their carnal desires."

"But Bishop, I have carnal desires. They overwhelm me some times. I find myself unable to think of anything other than, well, satisfying them. And they don't involve boys. Would it be better for me to find a boy at the singles ward to satisfy my desires?"

"Yes," the Bishop said. "Yes, it would."

"Okay. Maybe I'll come to that dance. That Mickey Crusoe is pretty hot. Maybe I'll come to the dance and see how he feels about carnal desires."

"Well, no," Bishop Jensen retorted. "You can't just, um, have sex with a boy. You have to get married."

"But you just told me it would be better if I did it with a boy than with a girl. Which is it, Bishop?"

"Neither, then. You have to wait for marriage, and you can't marry a girl, so it has to be a boy. After you marry him."

"Well, there's no way I'm going to marry Mickey Crusoe just so I can sleep with him. I guess I'll just stick to sleeping with girls."

"You are still invited to come to the singles wards," Bishop Jensen said. "Heavenly Father still loves you."

Jensen paused, took a deep breath, held out his hands, palms up, and implored Iris.

"Iris, you know how much I care about you and your family, I really do. I don't say these things to hurt you, or to tease you. I know you don't like to hear this, but I believe there is a curse over this valley as old as the Lamanites. It affected Rex Jex and Clive Smythe, and it may have affected even my own Great Grandfather, Ephraim Jensen. It places little devils in people. Satan puts little devils in people and they are drawn to their own kind. Satan makes them want to be with their own kind, and to spread the temptation to others. I have read my great grandfather's journals, and he wrote of spirits, and of being watched, and of being infused of the spirits, the ancient spirits, spirits of the antelope and the ancient Mokis. I think those little devils entered him. They may have killed him, you know. He was killed by a falling tree in a big windstorm. My great grandmother Cora thought those spirits killed him. She really did."

He blinked, turned to leave, then turned back.

"Please be strong, Iris. Faith can help. You know I will be there for you."

Iris could see a tear forming in Bishop Jensen's eye, and while she did not doubt his sincerity, she wanted nothing more to do with him.

"Thanks Bishop," Iris said, "but you are just too much sometimes. Curses and Satan. Sheesh."

She turned to go back into the house.

"Tonight's election night. I've got to make up my pickle slaw and then take a shower before the whole thing starts. I kinda have to run the thing, you know. I have to shave my legs, and I think I'll shave my hoohoo, too. See ya!"

Bishop Jensen stood on the doorstep for a few minutes, uncertain of what had just transpired. He thought of the delicious slaw that Iris's family had brought to potluck dinners for years, and he tried to stop thinking about Iris's hoohoo.

### Dill Pickle Cole Slaw

One medium-sized head of cabbage
One medium-sized sweet onion
Two medium-sized dill pickles
Two ribs of celery
One half cup of mayonnaise
One quarter cup of dill pickle juice
Salt and pepper to taste

Chop the onion, celery, and pickles and place them in a large bowl. Add the mayonnaise and pickle juice and stir to combine. This step allows the flavors to meld.

Chop the cabbage as finely or coarsely as you desire. Add to the bowl with the other ingredients. Stir to combine. Refrigerate.

The flavor improves if it sits in the refrigerator for an hour or two. Excellent when served with barbecued meat or on sandwiches.

# Chapter Seven

# Pronghorn Guide

Pioneer Times—circa 1855 – 1865

"There's quite a bit of water running in the wash. Does it always run like this? Does it run year-round?" Bill Baggs asked Tickup, as they approached the side stream as it entered the main stem of Lost Valley.

"It will be dry by the end of the summer," Tickup answered. "But the water will run for at least another month or two."

The two friends followed the cliff-walled canyon as it cut through the sandstone rock that capped the mesa adjacent to Lost Valley. The spring came early to the mountain valley, and the settlers and their Ute Indian hosts welcomed the returning warmth and the eruption of green vegetation celebrating the end of a long, harsh winter.

Tickup led the way, and the two friends rode quietly along the narrow game trail that ascended the canyon floor, stopping occasionally to examine something of interest, or for Tickup to point something out to Bill and to answer his questions. Baggs was serving as an unofficial surveyor for the settlers, having had some experience in Tennessee and Pennsylvania working with mapping crews. He had been very explicit with Tickup that his task was to make maps so the land could be divided up into ranches for the settlers. Tickup and Wopsock had agreed, over the course of long conversations in the snowbound settlement, that they would work with the settlers and assist them in settling the valley in exchange for lands for themselves, and for certain lands to be set aside for common use by the Ute people. Tickup knew, from his experiences in Colorado, and from his work with Ouray and Wakara and other tribal leaders, that the advancing flood of settlers would not diminish and could not be overcome. He chose to work with the settlers to try to secure a reasonable future for his family. He also knew that he would not be treated as an equal, and that his efforts would likely be wasted, and that land he obtained would likely be stolen, no matter what assurances he received. He was a pragmatic and optimistic man, and his educational background and command of the English language gave him opportunities not afforded to all Native people. He trusted Bill Baggs and did not trust the Indian Agents his tribe was forced to work with, and he thought that perhaps he could make something positive happen here in Lost Valley, the valley he and his family referred to as Tabyako or sometimes as Hideout Valley.

About midday the men stopped to water their horses in the stream. Baggs took a compass and a notebook from his saddlebag and started making some notes and drawings on the topography. He took compass sightings on several prominent landmarks and sketched the general lay of the canyon and the stream. Tickup tended to the horses for a few minutes, then walked to an open, sage-covered area, away from the cottonwoods and willows along the stream, and below the piñon and juniper trees that covered the slopes. He stood quietly, looking up the canyon, then down, turning, looking all around. When Bill Baggs finished making sketches he took his canteen to the creek, filled it, drank, and joined Tickup.

"Water?" he asked, offering the canteen to his friend.

Tickup nodded, took the canteen, and drank. He handed the canteen back to Baggs, still staring into the tree-covered slopes above them.

Baggs stood quietly, seeing that his friend appeared to be pondering something. After a few minutes, Tickup spoke.

"There are people all around us," he said. "I see them moving around in the trees, along the rocks. They are by the stream, and even here, next to us."

He gestured toward the slope rising in front of them.

Baggs looked around, intently trying to see who Tickup was talking about. He hadn't expected to see anyone at all in this canyon, and was startled to hear Tickup speak of people, maybe people hiding, sneaking up on them.

"Where? I, I don't see anything," he said, turning in a circle. "I haven't seen anyone."

"Not living people, not people with bodies," Tickup answered. "Shadow people. Lurkers. I see their shadows. I see light when they move," he said, sweeping his arm toward the nearby thicket of vegetation along the stream.

Bill cocked his head and followed Tickup's gesture with his gaze. He saw leaves moving in the slight breeze, and changes in the light as it reflected from the water, and from the waving silvery leaves of the willows. He squinted his eyes and looked all around.

"I, I don't know. I don't see anyone."

"Maybe you can't see them. They let some people see them, and they hide from others."

Tickup stepped forward and took some leaves from a tall sagebrush plant, then bent over and picked a few grass stems. He took something from his pocket, reached both hands forward, and began speaking in Ute. He turned in a circle, gestured with the bundle of leaves in his right hand, and sprinkled something from his left. When he completed the circle, he stood for a moment, said a few more words, bent down, placed the leaves on the ground, and turned to Bill.

"Come on, I want to show you something."

He started walking up the slope, trending first to the right, then turning left and angling up across a talus slope. Bill could see that they were approaching the foot of the cliff. As they rounded a portion of the cliff that jutted out above the canyon, they entered an overhanging area, where the stone had eroded back into the cliff, forming a large, sheltered area, like a wide, shallow cave. Tickup stopped, held his arm out to the side to signal Bill to stop, and began singing in a very low, barely audible voice.

After a few minutes, he turned to Bill.

"This is a place that is very special to me, and to my family. This one of Wanzi's homes. The Antelope Watcher. The Pronghorn Guide. Like the one in the cave. This is one of his homes. You remember that he is a watcher. A helper. He shows us things. Tells us things. I was talking with him down below, and just now. If you listen, he will talk with you."

Tickup stood very still and closed his eyes. Bill saw what Tickup had done, and did the same. The men stood in silence, and Bill listened to the breeze, the wrens and swallows flying in and out of the shelter. He could hear his own breathing, and felt a gust, like a puff of breath, against his face, coming from toward the back of the shelter. He saw lights moving beyond his closed eyelids, and a very peaceful feeling came over him. Tickup began singing again in a very quiet, breathy voice, and Bill felt that he knew the song, that he was singing along with Tickup. When the song ended, Tickup reached over and put his hand on Bill's shoulder.

"See him?" he asked. "See the Pronghorn Guide? Do you see Wanzi?"

He gestured toward the sandstone face at the back of the shelter.

"Oh yes. Oh my!" exclaimed Bill, stepping forward to view the figure painted in red on the sandstone back wall of the shelter. The deep dark red boldly executed lines stood out from the buff-colored sandstone. Bill looked the figure up and down, noting that it obviously depicted a male who appeared to be wearing some sort of a necklace or chest ornament made up of two three-pronged fork-like elements, one on each side of the chest. Coming from the figure's head were two pronged, horn-like protrusions.

"It's upside down," Bill said, still looking intently at the figure. "He's upside down, like the little one in the cave," he said, turning toward Tickup.

Tickup nodded, and said something in Ute.

"Wanzi watches this place, this canyon. He helps lost people find their way. He helps us find things. He helps us know things. He is very strong. Very powerful. He is a helper, but he can be an enemy, too. My father talked to him. And I do, too. I talk to him. Sometimes in the Fall we say goodbye to the Pronghorn Guide when he goes away for the winter. There are some songs we sing to him, and a special dance. The leader wears a hat with pronged horns on it."

Tickup reached into a bag he carried by his side and took out a small wooden object. He held it in his outstretched hand and spoke in

Ute. When he finished, he showed the object to Bill. It was a figure that looked like a small antelope, about the size of Tickup's palm.

"This is Wanzi. One of his forms. He is made from one piece of willow, and I have taken him from here to visit all of his homes. He has five homes. Now I return him here where he is happy, where he wants to stay."

Tickup walked to the rear of the shelter and stopped in front of a small oval indentation in the cliff face that had been chinked in with small stones. He removed a few of the chinking stones, and placed the stick figurine inside. He spoke in Ute, and replaced the chinking stones. When he finished, he turned to Bill and held out his hand.

"Here, this is for you."

Tickup placed a split twig figurine in the shape of a pronghorn in Bill's hand.

"It is like the one you put in the wall, over there," Bill said, turning it over and around in his hands.

"It is like that one," Tickup said. "This is Wanzi. You can keep him with you. He will help you, if you are good. He will help keep the little devils and water babies from entering you and making you do evil things. Keep Wanzi, and Wanzi will be your watcher. He will be your guide."

Tickup turned and motioned to Bill to follow him.

They walked toward the back of the shelter, and Bill followed his friend into a large crack in the sandstone. They made their way up through the crack and climbed up, over boulders and stones that were lodged in the crack, finally emerging on the top of the cliff. They climbed up onto a narrow fin of sandstone that angled away from the cliff, and Bill could see what appeared to be a masonry structure on a mushroom-like pedestal. Tickup walked to its base, then ducked down, and crawled up through an opening. Bill followed.

"What is this?" Bill asked, standing in the interior of the structure and turning around. "Look, you can see the entire valley from here. There are our horses down below!"

Tickup looked around over the top of the masonry walls.

"I guess it is some kind of a fort," he said. "This is from the Ancient Ones, not my people. Maybe they needed to hide from someone, I don't know. Our elders don't know. They are the same people who made the little houses in the cliffs, and some of the rock writings. We don't know much about them, except that their writings can be evil, can bring bad luck. That's why our healers kill some of their writings, some of their spirits, so they won't be at war with us."

"Is Wanzi, the Pronghorn Guide, is it, he, is he from the Ancient Ones?" Bill asked. "Did your people kill him? I didn't see a mark on the rock."

"He is from the Ancient Ones, but he talks to us, and to our healers. They don't kill the Pronghorn Guides. And they don't kill the Head Hunters either, or the snakes. They talk to them. They are ours now. They are ours."

Bill clasped the figurine to his chest, took a deep breath, and looked over the stone wall to the canyon below. A male antelope stood in the small clearing and seemed to be looking back, straight at him.

# Chapter Eight

# Beef Jerky

Present Day

"What's that?" Tom asked.

"Beef jerky," Ralph answered. "I make it myself."

"Could I try it?" Tom asked, reaching down and taking a piece.

"I don't know," said Ralph. "It's really spicy."

"Hey, I'm Latino, man," Tom said. "We live on spicy food."

"Don't say I didn't warn you," Ralph said, looking up from his camp stove as Tom put a chunk in his mouth and chewed away.

"Hmmm," Tom said. "It is pretty…." His voice trailed off.

Tom's eyes opened wide and he opened his mouth and took in a big breath. He pawed at his mouth in a panic and spit the jerky out. His breathing became labored and he sounded as if he were having an asthma attack.

"Here, have a drink," said Ralph, offering Tom a water bottle. "Take a drink and I'll get you a piece of cheese. That will help."

Seeing Tom in apparent distress, Kenny came over from where he had been setting up his tent.

"Everything okay?"

"Tom's dying from eating a piece of spicy jerky," Ralph explained. "I warned him."

"Spicy, Jesus Christ," Tom gasped. "I'm on fire! My tongue is melting! Jesus!" he sputtered, "Holy shit!"

He guzzled some more water and reached for some more cheese.

"Shit, man, what the hell kind of jerky is that? I want to see you eat a piece. Here, Ralph, eat some. Holy crap that burns."

"Well, I told you it was spicy," Ralph said.

"Spicy, shit. I know spicy," Tom said. "That crap's not spicy, it's, it's freaking ridiculous. You eat that shit? I want to see you eat some of it—just one piece. Here."

Tom reached for a piece of jerky and handed it to Ralph."

"Oh, I don't eat it," Ralph said. "It's way too spicy for me. I cook with it. It's what I use to season my camping beans. One little piece is good for a whole pot of beans. Beats having to carry spices."

"Well, you better get a Hazardous Materials symbol to put on that container. That's just nuts. What's on it anyway?" Tom asked.

"Mostly habañero chiles and hot sauce. And crushed red chiles. Nothing industrial."

Ralph, his friend Tom Pacheco, owner of Tom Pacheco's Lost Valley Automotive, and Kenny Clements, the museum curator from Salvation Lake State Park who had reported the rock art missing from Skull Creek, were camped by the road to Lighthouse Canyon. The next morning they planned to hike up the canyon to check on the rock art panel there. It contained one of the three figures Ralph knew about that depicted an upside-down human-like figure. Two of the three had been sawed off and taken away within the last six months. Law enforcement people from the county and from the BLM didn't seem too interested in investigating, so Ralph and his friends decided to check on the remaining panel themselves. Even though it was not a long hike, they decided to take a little camping trip and enjoy themselves while they checked out the one remaining upside-down panel.

After dinner they sat around the fire, occasionally talking, taking sporadic swigs on the bottle of George Dickel that Tom had brought along, and periodically listening as Ralph and Kenny played a few songs on mandolin and guitar.

"Why would anyone cut the figures off the rocks and haul them away?" Tom wondered aloud. "That's a lot of work. Think they're selling them?"

"They must be," said Kenny. "I bet the missing panels are already in some mansion in California or New York by now. I bet they're part of a big display with Anasazi pots and Mayan stelae and Egyptian mummies."

"Or Santa Fe. Or Albuquerque. Maybe at that guy Fenn's house. I heard he had a mummified finger on display at his house," added Tom.

"Or Tokyo. Or Qatar. Or Shanghai," volunteered Ralph. "No way to know. My question is why these particular ones. They are not especially artistic or beautiful. I think somebody is stealing them for something other than just beauty. I think they're stealing them for the power."

Ralph leaned over and put his mandolin back into its case.

"What do you mean power?" asked Tom.

"Well, the ones they are cutting off are rare, and they show a person upside-down. Why would a person be shown upside-down?" asked Ralph.

"Well, people call them the 'falling man' petroglyphs," said Kenny. "Maybe they tell the story of someone who fell off the cliff, like 'Here's Bob when he fell from the granary he was building,' just a picture of something that happened."

"Could be. We'll never know, since the artists died a thousand years ago, but they are unusual. The Utes call them Watchers. Say they have power, both for doing good and bad. They don't want the figures to look at them, so they stay away. And, the one right up here in Lighthouse Canyon has really big feet and hands with six fingers and toes on each one. Some people say big hands and feet on rock art depict powerful people, like Shamans. Maybe someone thinks these are portraits of powerful Shamans and they want to control that power."

Ralph picked up his instrument case and prepared to turn in.

"You know," he said. "Some of the first settlers in the valley thought the rock art had special powers. Old Ephraim Jensen wrote in his journals about the Antelope Cult—that's what he called it, right Kenny?—you know, based on the artifacts from Gooseberry that he collected—and which are now in the museum—but also the rock art. The upside-down man at Gooseberry has, or had, I should say,

"Some of the first settlers in the valley thought the rock art had special powers."

pronged horns, just like an antelope. You also know about the strange coincidence between the rock art being stolen and disastrous weather, don't you? The flood in Gooseberry that killed Mrs. Norris and her dogs? And the fire in skull creek? Both at the same time as the rock art was stolen. Some of the Utes I've talked to say there is no coincidence. They say someone is disturbing some powerful forces, and if it keeps up, things are going to get worse. Maybe a lot worse. I don't know. I tend to think the bad weather is just a coincidence. Has to be, right?"

They sat in silence for a while.

"Well, that puts a whole new spin on things," Tom said, taking a pull on the bottle. "And I was looking forward to crawling into my sleeping bag for a good night's sleep. Now I'll probably dream about Shamans and killer antelopes all night. And floods. Thanks Ralph."

≈ ≈ ≈

"Well, it looks like somebody has been here, very recently. They went straight to the panel and made a lot of tracks. Maybe just taking pictures, I don't know, but let's be careful and not mess up the footprints. Let's get some good pictures of them and measure them, and try to see if more than one person was here."

Ralph had never seen footprints by this falling man panel, and now that other similar works of art were disappearing, finding fresh footprints at this lesser-known panel concerned him.

"The more we can find out about who was here, the better chance we may have of catching whoever has been cutting these panels down. Everybody be careful. Look where you step, treat this place like a crime scene. Let's take lots of photos. If you're taking pictures of footprints, use something for a scale, like this little ruler I brought. Or a coin or a pocket knife. Keep your eyes out for any trash they might have left behind. Anything. Then let's see if we can tell how they got here."

Kenny, Tom and Ralph spread out, eyes to the ground, looking for any detail they could find that could help them find out who had visited the site.

"These footprints are fresh," Tom observed. "I bet they were made yesterday or at the most the day before. They're about the same size as my boot print, so the size is probably about a men's ten."

"We don't know that whoever made these prints is a criminal," Ralph said. "I just want to be careful, in case someone is casing the spot, seeing what they need to do to cut the thing down."

"There are at least two sets of footprints," Tom said, waving the others over. "There are the hiking boots over there, about size tens, but look at these—cowboy boots, and they're huge! Ralph, come over here. What size feet do you have?"

"Thirteen," Ralph said, holding his foot over one of the large boot prints. "Looks like about my size. Check and see if they go back and forth over each other's prints, like they would if they were here together."

They took pictures and measurements and notes, and found no cases of the hiking boot stepping on the larger cowboy boot prints. "I'm pretty sure Bigfoot was here after Hiking Boot guy. Or maybe he just followed him around. Hard to say, but it looks like the cowboy boot prints are just a little fresher."

They had just about wrapped things up and were ready to head back to their camp when Kenny hollered out.

"Hey, Ralph, come over here. What do you make of this?"

"It's scrap of paper with some numbers written on it," he said, handing it to Ralph.

Ralph took the paper and looked it over. In pencil he could see 17" x 39" written in pencil.

"Tom, take the tape measure and go back to the falling man. Measure its length and width in inches."

Ralph turned the piece of paper over and could see that it had printing on the opposite side. Only a few words remained: *ard Mixer Saturday night* on one line and *ther Boomgarden* on the next.

"Thirty-nine inches tall and seventeen inches wide," Tom hollered out.

"Shit. Well, someone was measuring the panel, and I don't think it was for scientific purposes," Ralph said. "And I think they wrote it on a scrap of paper taken from the church bulletin, the LDS ward bulletin."

"Well, that narrows it down, Tom said. "Only about half the county goes to that church."

Ralph shook his head.

"This is getting weird. Very weird."

He took his hat off and pushed back his hair. A cold gust of wind blew down the valley, chilling the men. Ralph looked up and saw dark clouds starting to form above them.

"We'd better go," he said raising his eyes to gaze at the darkening sky. "Those clouds don't look good. Getting mighty dark up there, and we have a ways to travel."

## Ralph's Beef Jerky

Take about two pounds of round steak, flank steak, or whatever cut you prefer. Place in the freezer for about an hour (makes slicing easier). Cut in thin slices against the grain.

Prepare a marinade: Place in a blender one cup of hot sauce such as Sriracha, Tapatio, or Melinda's, three or four habañero chiles, two cloves of garlic, a tablespoon of salt, a liberal amount of black pepper and a two tablespoons of crushed red chile flakes. Blend until smooth. Place the meat in a glass casserole and pour the marinade over the meat. Stir so all the meat is coated. Cover with plastic wrap and place in the refrigerator overnight.

Remove the meat from the refrigerator and drain the marinade from the meat. Pat the strips with paper towels to remove any remaining moisture. Place on a rack over a sheet tray and sprinkle the strips with habañero chile powder. Dry in 175°F oven for about two to three hours, until the meat is dried but still flexible and not crisp or crunchy.

Be careful! It is spicy.

## Ralph's Camping Beans

Cook pinto beans until tender. Thoroughly drain. Place on a sheet pan and dry in the oven or out in the sun. When completely dry, place in a plastic bag. When ready to use, cover with water and bring to a boil. Season with a piece or two of the spicy beef jerky.

# Chapter Nine

# Triangle Dancing

Pioneer Times—circa 1855 – 1865

The settlers realized that they were not where Brigham Young had sent them even before they arrived in the valley in which they settled. Over the course of the first winter, between exploring when the weather permitted, and from long discussions with Tickup and the other Utes, they learned that they had overshot somewhat, and had missed the Pachoose Valley completely. They found themselves in a valley the Utes called Tabyako, and which they sometimes called Hideout Valley. They found an easier way in and out of the valley than the treacherous Nettle Canyon, through which they had arrived. Much easier ingress and egress was available through the mouth of the valley, where Piñon Creek enters the Tavaputs River, upstream of its confluence with the Green.

When the spring thaws had opened up the trails, and communication was once again reestablished with the outside world, the isolation of their cold dark winter diminished. A road of sorts was established, and a few additional settlers began arriving, along with occasional itinerant cowboys in search of work, and crews brought in to help set up ranches and sheep operations. The settlers began referring to both the settlement and the entire valley as Lost Valley, honoring its discovery and the way they had felt through those first lonely months. They planted crops, expanded their homes, and settled in. They put in irrigation ditches with relative ease, simply digging out existing ditches that Tickup said had been made by the little people who had lived in the tiny houses in the cliffs long before his people had arrived. Spring came early and was especially warm. The moisture from the ample winter snowfall enabled crops and gardens to begin growing as soon as they were planted, and optimism was rampant.

The original families divided the valley into relatively equivalent sections, and drew lots to see who would claim each portion. Tickup and Wopsok were given first choice of lands, as well as full claim to the forested slopes of the eastern portion of the valley, where they told the settlers their families had used the piñon groves and hunting grounds for generations. The settlers determined that the open area near Piñon Creek where they had first built cabins would be community property, with areas for a town square, a park, church, and other public spaces. They laid out a grid oriented north-south and east-west for streets and ditches. Bill and Maggie Baggs drew the piece of property just north of the town square, and were able to move their original cabin to a new site on their own land without too much difficulty. Their property was next to Tickup's, and next to his was Bishop Jensen's place, just near the mouth of the small creek that ran through the red rock cliffs just to the east of town. The upper reaches of the drainage were thick with berries, and the creek soon became known as Gooseberry Creek. Bill Baggs did not tell the others the story of the pronghorn guide that protected Gooseberry Canyon, out of respect for Tickup and his beliefs.

As the first anniversary of their arrival in Lost Valley approached, the settlers decided to celebrate their good fortune with a picnic and dance in the area they had designated as the town square. Everyone would contribute what they could. They would butcher a steer and cook it slowly in a stone-lined pit, and eat fresh corn, melons, squash, bread, jam, and sweets. Music would be provided by Bill Baggs on guitar, Melvin Jones on mandolin, Mahonri Jensen on fiddle, and two cowboys who were working on Jensen's property playing banjo and accordion. Baggs was a pretty good singer, and they all knew the familiar and old time tunes of the day, so a good time was assured.

The picnic was a grand affair, attended by everyone from miles around. Long tables featured an abundance of food such as few in attendance had seen in recent years. Everyone contributed, including Tickup and Wopsok and their families, who wowed everyone with their smoked cutthroat trout with Indian Rice Grass. Everyone ate and ate. Children ate, ran and played, napped, played, and ate some more. As the sun began to set over the western mountain crests, the Lost Valley Players brought out their instruments, and filled the open area beside the stream and under the cottonwoods with the delightful sounds of dance music. Maggie Baggs was the first dancer, asked by Billy Buck Tittsworth. Soon all the available women and girls were twirling and two-stepping to the sounds of fiddle tunes and schottisches. Maggie did not get a moment to rest, for as soon as one dance finished, another man asked her for the next. And the same went for all of the handful of women. Soon, men were cutting in during the middle of a song, and competition for the few female dancers began to heat up. When a young cowboy cut in on Lily, Maggie's seventeen year old daughter with the flashing blue eyes and shiny dark hair, a bit of shoving and jostling took place. As the band wound down, finishing their sparkling rendition of "The Star of the County Down," Maggie stood on a bench and got everyone's attention.

"The band is going to take a short break. Everyone get something to eat and drink, and we'll start back up in a few minutes."

Maggie looked around and counted about thirty men, crowding in and wanting to dance. She knew that there were only twelve women and girls, and that there might be trouble. At that moment, she invented Triangle Dancing. After running a few things by the musicians, and getting something to drink, she again addressed the crowd.

"When the band starts up again, I'm going to teach you all a fun kind of dance my grandmother Lilian taught me. They used to do it in the old country where she was born. Prussia, I think. It's called Triangle Dancing."

She gestured toward her husband and Tickup, who were standing nearby.

"Come over here, boys. Let's dance!"

Maggie held out her hands and took her husband, Bill Baggs, by his left hand, and Tickup by his right.

"Now, grab each other's hand, and follow me."

Arranged in a triangle, she nodded to the band to start.

"First I do this," she called out, in a very perky and enthusiastic way. Still holding the two men's hands, she ducked beneath their clenched hands, and pulled them with her. They lifted their clenched hands over their heads, and their triangle now was reversed, facing outward. Maggie led them to the left, then to the right, and then again inverted the triangle. She then showed them how to duck between hands in sequence, kind of "rolling" the triangle. On the spot, she invented a number of intricate moves, and gave them each a name, such as up and under, twister, pig slapper, snapper-up, toe heeler, and goose flap. Before the men could feel awkward about holding another man's hand, they were laughing and having such a good time that soon everyone was giving it a try. Triangle Dancing quickly became a favorite activity in Lost Valley. At every gathering, especially during Lost Valley Days, Triangle Dancing was one of the most popular pastimes, and each year new moves were added, some successfully, some less so, but the activity was always fun, entertaining, and, most importantly, Maggie's quick thinking averted a likely rough outcome at the first Lost Valley dance, and set the community on a course that served it well for many years.

When outsiders saw Triangle Dancing, and reported it to others beyond Lost Valley, the innocent fun of the dance was not easily conveyed. Rumors spread far and wide about the strange dance of the Lost Valley folk, and there was talk that Maggie not only danced with two men, but that she was actually married to both a white man and an Indian. People talked about Lost Valley as if every woman had more than one husband, and in a land where marriage between a man and more than one woman was common, indeed, preferred, the forms of dance and perhaps marriage in Lost Valley were very suspect indeed.

## Maggie's Triangle Dance Cookies

6 ounces butter (1½ sticks)
1 cup sugar
2 eggs
1 teaspoon vanilla
3 cups flour
1 teaspoon baking powder
½ teaspoon salt
¼ cup water
½ cup jam


Cream together the butter and the sugar. Add in the vanilla extract and the eggs and beat until well combined.

Mix the flour, salt and baking powder, then combine with the butter mixture. Add the water a little at a time.

Form the dough into a ball, cover, and place in a cool spot for an hour or so.

Roll the dough to about ¼ inch thick. Cut into about 2 inch rounds and place them on a greased baking sheet.

Put a small amount of jam in the center of each circle, and pinch edges up into a triangle shape. Sprinkle with sugar if desired. Bake at 350°F for about 15 minutes until golden brown.

# Chapter Ten
# Porter Rockwell

Pioneer Times—circa 1855 – 1865

"They're coming! They're coming! Rockwell is coming!"

Cletis Baggs rode his pony as fast as he could through the town square, straight to the front door of his family's home and business, the Lost Valley Inn.

"They're at the Jensens's and they're headed here," he called out to his sister Lily, who was in the side yard hanging out laundry.

"Tell Mom! Where's Dad?" Cletis hollered.

Lily started running toward the house.

"He's irrigating, with Tickup," she shouted as she ran through the front door.

Cletis urged his pony to top speed and raced past the buildings toward the upper pasture. Rumors had spread through Lost Valley that Brigham Young would be sending his primary emissary and thug, Porter Rockwell, to visit Bill and Maggie Baggs. Rockwell was a well-known and feared figure, having been the last visitor many accused apostates had received. When Rockwell showed up, people often disappeared, or decided on the spot to move to California or Colorado.

That Bill and Maggie Baggs, and a few others in Lost Valley, including their closest friends Billy Buck and Mollie Tittsworth would be visited by Rockwell, or some other "Avenging Angel" of the Mormon church was not unexpected. They had been sent by Brigham Young to accompany Mahonri Jensen and establish a Mormon settlement.

Rockwell dismounted and pulled open his long duster to reveal his gun belt.

All had started out well, but getting lost, finding themselves on their own, and having a bit of time to think things over had led Bill and Maggie astray. They, and others, had found the leadership of Jensen to be lacking, and had felt manipulated, dominated, and unappreciated. Their faith wore thin, and they found fulfillment in a more personal kind of spirituality, influenced in no small way by the stories and practices of their close Ute friends, especially Tickup, and Tavibo, a friend of his who had visited a couple of times over their first year in Lost Valley. They knew that they would face the wrath of a vengeful leader, and dreaded the day the feared riders would enter the valley.

A cloud of dust surrounded the seven riders as they stormed up the valley. A few hundred yards behind rode Bishop Jensen and two members of his bishopric, the local church leadership. Porter Rockwell, a big, barrel-chested man with full reddish brown beard and long flowing hair, was a fearsome figure. He was loud, a braggart, quick to anger, and showed no mercy. He was also charming, sweet on the ladies, and liked a sip of whiskey now and then. He ran a roadhouse with a small distillery on the road between Salt Lake City and Provo, and profited greatly from the weariness and thirst of travelers. The men with him were a motley bunch of marginally reformed deserters, wife-beaters, murderers, rapists, and Indian hunters. The riders barreled into the small yard in front of the Lost Valley Inn. Rockwell dismounted, and pulled open his long duster coat to reveal his gun belt, with a revolver on each side.

Maggie Baggs came through the open door of the Inn, carrying a pitcher of lemonade. Lily followed behind her mother, carrying a platter covered with glasses and cookies.

"You men are surely parched from riding in this heat," Maggie announced, walking up to Porter.

She took a glass from Lily, filled it, and offered it to the large red-faced man.

"Go ahead, don't be shy," Maggie urged him.

"Well, um, maybe a drink would be nice," he muttered, taking the glass and looking Lily up and down. "Come on boys, have a drink,"

Maggie and Lily served the men, and urged them to move into the shade.

"Floyd here will water your horses." She nodded to her son, and the boy stepped forward to take Rockwell's reins.

"We're here to see your husband," Porter said. "It won't take long. Where is he?"

"Well, I believe he went up on the mountain chasing after some stray horses with our neighbor," Maggie answered. "I don't expect him until later this afternoon."

"Send someone after him," Rockwell said. "Tell him he has important visitors. We'll wait."

His eyes sparkled as Lily brought him another cookie and refilled his glass.

"And who are you?" he asked.

"I'm Lily," she replied, with a slight curtsey. "Lily Baggs."

Porter smiled and nodded, still looking her over.

"We can wait."

Rockwell and his men lounged in the shade, not having anything to do with Bishop Jensen and his bishopric, to whom they had paid a courtesy visit on their way in, but with whom they had nothing in common and no interest in pursuing small talk. The men chatted or dozed off under the cottonwood tree. Porter, not the type to lie about, poked around the Inn, looking in the sheds and around the dining room. Passing a small building behind the tack shed, he noticed some familiar smells and equipment.

"I recognize this. It's a still. You make whiskey?" he called to Lily.

"My dad does," Lily answered. "Would you like to see the barrels?"

Lily showed Rockwell the barrels where Bill Baggs matured his whiskey. Spotting a row of ceramic jugs, Porter nodded toward them and asked, "Mind if I try a sip?"

"Not at all," said Lily. "Dad's proud of his whiskey. He's from Tennessee. His family has made whiskey for ages. They're kind of famous for it, I hear."

Porter lifted the jug and took a swig.

"Mmmmmm. That's good. Better'n mine. Smooth, very smooth."

He took another swig.

"Very good."

"Mama's getting some supper together for your men," Lily told him. "We don't know when Papa will get back. She told me to ask if you would like to come into the inn and clean up or just relax or have some tea before supper."

"Love to," Porter replied. "Think I'll bring this," he said nodding to the jug, and giving Lily a little wink.

Porter sipped and sipped and sipped Bill Baggs's whiskey, and Lily waited on him hand and foot. She brushed up against him, touched his leg when she spoke with him, and looked him in the eye. And she made sure that his cup was always full.

Maggie served a meal of stewed chicken and corn to Porter and his angels, feeding the men under the trees, and Porter at the long table in the Inn. Porter ate little, drank heroically, and flirted with Lily. Maggie watched it all, and knew that her daughter understood what was going on. Lily lit the kerosene lamp and two candles just as the dimming afternoon light began to darken the dining room. As she leaned over the table to light the second candle, Rockwell reached forward and put his hand on her leg. Lily froze, and stood there quietly. She looked back at Rockwell, and saw the surprise come to his eyes when he felt the cold of Tickup's knife across his throat. Bill Baggs quietly closed and bolted the dining room door, and motioned to Lily to leave the room.

"Thank you, Daughter," he whispered to Lily as she turned toward the door.

Nobody ever told the story of exactly what happened that evening in the dining room of the Lost Valley Inn. Bill Baggs did not disappear, and his family was not run out of Lost Valley. The church never tried to take their land or their property, and Porter Rockwell never again visited Lost Valley. By all accounts, including Mahonri Jensen's journal, Porter Rockwell and Bill Baggs shook hands and took leave of each other as gentlemen do. Rockwell thanked the Baggs family for their hospitality, and he and his men rode off into the night, never to be seen or thought of again. Bishop Jensen did note in his journal that Rockwell seemed to walk awkwardly when he left the dining room, as if he might have hurt himself somehow.

## Stewed Chicken and Corn

Cut up and brown enough chicken for your guests in a large stew pot. When nearly browned add chopped onions and cook until limp. Cover with water. Add grated field corn, and salt and pepper to taste. Cook on low heat for an hour or two or more, adding liquid as needed. Serve at the consistency of a porridge, or thick soup. If you don't have field corn, use sweet corn, cut from the cob, added shortly before serving. It will not have the full flavor of the field corn, but will suffice.

# Chapter Eleven

# Trout Napoleon

Present Day

"So the sales rep from Acme Foods had been pestering me for ages to buy their pine nuts. He knew that we had several dishes with pine nuts on our menu, especially pine nut pie since it got written up in the paper a few years ago," Barbara said, wiping the salt and pepper shakers with a white towel. "I always told him I had a local supplier, but he kept offering me special deals, so one day when he came calling I had Tony give us both a blind taste test—Acme's pine nuts—from China, by the way—versus the piñon nuts I get from Old Man Squint's family. Ha! That test didn't last long. We both agreed instantly on which one was the best. I think he even said it was like comparing a fine merlot to Kool Aid. I'm not kidding, it was that dramatic. These are the best in the world."

"No argument here," replied Ralph, smiling as he chewed a bite of his dinner. "This trout is one of the very best meals I've eaten anywhere. Period. I just love it."

"One of my favorites too," Barbara replied, moving to the next table and refilling the napkin dispenser. "Did I ever tell you how I learned to make it?"

"I don't think so. Is it French?"

"Oh, no, not by a long shot. I learned it from Napoleon Foster, a Paiute man, one of Squint's pals." Barbara smiled. "I wonder how many people make that same mistake! Thinking I have some fancy

French dish on the menu!"

"No, I got it a long time ago. You know how I like to go and visit Squint's family during pine nut season? Well, one year I went out with them, and Squint's buddy Napoleon Foster was up there with him. Napoleon was a cool old guy. He said he was too old to gather nuts, so he just fished all day. That was fine with everyone else because he was a good fisherman and they liked the trout. Well, he made this dinner, he called it pine nut trout, and I ate with them that night and I really thought I had died and gone to heaven. It was the best meal I had ever eaten, and I couldn't stop gushing. Maybe it was just because I was tired and hungry and back in the woods, but I will never forget that dinner. I still think about that day every time I make it here at the Café."

She put the napkin holder down on the table and moved to the row of booths.

"Did you know that Squint was the grandson of Tickup—the Ute on the monument in the park. The one who helped the pioneers the first year here in Lost Valley?"

"No, I'd never heard that," answered Ralph. "I thought Squint was a Paiute."

"He was part Paiute. Tickup and his wife Mincy were Utes, and their son Clifford Lone Bear was a holy man for a long time, pretty famous, too. He married a Paiute woman, I think her last name was Tom, and Squint was their son. They had several kids. One of Squint's sisters was chair of the tribe for a while."

Ralph nodded and sipped his coffee.

"Looks like you've got a couple of late customers." He nodded toward the door.

"Oh good, it's Rupert and Betsy. I've been expecting them. That's why I have pine nuts on my mind. They're bringing me a sack full."

Barbara hurried toward the door. After letting her guests in and taking their delivery to the back, she showed them to the table with Ralph.

"Ralph, I'd like you to meet Rupert and Betsy Perank. Rupert is Squint's grandson. They're my pine nut suppliers. Best pine nuts anywhere. Rupert and Betsy, this is my friend Ralph."

Ralph stood and greeted the guests, and gestured for them to join him. Barbara waved to Iris and ordered coffee and pie for Rupert and Betsy and joined them all at the table. She told the story of the taste test, which they had heard a number of times, but which they still enjoyed hearing.

"So, Barbara tells us that you wrote a book on the rock writings," Rupert said to Ralph. "You know, Betsy's uncle wrote a book about the ancient writings. His name was Martineau. Ever hear of him?"

"Oh, sure," Ralph replied. "I never knew him, but I read his book. Interesting stuff."

"Yep, a lot of people think he was pretty wacky with his interpretations of what it all means," Rupert said. "I don't know, maybe he was on to something. I don't know."

"Did you know that someone has been cutting down rock art and stealing it?" Ralph asked Rupert and Betsy.

They shook their heads.

"Someone has been sawing the figures off the cliff faces. They've taken two that we know of, and they are only taking one kind. The upside-down people. Some people call them the falling man figures."

Rupert and Betsy looked at each other and spoke in Ute. Ralph thought they might be arguing. There was a rather long silence as everyone ate pie and drank coffee. Finally Rupert spoke.

"We call the upside-down men Watchers. Sometimes people call them Long Lookers. Some Navajos call them that. The ones with Antelope horns are Wanzi—that's just Ute for male pronghorn, but Wanzi is a spirit too," he said. "They are very old—from the Moki people, the people who were here before our people. They have power. They can help you. Or harm you. They can bring rain. Or wind, or snow. We try to respect all the writings, because they are sacred or magic. Whoever put them there, even if it was a Paiute or Ute, they put them there for a reason, and others might not know the reason. They might be good magic, or maybe bad. Who can tell? But the falling ones—the Watchers—we don't like to have them look at us, so we don't go near them."

He looked at his wife, and she nodded.

"My great grandfather, Clifford Lone Bear, he talked to the

Watchers," Rupert continued. "They watched over him. But some people, they have been killed by the Watchers. Some people say that Mrs. Norris was killed by the Watchers. You know, the woman who was killed in that flood out in Gooseberry. Her dogs were killed too. The healers say she was killed by a Watcher."

Ralph and Barbara sat quietly. Rupert was still young—in his 30s, but he was already becoming known as a medicine man, and he was widely respected. The seriousness in his voice was very apparent to Barbara and Ralph, who both sat quietly.

They ate in silence for a few minutes.

"This is delicious pie," Betsy said, scraping the last of hers up with her fork. "The pine nuts are good, but you sure make them into some great pie."

"Thank you," Barbara smiled. "Would you like another piece? More coffee?"

She started to rise.

"Oh, no, no thank you," Betsy said, looking over at Rupert. "We need to get home. Got work tomorrow."

"Well, thank you for the piñon nuts. I'll write you a check right now," Barbara said, rising and heading for the kitchen.

"Just one more thing," Rupert said. "Maybe this is nothing, I don't know, but when you told us about somebody stealing the old writings, it reminded me. We've been seeing these footprints around the ruins and writings lately. And somebody has been digging around in some of the caves and places where the old ones and the Mokis lived. Somebody with really big feet. Wears these giant cowboy boots. I've seen his footprints a lot lately. Just thought that might mean something. I don't know."

# TROUT NAPOLEON

## Trout Napoleon

Adapted by Barbara Haywood from a recipe she learned from Napoleon Foster.

Four fresh trout fillets (skin on, bones removed)
½ cup toasted pine nuts, crushed
¼ cup bread crumbs
¼ cup butter or bacon grease
Salt and pepper

Place fillets on a greased baking sheet or in a greased Dutch oven. Mix all ingredients but the trout in a bowl. Place pine nut mixture on the trout fillets and press down. Bake the fillets in a hot oven (400°F) for 10 – 12 minutes. The crust should be slightly browned, and the fish cooked.

# BARBARA'S DESERT CAFE

# Chapter Twelve

# Old Ephraim

Turn of the Century—circa 1890 to 1910

Ephraim Jensen, the son of Mahonri Jensen, one of the founders of Lost Valley, was well known for being the town's gregarious Postmaster for over fifty years, managing the small post office, which took up a corner of his business, Jensen's General Store. On display in the front window for most of those fifty years was a fabulous array of Indian artifacts that Ephraim and his pal Nephi Madsen had dug up in the hills around Lost Valley. Although the early settlers had noticed the "forts" on pinnacles above the valley, the many pecked and painted figures on the sandstone cliffs (which the locals called hieroglyphs), and even the ancient irrigation ditches, which the first settlers dug out and used for their own irrigation, Ephraim and Nephi were the first to snoop around in the old ruins and caves, and the first to dig in the dusty dry deposits that held the secrets of the ancient past. The fantastic and mysterious things they found profoundly affected them, and some say, exacerbated the curse allegedly placed on the town and valley by Brigham Young in retaliation for the mistreatment of his emissary, Porter Rockwell.

Ephraim and Nephi started out by picking up an occasional arrowhead or potshard, and marveling at the fine craftsmanship and beauty embodied in the pieces. They tried to learn about the old ones, and found that not much was known, although their scriptures, the Book of Mormon, gave them some understanding of those who had come before. Ephraim and Nephi, like many others at the time, attributed the magnificent artifacts and striking art to a high culture, long gone, for, according to common knowledge, the modern Indians were incapable of such fine craftsmanship and symbolic expression.

Townsfolk and neighbors learned of the friends' fascination with the past, and soon the storefront filled with a variety of odd and mysterious and common and mundane artifacts of the past, including ceramic vessels, baskets, strings and rope, stone points and knives and scrapers, arrows, bows, throwing sticks, rattles, digging sticks, leather moccasins, and more. Each piece was a marvel to Ephraim, who cataloged the artifacts in a special notebook, recording where every object had been found, by whom and when, and what other objects were found with or near it. He made detailed, scaled pencil sketches of many of the objects, and speculated about the use and significance of each. He was certain that they had been made by a now-extinct race much superior to the local tribes, because none of the modern Indians made such fantastic things, and when he asked them, most did not know what the objects were, and were not comfortable talking about them.

Just a short way from town, in the lower reaches of Gooseberry Canyon, on the tip of a knife-edged ridge extending out into and above the canyon floor, stood a stone structure, constructed of dry-laid natural stone masonry, enclosing and walling off the end of the ridge. It was known locally as the Indian Fort, and a few cowboys had made their way down the ridge and up through a tight passage in the sandstone into the center of the structure. A three-foot round sandstone slab sat to the side of the opening and could be slid into place to close it off. The floor of the structure was clean sandstone, and a person could stand inside and peer over the gradually tumbling walls, which stood about five feet high. Nothing had been found in the fort, and people thought it must have been a lookout or defensive structure of some kind.

Ephraim and Nephi had noticed an overhang that produced a sheltered area below the fort, and one summer afternoon they decided to investigate it. They scrambled up the steep talus slope from the creek bed below, and when they got to the overhang, they were surprised to see how large it was; the overhanging rock sheltered an area of at least fifty feet wide by twenty feet deep.

"Whoa, look at that!" Nephi exclaimed, awestruck at the sight of a nearly life-sized figure painted in red on the sandstone wall at the back of the overhang. "He's upside down."

Both men studied the painting, and were captivated by its detail, and the powerful depiction of a human-like figure, clearly male, with what appeared to be forked horns coming from his head, and two trident-like shapes hanging on his chest. And, he was upside down. Nephi bent sideways and craned his neck, trying to see the figure as it would have looked if upright.

"He's scary-looking," he said. "I wonder why he's upside down."

"Maybe somebody fell off the cliff, and they made this picture of him," Ephraim mused.

"I don't know," replied Nephi. "He's a mighty powerful-looking person, like a spirit. And being upside-down makes it even more strange. I'd wager that he is up there to protect this place, or to scare people away."

"Maybe," Ephraim nodded. "It does seem like it's more than just a picture. I feel like it's giving a warning or something."

The men stood for several minutes looking and thinking. The lone figure was the only decoration on the wall of the shelter, and it dominated the space.

"Well, if I had to spend the winter out here with no house, this is where I'd camp," remarked Ephraim. "Nice roof, and it would get good warmth, facing south."

"You're not the first one to think so," said Nephi, bending over and pulling a hand-sized fragment of an ancient basket from the sand. He brushed it off and turned it over and held it in the sunlight for a better look. "I bet this place if full of this kind of stuff."

"You're right, Neph," Ephraim said. "Look at this."

An arc of what appeared to be leather protruded from the sand, bright red in color with black tic marks around the edge. Ephraim brushed the sand away.

"Aye Golly!" he exclaimed. "Look at how big this thing is!"

Neither man spoke, or even really breathed as they looked at what the sand of the rock shelter revealed. As he carefully brushed the sand away with his bandanna, they could see that it was at least three feet in diameter, circular, and painted with a stark black figure on a bright red background. A hollow-eyed figure stared at them from the exposed portion, and what appeared to be forked horns rose proudly from his head. As Ephraim brushed more sand away, and lifted the edges to reveal more of what he was exposing, they realized that it was a heavy leather disc with a single ghost-like figure painted in the center. Black tick marks marked its circumference, and the imposing black figure on the red background both attracted their gaze and frightened them.

"It's the same feller that's on the wall," Nephi whispered.

"Look, there's a handle on the back," Ephraim exclaimed. "It's a shield."

He held it up for Nephi to examine, but Nephi was not looking at the shield. He gasped and stepped back, and put his hands to his chest. Ephraim too stepped back quickly, as he didn't know how to interpret Nephi's action. Had he seen a snake?

Both men looked down at the sandy floor of the rock shelter, right under where the shield had lain. A human face looked up at them, its dried skin pulled back, exposing its gaping jaw as if frozen in a death scream. Both men looked in horror at what they had uncovered, unable to take their eyes from the skull, which seemed to be the frozen, mummified embodiment of fear.

"Blessed Heavenly Father," Ephraim whispered, just loud enough for Nephi to hear. "There's three of them."

# Chapter Thirteen

# Ancient Ones

Turn of the Century—circa 1890 to 1910

Ephraim and Nephi left the artifacts and remains as they found them, and returned home. Without telling anyone what they had found, and only letting their wives know where they were headed, the next day they set out early in a small wagon pulled by two horses. They brought along shovels, blankets, and a tarp. When they reached the canyon they made their way to a small clear area below the shelter, unhitched and tethered the horses, and headed up the hill.

The men worked carefully and quietly and a little timidly as they removed the dusty, sandy soil from around the artifacts and the skeletons. The remains had been placed in a small circle, facing inward, with their legs pulled up in front of them as if sitting on the ground. The shield was over the center of the small circle, and as they removed it they could see that it covered a large piece of loosely woven fabric, upon which lay what appeared to be a hat or headdress. Bright orange and black feathers were attached to a leather and fabric band, and several dozen exotic looking seashells trailed from the headdress on twisted thong streamers. Ephraim sketched the hat and the fabric upon which it lay.

"It looks like it could have been made this morning," Nephi whispered. "I think those are flicker feathers."

When Ephraim had finished sketching and describing the find in his journal, the men carefully lifted the headdress and placed it on one of the blankets they had brought. Nephi moved it away from the area where they were working, and they began lifting the delicate fabric that lay exposed beneath where the shield had been removed.

"It's like a shirt, or maybe a cape," Ephraim exclaimed.

He lifted the garment and held it out so he and Nephi could look at it.

"Not like we'd make today, but pretty well-made," Ephraim observed. "Looks like it's about my size, too."

Underneath the garment they could see a circular outline, about the diameter of Ephraim's outstretched hand. Nephi brushed the sand away and they could see the bottom of a basket protruding from the dusty sand. He carefully cleared the deposits away from the basket and lifted it free. He brought it up so he and Ephraim could look at it.

"It's perfect, a perfect little basket," Nephi said.

He turned it upright and exclaimed "Look, it's got a pot inside it!"

Nestled perfectly within the basket that was about the size of his head was a gray ceramic vessel of about the same shape as the basket. Inside the pot they could see what appeared to be loosely packed strands of juniper bark, within which was nestled a small leather bag.

"Let's see what's in the bag," Nephi exclaimed.

"We will," Ephraim answered. "Just give me a minute to take some notes and make a drawing. I don't want to miss anything, or forget something about how we found all this."

When Ephraim finished his sketch, the two friends removed the juniper bark packing from the pot and pulled out the pouch.

"There's something in it, something loose," Nephi said, feeling the sides of the pouch.

He slipped back the thongs holding the pouch closed and expanded the opening. The men looked at each other and Ephraim nodded. Nephi cupped his hand and poured some of the contents into his palm.

"Corn," he observed. "Dent corn, with little dimples in each kernel. I bet it was their seed corn."

"Or corn for a special ceremony or prayer," Ephraim added.

The men found no more artifacts beneath the basket and pot, and they smoothed the earth back around the hole they had created.

Ephraim carefully sketched and described the three bodies that encircled the area from where the artifacts had come. They brushed some of the sand and dust from around the remains and thought about removing them as well.

"It looks like a little family," Ephraim noted. "That one is surely a child, and the other two are adults. One's bigger than the other. I think it's a little family, father, mother, and child, sitting in a circle."

"I don't like this," Nephi said, quietly. "We shouldn't be digging around them anymore."

"I agree," said Ephraim. "Let's cover them up."

They took sand from around the shelter and covered the three individuals. Both men stood in silence when their work was complete.

"I wonder how long they've been sitting here," Ephraim wondered aloud. Nephi shrugged.

The men had just started picking up the blankets and packing them to carry down to the wagon when Ephraim stood and walked over to the back wall of the overhang, just a few feet from the upside down pictograph.

"Look at this," he said to Nephi. "This just didn't happen. Somebody did this."

About chest high on the back wall of the shelter was what appeared to be a small nook in the sandstone face that had been chinked in with small stones. Ephraim looked at Nephi, shrugged, and began removing the chinking stones. Despite the poor light in the shelter, they both quickly realized that the nook held the skull of a male antelope, upon which rested a small figurine made from one split piece of willow, in the shape of an antelope.

"Hmmmm," Ephraim said, lifting the skull from its resting place, "He's a big one. And this little stick figure, he's an antelope, too. See the forked horns?"

Nephi nodded, and looked back in the nook, standing to the side to allow in more light. He reached in, and on the floor of the nook was a tangle of cord, with some stick-like objects underneath. He pulled the items out and laid them in his palm. The men looked at the objects—a carefully made looped cord, with two spindly, forked pendants hanging from it.

"Looks like bird feet," Nephi mused, "tied on to a string."

"It's a necklace," Ephraim observed. "with parts of two bird legs and feet. Probably hung like this."

He held the cord up to his chest, and the two legs dangled on his chest, the three toes of each splayed out. Dried skin held the bones and toes, and even the claws, in place. Ephraim turned the cordage and two pendants over in his hands, noting the finely made twisted string, and the tiny holes in the bird bone through which the cordage passed.

"Yep, it's a necklace," Nephi said, giving Ephraim a wide-eyed look. "A pretty fancy one. Like the one that upside-down feller's got on."

Ephraim returned his glance and nodded. Ephraim wrapped the necklace and the split-twig antelope figurine in his bandanna, and Nephi rolled them and the skull in one of his old, worn shirts, and began carrying the artifacts down to the wagon. It would take them three trips to bring everything down.

# Chapter Fourteen

# Doggie Treats

Present Day

Barbara Haywood pulled her big black Ford F-250 extended cab pickup in front of the gate to Ralph's yard. Ralph, Kenny, Tommy and Iris sat in lawn chairs sipping beer and munching on chips and salsa.

Barbara got out of the truck and went to the back, where she opened a small door in the fiberglass shell over the bed and pulled out a long, narrow plank with short rails along the sides. She walked it out until it stopped, and placed the end of the plank on the ground. She then went back to the shell and slid open a small door that covered the opening.

"Come on, pups," she called.

Out of the opening streamed a relatively orderly but very rapid flow of tiny dogs of every color imaginable. When they reached the bottom of the plank, they all immediately ran to Barbara's feet, where they sat, and attentively awaited her instructions. When the last tiny dog had exited the truck, and Barbara had completed a quick inventory of those present, she turned toward the gate, and said, "Come on, pups."

The little herd ran with her, and then ran past her into the yard, where they spread out, thirty noses to the ground or in the air, thirty tails wagging, chasing, investigating every odor, every object, every nook and cranny in the yard. A nearly white dog leapt high in the air, caught a moth in its mouth, and gulped it down. Others made their way toward Ralph's garden, where they would hunt down and consume any grasshopper, mouse, tomato worm, or other living creature in

"Of course, they have names."

their size range they might encounter.

Kenny stared in wide-eyed wonder.

"Holy crap," he exclaimed. "How many of those things does she have? What are they, Chihuahuas?"

"Yep," Ralph answered. "They're Chihuahuas. Barbara runs a kind of Chihuahua rescue operation. She has plenty of room for them, and she has all kinds of good food from the restaurant for them so she's accumulated quite a family."

Barbara walked up to the group, gave Ralph a kiss, and sat down in a lawn chair.

"Beer?" Ralph asked, opening the cooler.

"Indeed!" Barbara answered. "What do you have?"

"Well, I know how you love the IPA from Ska Brewing, so I brought a case of their Modus Hoperandi when I came back from Durango last week. Will a Modus do?"

"Ralph, you are my dream guy," Barbara smiled. "I would love one."

"I have never seen so many Chihuahuas in one place before," Kenny said, looking around at the roaming pack. "And they seem to be so well-trained. I didn't even think you could train a Chihuahua."

"Oh, sure you can," Barbara answered. "Most people don't spend any time training their dogs anyway, no matter what breed they have. And most Chihuahua owners don't bother. They just let them do whatever they want to do, 'cause, what trouble can such a little dog get into, anyway?"

She took a sip of her beer.

"Wonderful," she said. "Tastes like grapefruit juice."

"Chihuahuas are actually quite intelligent and trainable. My pups mostly train each other. I have a core of dogs who are really the leaders, and everyone else follows them. See that little white dog hopping around on three legs? That's Cookie. She's fourteen years old and the undisputed Queen of this pack."

"So, can you tell them all apart?" Kenny asked. "Do they all have names?"

"Of course, they have names!" Barbara exclaimed. "They're my pups, my pals. Here, I'll introduce you."

"That's Bill, and right behind him is Sally Ann. And the yellow one is Dolly, and by her are Jim and Jesse, and Sara and Jimmy. Over there are Lester and Howdy and Alice and Hazel and Stringbean. On the lawn playing in the sprinkler are Emmylou and Chubby and Birch and Weeds and Rhonda and Maybelle. Sonny and Bobby are chasing Dale Ann and Alison. Doc and Merle and Earl are over by the rosebushes. There are a few more in the garden, but don't worry, they all have names, and they all know their names and answer to them. They're a lot of fun."

A loud, deep bark startled everyone. It was coming from the back of Barbara's truck.

"Jeez," Barbara exclaimed and she rose from her chair and started for the truck. "I forgot about Zac."

She went to the back of the truck and opened the door to the shell.

"Come on boy," she said, and over the tailgate leapt a large, powerful, beautiful red Doberman. "Sorry Zac," Barbara said. "Come on in."

The graceful dog trotted toward the roaming Chihuahuas, and they all greeted each other and Zac scanned the yard and glided around its perimeter, as if checking to make sure everything was okay.

"What is that, a Chihuahua from the Nevada Test Site?" Kenny asked, laughing.

"Well," Barbara answered, taking her seat. "He's the real leader of the pack. That's Zac. He treats the Chihuahuas like they're his children. Don't make the mistake of hurting one of the little ones, or you will have to answer to Zac. He loves them and takes care of them. And they absolutely adore him. He is their God."

"I'll go fire up the grill," Ralph said, rising from his chair and heading for the patio behind the two-story mobile home.

"It is always a treat to have someone else do the cooking," Barbara said. "I love working at the café, but it sure is nice to have someone else feed me once in a while."

"How long have you owned the café," Kenny asked. Seems like it must have been there for a while."

"Oh, I've owned it for much of my life now," Barbara replied. "I'm originally from Colorado, and after I graduated from college I was driving to visit my cousin in San Francisco, taking the back roads and scenic route, and frankly got kind of lost. Seems appropriate that I got lost and wound up in Lost Valley. Anyway, my VW bug broke down. The clutch or transmission was going out, so I took it to Tom Pacheco's garage."

She nodded toward Tommy, who smiled.

"It was going to take a couple weeks to get the parts and complete the work, and I didn't have much money, so I didn't know what to do. I went to the café for something to eat and there was a help wanted sign in the window. I went in, asked about the job, and I've been there ever since."

"Was it named Barbara's Desert Café then, or what was its name?" Iris asked.

"It was just the Desert Café then, and it was owned by the most wonderful man I have ever met, a great guy named Jimmy Nelson. He had owned the place for about forty years when I came along. He was a very sweet man. He always had a twinkle in his eye. He worked long hours every day, but always had a smile for everyone. He was sort of like a kid in some ways, innocent, but curious, and, well he just took delight in little things. He loved showing me his secrets in the kitchen. I learned lots from Jimmy, not just about cooking and running a restaurant, but about how to be a better person."

"He sounds like a great guy. My mother remembers him and has told me about him. Whatever happened to him?" Iris asked.

"Well, he was around seventy when I met him, and he was winding down. He came into the restaurant every morning at 5:30 am and stayed most nights until 7:00 pm or so. He usually took a nap in the afternoon in a cot he kept in the back office. I don't know how he kept it up for so long. Anyway we really liked each other, and his son Norman wasn't interested in the restaurant business—I think he was a hairdresser in Rock Springs or something. About three years after I started, Jimmy asked if I wanted to buy the business. He gave me very generous terms, and I borrowed some money from my parents for the down payment. A few years later I inherited a little money when my Aunt Lou died, and used that to pay off most of what I still owed. Jimmy died a few years later. He was walking his dog Suzy, who was old as hell herself, and he just sat down on a bench in the park and died. Heart gave out. I still miss him. He was like a second father to me. And you know what? His wife took Suzy home and she curled up on her rug and when Gertrude checked on her later that day she had died, too."

Tears welled up in Barbara's eyes.

"I don't know why that always makes me so emotional. I was terribly sad when Jimmy died, and I missed him an awful lot, but the thought of his little dog just lying down and dying always makes me cry."

Iris walked over to Barbara and gave her a hug.

"You really seem to have loved this guy Jimmy."

"He changed my life. I have no idea what I would have ended up doing without him. I got my degree in sociology, and there are not a lot of jobs for sociologists. It always amazes me how little things like your car breaking down can set a course for you that affects everything you do for the rest of your life."

"Did Jimmy use local products and do things for the community like you do?" Iris asked.

"Well, Jimmy did lots for the community. The Locals Special was something he started long before I came here, and I started buying from locals because at first I didn't have the cash or credit to buy from the big distributors, so I started dealing with people I knew—gardeners and farmers—trading them meals for their products, and asking for time to pay. My first deal was with Mrs. Bess for tomatoes and lettuce from her garden. I started buying lamb from the Samaniego Brothers, beef from the Tickup Cattle Company, corn and other vegetables from the Everetts and others, and it has just built from there. It's been great for both the restaurant and for the local farmers and ranchers too."

"What's the Locals Special," Kenny asked.

"Can't tell you, Kenny," Barbara laughed. "You haven't lived here long enough!"

"Aw heck."

Kenny looked down and feigned humiliation.

"Oh, okay, I'll tell you," Barbara said. "Each day we prepare a meal and make it available to locals for about the cost of the food. It's something Jimmy started doing years ago when he saw people going hungry. It's usually something like chicken and dumplings, meatloaf, beef stew, chile, stuff like that. You have to be a local and ask for it. We also work with the local religious leaders—Father LaPenske, Bishop Jensen, Reverend Jones, to provide meals for needy people or travelers. They give out little vouchers and then reimburse me for them. Works out okay. Nobody really abuses it and it really does make us feel like part of the community."

"Wow, that is so cool. You are just amazing," Kenny said.

"She is amazing," Iris said. "But that doesn't mean that she's easy to work for. Some days she works me half to death. Of course, she's working that hard, too."

"The restaurant business isn't something for a lazy person, that's for sure," Barbara said. "I get there at 5:30 or 6:00 am, light the griddle, get the pancake batter mixed, and start two big stock pots—one with vegetables, one with chickens. I learned that from Jimmy. He never wasted anything. He would save the ends of celery and onions and carrots, things he trimmed from vegetables—not bad spots, just the parts you usually trim. The next morning he would put all those plus some more vegetables and herbs in two big pots, one with several chickens, and start them simmering. They produce the stocks that we use for gravies and sauces and soups, plus the chicken meat is what we use in all kinds of things—chicken noodle soup, chicken salad, enchiladas, whatever. We cook and serve all day, and clean up after dinner. The last person leaves at around 9:00. It's a lot of work."

"She ain't kiddin'," Iris added, nodding her head. "She ain't kiddin'."

"Here puppies," Barbara called out, reaching into her bag. "Who wants a treat?"

## Doggie Treats

Preheat oven to 400 °F.
1 ½ cup whole wheat flour
½ cup cornmeal
½ cup rolled oats
1 cup chicken stock, broth, or water
½ cup bacon grease or other fat or oil
1 egg
dash of garlic powder

Blend dry ingredients. Add wet ingredients and mix well. Roll out to about ¼ to ½ inch thick. Cut into your favorite shapes, or use a cookie cutter. Place on greased cookie and bake for 20 minutes. Turn the biscuits over and bake for an additional 15 minutes. Allow them to cool before giving them to your pups.

## Barbara's dogs

| | |
|---|---|
| Zac | Dawg |
| Cookie | Weeds |
| Bill | Isom |
| Birch | Hazel |
| Lester | Alice |
| Earl | Dolly |
| Jim | Emmylou |
| Jesse | Alison |
| Howdy | Gillean |
| Chubby | Bessie Lee |
| Stringbean | Sally Ann |
| Sonny | Rhonda |
| Bobby | Dale Ann |
| Jimmy | Maybelle |
| A.P. | Sara |
| Tim | |

# Chapter Fifteen

# The Guardian of the Canyon

Turn of the Century—circa 1890 to 1910

As Ephraim and Nephi made their way with the last load of artifacts down the talus slope toward the creek bottom, they noticed a single puffy dark cloud moving rapidly up the valley.

"Looks like that little cloud is in a hurry to get somewhere," Ephraim chuckled.

Within just a few minutes the cloud had reached them and a fierce wind struck, blasting them with sand and dust. A bolt of lightning struck a boulder not fifty feet upslope from the two men, and the clap of thunder was deafening. Rain fell in sudden sheets as though dumped from giant buckets and Ephraim and Nephi ran madly down the slope, stumbling, falling, rolling, getting back up, and running more. Lightning struck all around them, hitting a juniper just in front of Nephi causing him to dive flat into the rocky slope and curl up into a ball. Ephraim leapt over a small ledge and hunkered down beneath an overhanging stone. Within ten minutes, the storm was over.

"Ephraim, Ephraim," Nephi called. "Are you safe?"

"Over here," Ephraim replied. "Whoa, that was something! Have you ever seen such a thing?"

"Never," Nephi replied, brushing himself off. "Never. Never. I thought we were goners. I thought that storm was going to kill us."

"I think it *was* trying to kill us," Ephraim said, standing up and looking around, somewhat warily. "Or to at least scare us to death."

"It worked," said Ephraim. "It worked."

When they neared the wagon, which they had left beside a large piñon tree just above the creek bed, Ephraim let out a disgusted snort.

"Horses are gone."

As they reached the wagon, Ephraim placed the antelope skull, the pronghorn figurine, and the bird-foot necklace, wrapped in an old shirt, under the tarp with the other artifacts. Nephi walked to the top of the knoll and scanned the surrounding area for the horses.

"All that thunder spooked them," he muttered. "Bet they ran all the way home. I would have."

Having no other options, the two friends filled their canteens from the water jug lashed in the corner of the wagon bed, and prepared to hike out of the canyon. As they started walking, a large male antelope crossed the creek bed and stopped in the middle of the trail. He turned his head and looked straight at the two men for several seconds before walking slowly down the drainage. The men looked at each other and Ephraim shook his head and shrugged.

They wearily trudged the eight miles back to the road, fighting blustery wind and occasional driving rain that forced them several times to hunker down and take shelter until it passed. The antelope walked ahead of them, looking back periodically, but continuing along the only route back to the settlement. Just before they reached the road he turned, looked at them one last time, and headed upslope across a sage flat. The men shared another bewildered look and continued on. After another mile or so of walking they got a ride from Lowell Norris, who was heading into town from his place out in Three Mile Gulch. Just after Lowell dropped the two men off at the end of the short road that led to Nephi's house a fierce gust of wind swept through the valley, sending Ephraim's hat bouncing down the road, and nearly blowing them over. Nephi and Ephraim leaned into the wind and struggled to walk the last few hundred yards to the house.

Nephi's wife Cora opened the front door as the men walked up.

"Get in here you two. We've been worried sick."

Ephraim's wife Vesta helped hold the door open against the gale.

"Come sit down," Cora said, taking the men's hats. "Are you all right? When the horses came running in all lathered up I got worried and sent Cleon to get Vesta. Now he's gone to get Rulon and Eldon and some others to go look for you. And now this awful weather has blown in. I hope they all have the sense to find shelter somewhere."

"We'd better go find them before they head up the canyon looking for us," Ephraim said, rising. "We'll just head over to Rulon's. I bet they are there, waiting for the wind to die down a little."

"You just sit right down and have a little Brigham Tea," Vesta announced, taking charge. "The men would come here first before heading out for the canyon. You just wait here until the wind dies down. Nobody's heading for the mountains in this hurricane. Here—have some tea, and tell us what happened."

The wind blew all night, and caused considerable damage to roofs, fences, sheds, and trees all over the valley. During a brief lull in the wind, Ephraim rode to Rulon Fife's place and found the searchers before they could attempt to brave the storm to look for their friends.

In the morning, Ephraim and Nephi headed up to Gooseberry Canyon, trailing the two cart ponies. As they made their way up the road toward the mouth of the canyon, a large male antelope stood facing them in the middle of the road. When they were within 30 yards, he turned, and trotted down the road. When they reached the mouth of the canyon, he turned, and without hesitation, headed straight up the canyon. Nephi and Ephraim looked at each other, and resolutely rode on. The antelope stopped in the center of the path as they neared the spot where they had left the wagon. He turned, looked straight at the two men, paused for several seconds, moved to the side of the canyon, and allowed the men and horses to pass. Ephraim and Nephi looked at each other again, and without talking, communicated something more profound than they could have with words. They felt the presence of something greater than themselves, and they were awestruck, bewildered, but they knew what they needed to do.

When they reached the wagon, they tethered the horses, and again, without speaking, both went to the wagon, untied the tarp, and Ephraim lifted up the corner, and brought out the shirt that held the antelope skull, the split-twig antelope figurine, and the necklace. Nephi nodded to Ephraim, and the two men headed for the shelter. Inside the shelter, just in front of the nook in the back wall, they stopped and knelt. As they unwrapped the artifacts, Ephraim looked around, and then over at Nephi.

"The little antelope, where is it?"

He lifted the antelope skull and the necklace and looked through the bandanna and the shirt.

"We wrapped it up with these other things, didn't we?"

Nephi nodded.

"It was in with the necklace. It's not there now? Where could it be?"

The two men stood and looked all around where they had been standing, and around the area where they had dug.

"Not here. I don't know what could have happened to it. We didn't open the wrappings back up until now. How could it have fallen out?"

"I don't know," Nephi replied. "I don't know."

The two men replaced the skull and necklace just as they had found them. They didn't know what had become of the small antelope effigy, and they knew that something would be missing when they closed the opening back up. They replaced the chinking in the nook, and when it was closed up just as they found it, they both knelt in silent prayer.

The two friends told only their wives of their experience with the bird foot necklace, the effigy, the antelope skull and the antelope that guided them. They swore each other and their wives to secrecy. They recorded what had happened in their personal journals, and wrote that they had felt the presence of something great and powerful that day, and that they thought they had made things right by replacing the skull and the necklace. They worried about the lost effigy, and despite looking carefully along the trails and in the wagon, never again saw it. For years afterward, each time Ephraim or Nephi went into the canyon, a large male antelope greeted them, and made sure they knew that they were being watched. They never again experienced the kind of wrath that had descended on them that first day, and they never felt that the antelope intended any more than to greet them and to remind them of its presence. Neither man ever hunted antelope again, and both men felt a lifelong connection to the fleet and mysterious animals. They saw them as guardians and guides, and both men spoke to the pronghorns, asked them for guidance and friendship each time they saw one, hundreds of times, for the rest of their lives.

## Brigham Tea

Pour boiling water over the dried stem-like leaves of the Mormon or Brigham Tea plant (*Ephedra viridis*). Use a handful of the stems for each cup, and let them steep for ten minutes or so. A teaspoon of sugar, or of jam, in the tea cuts the harshness of the brew.

# BARBARA'S DESERT CAFE

# Chapter Sixteen

# Election by Stochastic Process

Present Day

Iris Cain was not elected to the office of mayor; she was randomly selected, according to Lost Valley City policy and tradition. Her name, along with those of all qualified registered voters, had been placed in a large mesh-sided hopper, the same one used to choose the winners in the Lost Valley Days Grand Prize Drawings, and spun around a few times. Students from the Lost Valley Elementary Kindergarten class reached in and each selected a single name. The names of the new mayor and other office-winners were read aloud by the students, with some help from their teachers.

Above the proceedings hangs a banner with a statement of the town's political philosophy: "Vote on issues, not politicians." The mayor and town council are chosen by drawing from a pool of registered voters, minus those who have recently held office, and those who choose to opt out. More specialized career positions, such as chief of police and city attorney, are selected by the town council.

The second Monday of January, April, July, and October is Election Day in Lost Valley. The town throws a big pot-luck dinner in the school gymnasium, and registered voters exercise their civic rights and duties to select the course of action on a variety of issues of concern to the town. Typical issues on the ballot include zoning changes, deciding what kind of new bleachers to build at the ball field, approving appointments to town committees, determining how many chickens will be allowed per household, setting fees for using the town dump, selecting the theme and budget for the Lost Valley Days Parade and Pageant, and other variously weighty and sometimes small but never insignificant matters.

At the April election, Mayor Iris presented, on behalf of the Mayor's Office and the Town Council, an explanation of the major issue before the town at that evening's election: whether to form a sewer district and get state and federal grant money to build a modern, large-capacity sewer system, or to not approve forming the district, and stay with the current and traditional system of individual septic tanks for residences and businesses.

"Thank you all for coming out tonight," she began. "I know you're ready for some dinner, but we have a very important issue before us tonight, and I know that many of us have strong opinions about the sewer proposal. We all also know what this means—if we agree to get outside money and build a sewer system, we will all be free of the hassle of dealing with septic tanks. Nobody likes dealing with septic tank problems. I sure don't!"

Cheers rang out, followed by a loud clear shout, in Delbert Bess's easily recognized, somewhat theatrical voice: "I dig septic tanks!"

Which was followed by another loud cheer, acknowledging the work of the poet, who was also the town's only plumber.

"Well," Iris continued, "we all know that this isn't about septic tanks or sewers really. It's about our town. It's about growth and development. If you like Lost Valley as it is, with small businesses and quiet streets, then vote no on the initiative. If you want big chain motels and restaurants moving in with jobs and tax contributions, then vote for the sewer. The town council is split on the issue—half support it, half oppose. I oppose it, but I have only one vote. Now we will hear from Representative Knoll speaking in favor of the initiative, and Kenny Clements speaking against it. They'll each have five minutes, then we'll vote. It's the only item on the ballot, so we should know the outcome by the time we're finished eating dinner."

"Dear friends," State Representative Robert Knoll, dressed in a dark blue suit, white shirt, and red-white-and blue striped tie, began his presentation, "We are so delighted to have you all come out on this most important occasion." He stood with arms folded, and addressed the group in a droning fashion. "Our town is being left behind by the modern world. We are being neglected, because people, good American people with money in their wallets, race by on the highway and don't even blink as they pass us by. They speed past our valley and share their riches with the good people of Beaver, and Bicknell, and Manti and Moab. They don't even know that we exist. They might, if we were not ashamed to raise our heads. If we were not weak and tired and misled by our shameful and cursed past we could reap great riches from the travelers as they pass through, from the visitors who want to see our great beauty, ride their ATVs on our magnificent trails, hunt in our mountain meadows, and yes, even to come and enjoy our pageant. Without a modern sewer system, we are nothing. We can't even have a modern motel or restaurant. Vote for jobs. Get your kids a good job at a good American business. Let's join the twentieth century! Approve the sewer initiative!"

LaVar Jensen stood and clapped vigorously, and was joined by an enthusiastic group who clapped and cheered in support of Knoll's position on the sewer initiative.

Kenny Clements stood from his seat at one of the many tables set up for the dinner. His t-shirt had a picture of a dog hanging its head out of a car window holding a guitar while speeding down the road.

"I like sewers," he began. "Can everybody hear me? Okay then. I like sewers. They've been around since Roman times. They're good for sanitation and public health. Anybody here who doesn't like sewers?" he asked.

No one responded.

"But as Mayor Cain said, this isn't really about sewers. I don't want a sewer system in Lost Valley because I don't want a Holiday Inn Express. I don't want a Country Crock. I don't want an Alco, or an Applebees or a Wal-Mart. Those things will only kill our local businesses and bring us nothing but quantity in return. They will kill Barrett's Food Town. They will kill Barbara's. They will kill the Hobby Shop and Tom's Automotive, and the Walking Owl books. They will kill everything I love about this town. I say no to the sewer, and encourage everyone to vote with me. And by the way, Representative

Knoll, we left the twentieth century a while ago, and I don't miss it. Vote no!"

Ralph leapt to his feet.

"No sewer, no sewer," he chanted.

He was quickly joined by a number of enthusiastic voices.

"Quiet everyone, please quiet down," Mayor Iris Cain rapped her knuckles on the table in front of her. "It is time to vote. The poll is open," she announced. "So is the food line, and remember, after the vote is announced, we will have Triangle Dancing, featuring music by the Lost Valley Players!"

Voting commenced immediately. Voters formed a line by the basketball hoop under the scoreboard, and non-voters, mostly kids, formed a line by the long tables filled with steaming platters of food, vast expanses of salads and desserts, and rolls and breads of every variety imaginable. The city provided barbecued turkey, (in December it was ham, July leg of lamb, and October roast beef) soft drinks, coffee, and hot water, and the voters brought the rest.

At 9:00, Iris took the microphone to announce the results of the election.

"Well, we had 132 ballots cast, a new record for our community, over ninety-five percent! Congratulations to all of us! I know that not everyone will be happy with the outcome, but we can all be encouraged by the turnout. Well, I guess there's nothing to be gained by dragging it out any longer. The vote was 94 to 38. The sewer is defeated."

A cheer rang out through the gymnasium.

Iris cheered, along with most of the people in the room. Bob Knoll stormed out. He was joined by LaVar Jensen, who railed about the fools who voted against economic progress and who were continuing the curse.

After dinner the fiddle tunes and old-time murder ballads and love songs performed by the Lost Valley Players filled the gym. Ralph called out the dance steps for the triangle dancers who twirled and spun the night away.

## Lost Valley Barbecued Turkey

Cut the turkey into manageable pieces, approximately 1/3 to 1/2 pound each. Marinate the turkey overnight in a mixture of equal parts cola and soy sauce. Cook on a barbecue grill over moderate heat until done, turning frequently. Baste while cooking with more fresh marinade.

# BARBARA'S DESERT CAFE

# Chapter Seventeen

# The Lighthouse Canyon Watcher

Present Day

"Hey Ralph, did you hear about the landslide?" Kenny seemed to be hollering into the phone. "The one up in Lighthouse?"

"Hold on Kenny. Let me pull over," Ralph replied.

He maneuvered his truck to the side of the road.

"There, now. What about a landslide?"

"Well, with all the rain this spring, and that storm over the weekend, I guess a pretty big mud and debris slide came off the side of Lighthouse Canyon just below Billy's Wash. Right where the Falling Man is. The Watcher in Lighthouse!" Kenny said. "I guess it's dammed up the creek and everyone's worried that the dam will break and cause a serious flood. I'm about to head out there with some people from the Natural Resources Department and the Forest Service to see what needs to be done. I convinced them to bring archaeologists in to make sure they didn't damage the Falling Man site. Or any other significant ones, if it can be helped."

"Shit, Kenny. I hope the site is okay. I mean, well, I hope the slide and flood haven't damaged it. And that the engineers don't hurt anything trying to deal with the landslide. And shit. This really scares me, if you know what I mean."

Ralph held the phone to his ear and shook his head.

"I shudder to think," he said. "I mean, what if. What if."

"I know Ralph," Kenny said. I've been thinking the same thing. "I hope some asshole hasn't stolen the rock art, and that this landslide is just a natural thing, completely unrelated. That's what I hope."

"Um, would it be okay if I go out there with you, or meet you there?" Ralph asked. "I'm sure the authorities don't want people getting in the way or getting hurt, but I'd sure like to go out there. Even if it's just to prove that this craziness about the weather is just a coincidence, and get back to the business of catching a thief."

"Hell, just come with me," Kenny said. "I'm meeting the Forest Service archaeologist Elmer Schmitt on the bench road, and we're going in from above, so I don't think we'll be in the way of the engineers. They'll tell us if we are. They know we're coming, and I'll just make sure that they know that you're with Elmer and me. You're a consultant. A volunteer."

"Thanks Kenny," Ralph replied. "Is there time for me to run to the house and get some boots on and pick up some gear? I'm almost there, anyway."

"Sure, Ralph. I'll come by in about a half hour and pick you up. How's that?" Kenny asked.

"Perfect," Ralph replied.

≈ ≈ ≈

The Bench Road on the mesa above Lighthouse Canyon was rutted and muddy from the recent rains. Kenny drove the State Parks pickup slowly and deliberately, and he and Ralph made their way to the parking area and horse corral at the Upper Lighthouse Canyon trailhead. Elmer Schmitt was already there, standing in front of a Forest Service pickup, sipping coffee from a thermos cup.

"Mornin', Elmer," Kenny said as he smiled and reached out his hand to Elmer. "You've met Ralph, haven't you? Ralph Carter, this is Elmer Schmitt."

Ralph stepped forward and shook hands with Elmer.

"We've run into each other a time or two," Ralph said. "Nice to see you again Elmer."

Kenny spread maps out on the hood of the pickup, and they discussed the site that they were going to visit. The Lighthouse Canyon Falling Man was only one pictograph in a series of several dozen rock art elements along that section of the canyon and there were associated buried archaeological deposits that were of concern as crews attempted to minimize further damage and danger resulting from the landslide.

"Those crews that we passed on the road coming up are mostly surveyors and engineers going in to look at the slide to see how big it is, whether it is stable, and whether it can be removed without causing a catastrophe downstream," Elmer said. "They will all be downstream of us, I think. We may have a lake rising below us in the canyon, but we'll be upstream of the landslide and dam. Should be okay."

"We've all been to the site, haven't we?" asked Ralph. Kenny and Elmer nodded. "Good. Unless the trail has washed out or something, we should have a pretty easy hike down. Maybe a half-hour hike, no more probably."

The three men went to their trucks, organized their gear, hoisted their rucksacks, and headed down over the rim into the canyon.

"This doesn't look too bad here," Kenny remarked as the trail emerged from a large boulder field and snaked up against the cliff face.

A small panel of petroglyphs depicting nine bighorn sheep facing up canyon, and one facing down canyon, stood out on the dark patina of the sandstone wall.

"Looks like there's been plenty of recent rain, but nothing out of the ordinary. Nothing damaging."

"Let's hope it's all like this. And that the engineers can find a way to get that dam down without wrecking everything downstream," added Elmer.

The upper portion of the site appeared to be in very good condition. The storm had caused no significant damage, and the team found no cause for alarm. Kenny and Ralph looked at each other and their faces reflected a shared concern as they rounded the cliff face just above the Falling Man panel. Ralph walked ahead of the others, and all was silent in the canyon except for the sounds of their boots on the rock-strewn path. Kenny paused to adjust his pack strap just after rounding the corner, and he looked ahead to Ralph. He and Elmer stood and watched Ralph as he neared the panel. Ralph said nothing, but he didn't need to. Kenny watched as Ralph approached the panel, looked at it for a moment, and slowly sank to his knees. He covered his face with his hands, and leaned forward, nearly touching the earth. Kenny knew what he would see. The Falling Man had been stolen. Another Watcher was gone.

When Kenny and Elmer reached Ralph, they could see that the Falling Man had been sawn from the rock art face, like the others.

"Just like the ones in Gooseberry and Skull Creek," Kenny said. "Gotta be the same person. Gotta be."

"Let's not walk around too much, since there might be some clues about who did this," Elmer said, "but I doubt we'll find much in the way of tracks or small clues since there's been so much rain, but let's be careful anyway."

Elmer, who was trained in archaeological site damage assessment and vandalism investigation, surveyed the scene, took photographs, and looked for evidence.

"There's not even any rock dust left around the cuts and underneath," Ralph said. "The rain washed everything away. Thief couldn't have asked for anything more." Looking up, he remarked, "You know, I bet whoever did this might have lowered their tools over the cliff from above. I bet they brought their gear to right above here on an ATV or something, and lowered it down. You sure couldn't haul a rock saw or whatever they're using down that path on your back."

"And back up, and haul a hundred pound slab of rock too," Kenny added.

"I'm finished here," Elmer said. "I guess we should continue down and check on the rest of the sites. When I get back to the truck I'll call this in to the Rangers. They'll want to continue the investigation, and they'll probably want to check out the top of the mesa, to see if they can find tracks or anything that will give them an idea about how the thief did this. Especially since this is the third one just like this stolen in, what, the past year?"

Ralph and Kenny nodded. The three men lifted their packs and continued their survey down the canyon toward the landslide that had dammed the creek.

≈ ≈ ≈

"This is really too much," Ralph said, hunching over his coffee in the back booth of the café. "This weird correlation between extreme weather events and damage to the falling man rock art panels. I'm not the type to believe in some kind of ancient curse or magic or anything, but this is too weird. I don't know how to think about it. Just don't know how or what to think."

He ran his fingers through his hair, pushing it back, sat up, brought his coffee to his lips, and took a sip. He looked over at Barbara, sitting beside him in the booth, and shook his head.

"I just don't know," he said.

He reached his arm over and put it around her. She snuggled closer, gave him a reassuring smile and nodded her head.

"You're not the only one, Ralph," she said. "This is affecting a lot of us. It's getting scary. It really is."

"Well Ralph, I'm not the type to believe in magic or curses either," said Kenny from across the booth. "But I've been reading a lot of the old journals and things from the pioneer times, things about the Utes, you know, and well, this has been going on for a long time. It didn't just start last summer. It's been going on for a long, long time."

Kenny thumbed through some papers in a folder he held in front of him.

"Here, listen to this. It's from an interview with Bill Baggs, one of the first pioneers to arrive in this valley. He said that the Ute Tickup—you know the one who helped the pioneers—he's in the memorial in the park?"

Ralph and Barbara nodded.

"Well, Tickup and Baggs were great pals, and Tickup showed Baggs all kinds of things around here, including the rock art. Baggs said that Tickup showed him rock art in Gooseberry of an upside down man. He said that Tickup said the one in Gooseberry was a Watcher, a Guide, and that he would help people, but he could also bring storms and lightning if people were bad. He said Tickup gave him a little antelope fetish to keep with him, to help protect him. I think it was a split twig figurine of an antelope. We have one in the museum collection at the state park. I think it is from the same site.

Maybe it's the one Tickup gave Baggs, who knows."

Kenny continued to look at the papers.

"We've known they were called Watchers and Guides. Guess I didn't know that the Utes said that they controlled the weather," Ralph said. "Still doesn't mean that they can control the weather. Doesn't make sense. The jet stream controls the weather. Storms coming from the Pacific control the weather. Not some mythical Antelope God. At least that's what I think I should think. I mean, this is three for three now. Man. Man o man."

Ralph looked at his coffee cup and shook his head.

"Oh, Christ," Kenny exclaimed. "I never noticed this before. Shit. Baggs says Tickup showed him another upside down man. A tiny pictograph with birds flying around it. Have you ever seen that one Ralph? A pictograph of an upside down man ringed by tiny birds?"

Ralph leaned forward in his seat.

"What? No, I've never seen or heard of one. Where is it? Did he say where it was?

"Um, somewhere near Tickup's Cave, I guess." Kenny said, reading. "Maybe in the cave. It isn't clear. Says the whole thing—the man and the seven birds surrounding him is about the size of his outstretched hand. Tiny. Said the man is red and the birds are green."

"No, I've never seen that figure. I'd remember seeing that. And I don't remember ever reading about one like that. There are those tiny birds over in Six Mile on that Barrier Canyon style panel, but nothing like that around here that I know of. And he says it's near Tickup's Cave?"

"Yep, says Tickup showed him a lot of rock art that first time they went to the cave. Told him about how the Ute Healers "killed" the Moki rock art figures that they were afraid of. But they didn't kill the Watchers. Oh, hell, listen to this. He says that the little figure was red and had antelope horns, just like the one in Gooseberry. Said he was called Wanzi, and he was the Antelope Guide or Watcher, and that the little one, the tiny little one, he was the main one. He was apparently the most important one. His place was the most powerful place of all."

"We've got to go look around at Tickup's Cave. I've been to that cave twenty times, and I've never seen that pictograph. Maybe it is around the corner or hidden in a crack or something. Shit, if the thief knows about this, who knows what could happen. I mean, if somebody messes with the main Watcher. Well, like I said, I'm not the type to believe in magic or curses, but let's just say, I don't want to test my beliefs by courting some huge natural disaster. We need to look for this Wanzi and protect him."

# BARBARA'S DESERT CAFE

# Chapter Eighteen

# Rapture

Turn of the Century—circa 1890 to 1910

The lightning, the rain and windstorms, the runaway horses, and the general uneasiness that came from knowing that they had disrupted something significant and powerful left Ephraim and Nephi bewildered, timid, and nervous. They had placed the antelope skull and bird foot necklace back in the niche in the back of the rock shelter, and had replaced the chinking, blocking the opening and once again sealing off the cavity. They never did find the small antelope figurine that had been in the nook with the other items when they first opened it. The frightening events following their day of removing artifacts from the shelter had subsided, but the effect of the onslaught continued. Would that be the end of it, or could the wrath of the ancients descend upon them again at any moment?

The chronic occasional dry cough Ephraim had nursed since he had worked in the dusty grain mill in Thurber as a teenager grew worse. His wife, Vesta, worried, and each evening brewed him a concoction of hot chicken broth, garlic, and red chiles steeped together until extremely spicy and pungent.

"You are a dear to care for me so," Ephraim smiled as Vesta brought him a steaming cup of the aromatic broth. "If you put one more pinch of chiles in this, though, I might burn the skin right off my tongue."

He appreciated the care Vesta was giving him, and it did seem to help somewhat with the cough, at least while he was sipping the broth and for a short time afterward, but he worried that he would never be rid of the troublesome affliction.

As the weeks passed, and their terror gradually subsided, Ephraim and Nephi decided that they should unpack the artifacts they had brought from the shelter, clean them up, and record them in the ledger Ephraim kept of all the items they had collected.

One late summer Friday afternoon, as the work of the week was winding down, Nephi came to Ephraim's store and post office, and the two men cleared off the long table used for measuring out cloth and other items, and brought the tarps and blankets that wrapped the artifacts in from the storage shed.

First, they carefully unwrapped the shield. They were struck by its size, heft, and by the intricately and finely painted designs, and especially by the striking central figure.

"I can see a lot in this light that I missed when we looked at it in the cave," Ephraim remarked as he added to the sketches and notes he had made when they had found the artifacts. "Look at this—his horns are forked. See these little hooks coming from them? I think he has antelope horns."

"Like the skull in the hole in the rock, and the little figurine, the one we lost, and the upside down feller. He has forked horns too."

Nephi nodded.

"Like he's wearing an antelope skull hat."

"Or he is part antelope," wondered Ephraim. "Or an antelope spirit. Or a god."

The friends pondered the meanings of what they had found, what they had encountered. Ephraim sketched and took notes for each of the objects they unpacked, and they marveled at the skill and workmanship represented in each artifact. As they finished with each one they carefully wrapped it in clean, new flannel cloth, and nestled them in the cedar-lined chest that had belonged to Ephraim's grandmother. As they were just about to wrap and store the last two objects, the cape and the feathered hat, Ephraim held the cape up in front of him.

"It's about my size," he observed. "I think I'll just see. Help me out."

He handed the cape to Nephi and turned around.

"Just drape it over my shoulders."

Nephi placed the cape over Ephraim's shoulders, and Ephraim drew the ends close across his chest.

"Now the hat," he said, nodding toward the feathered band.

Nephi took the artifact by the strings that came from the ends of the soft buckskin band that held the upright feathers. Stepping behind Ephraim, he pulled the cloth tight across Ephraim's forehead, and tied the ends together in back of his head.

"How's that?" he asked.

Ephraim stood still, staring straight ahead. He did not reply, and did not move.

"Eeph?" Nephi said, "Eeph, how's that?"

He walked around to face his friend. Ephraim stared straight ahead, eyes wide open and unmoving. Nephi stopped and looked at his friend. He, too, stood still, aware that something unusual was happening. The men stood there for a long time, unmoving. Slowly, Ephraim's arms raised out to his sides, then came forward and embraced Nephi's shoulders. The men looked into each other's eyes, but remained silent. As the minutes passed, a warm breeze blew through the open door of the store and ruffled the flicker feathers on Ephraim's head. The shells hanging from the feather hat tinkled, and the fibers at the edges of the cape fluttered. Ephraim relaxed, and he let go his grip on Nephi's shoulders. His hands dropped to his sides. Ephraim sighed, and turned around.

"Undo the hat, would you?" he asked Nephi.

Ephraim and Nephi moved silently as they wrapped the cape and feathered hat in flannel and placed all the artifacts together in the cedar chest. When they finished, they again looked at each other.

"I felt something," Nephi began.

He shook his head.

"Something."

Ephraim nodded.

"I've never felt anything like that. I felt as if I was being lifted up by light. I felt light, and, I, I don't know, everything looked like it was glowing. Everything was beautiful. Even you, Nephi, you looked like

"I felt as if I was going to heaven."

you were, I don't know, lit by moonlight. I don't know. I felt good. I felt like I was going to heaven."

Ephraim started to cry.

"What have we done? What are these things?"

Ephraim and Nephi knelt in the center of the store and prayed.

## Vesta's Healing Broth

For each cup of chicken broth add one crushed garlic clove and one teaspoon of crushed dried hot chiles (adjust the amount of garlic and chiles to your personal taste, but use as much as you can be comfortable drinking). Bring to a boil, remove from the stove and let steep for a few minutes. Strain into a cup and sip. Good for coughs, head colds, and runny noses.

# Chapter Nineteen

# Healing

Turn of the Century—circa 1890 to 1910

In the weeks following their unusual experience with the cape and bird feather hat, Ephraim and Nephi pondered whether to return the artifacts to where they had been found. Although they experienced no more frightening events, they had not opened the cedar chest or even looked at the artifacts since Ephraim's first experience wearing the cape and hat. One evening, Nephi and Cora were visiting with Ephraim and Vesta at their home. Vesta had prepared Brigham tea, and served it to the guests. She filled Ephraim's cup with her special broth.

"My broth must be working," she remarked. "I haven't heard you cough lately."

Ephraim and Nephi immediately exchanged a silent and knowing glance. At that moment they realized that Ephraim's cough had disappeared the day he had worn the ancient garments. At the same time, Nephi remembered that the sore on his arm that he had suffered with and nursed for months had healed. The men knew then that the artifacts—the garments in particular—had special power, the power to heal.

Some men might have seen great riches or fame in their futures. They might have sought to join a circus, or start a clinic, or to pitch themselves as saviors and prophets and healers. Ephraim and Nephi could have used their discovery to improve their lots in life, to seek fortune, to boast of great powers. But they did not. It did not cross their minds. It would not have, because they had experienced something that so profoundly moved them, it was not something that could even be communicated to another person, let alone sold or prostituted. They both knew that they had been entrusted with something, something that was not made by them, something that they did not understand, but which had been granted, or loaned to them. They knew they had narrowly escaped with their lives when they had violated something sacred, and they had felt the angry power behind the lightning and the wind. But they had also felt the positive, healing power of the garments, and they knew both of those feelings from their own faith, and they were certain that the powers in the artifacts and garments were the same powers they felt in their own familiar sacraments and rites.

Ephraim and Nephi vowed to tell no one about the great powers of the garments, even their wives and spiritual leaders. They agreed that as long as they both lived, Ephraim would take out the garments and wear them once a year, on the anniversary of their discovery. They agreed that if Nephi survived Ephraim, he would carry on the tradition.

Ephraim and Nephi made a further pact that the garments' healing powers would be reserved for rare and important special occasions and uses, times they agreed both of them would know, or receive a sign. They used them only twice, when performing healing blessings for members of the community in grave need—once when the twin babies of Cletis Baggs were burned in a fire that destroyed their home and killed their mother, and once when Nephi's own grandson's forehead was smashed in when the roof of the salt mine collapsed, sending stones flying like missiles. In both cases near-miraculous healing occurred, which Ephraim and Nephi attributed to prayer and sacred blessings that brought God's mercy, never mentioning the special and mysterious garments or the powers of the ancient peoples and spirits.

# Chapter Twenty

# Dutch Oven Beer Bacon Chicken

Present Day

"Wow, there are a lot of people here," Barbara exclaimed as Ralph steered his pickup into the camp area staked out by Kenny and Tom. "There have to be twenty camps."

"There are usually a couple hundred people at these get-togethers," Ralph replied. "There are a lot of rock art fans. People come from all over. And you never know, there are always some who come from really far away—France, Australia, all over the place. Even New Mexico," he chuckled.

Since exiting the interstate in the middle of the San Rafael Swell in central Utah and leaving paved roads behind, Ralph and Barbara had driven first on graveled roads, then on two-tracks as they headed for the gathering. They were pleased to see small paper signs with a rock art figure and an arrow placed at intersections that might be confusing to newcomers. Pulling in to the large meadow loosely referred to as Head of Sinbad, they were joining members of the American Rock Art Association for their annual summer camp out and symposium.

"Look at them, just look at them," Barbara grinned with delight. "Desert Rats, true Desert Rats!"

Clad in everything from Levis and cowboy boots to khaki shorts and jungle shirts, the people who made up the gathering seemed to have something in common that went much deeper than their choice of dress—they were uniformly tanned, rugged, and bright-eyed. The kind of people who have spent their lives out of doors hiking and exploring, and who take great pleasure and delight in discovering and seeing artistic and cultural expressions from the remote past. The kind of people who will stay up all night exchanging stories of astounding experiences they have had with ancient art and who will be up at the crack of dawn to see rock art panels in the splendid first light.

Tom Pacheco saw them pulling into the camp and waved to direct Ralph to a suitable place to park.

"Hi, Tom," Ralph called out as he exited the truck. "Nice spot you have here!"

"Sure is," Tom answered. "Course there ain't a bad spot for miles. There's a flat place for your tent over by that juniper," he said, pointing. "And we have the kitchen set up over here between my truck and Kenny's jeep. Hey Barbara!"

Tom walked to greet Barbara with a hug as she rounded the rear of the pickup.

"Did you bring your pups?"

"Just one, just Zac, the big feller," Barbara replied, opening the tailgate and putting Zac on his leash. "Iris is looking after the pack back at my place. Think I had better keep Zac leashed up until I see what the dog situation is like. Don't need any scuffles."

She clucked her cheeks and Zac, Barbara's eighty-pound red Doberman leapt from the truck and looked alertly around.

"I think he'd like to find a good sagebrush to water," Barbara said to Tom as she followed Zac back down the two track.

After setting up their tent and getting settled, Ralph and Barbara strolled around the large, undulating sage flat that was ringed by sandstone outcrops and piñon-juniper forest. Small camps, each with from one to five or six vehicles were scattered out over a quarter-mile diameter area. Near the center of the encampment was an open area that had a large sunshade suspended from poles, and a flat utility trailer set alongside as a sort of stage. As the afternoon drew on, people started gathering near the stage, and a fire was kindled in a large, stone-ringed fire pit. Ralph seemed to know most of the people he encountered, having been a member and officer of the organization for over 20 years.

At about five o'clock, a tall woman started ringing a large iron triangle, the signal to gather at the stage. People drifted in, some carrying chairs, some with picnic baskets, some with wine or beer. A few had dogs, many had cameras or binoculars around their necks, and some had photographs or drawings to add to the display boards by the stage.

"Welcome everyone, welcome rock art lovers, ARAA members. Welcome to the Head of Sinbad," a tanned gray-haired man addressed the crowd using a battery-powered bullhorn.

After a few introductions, he outlined the schedule for the evening and for the rest of the weekend. Then leaders of each of the eight field trips scheduled for the morning got up and read lists of names of people signed up for each, explained where they would meet and what to bring. Ralph was invited to the stage following the tour leaders.

"Good afternoon everyone. It is great to be here in this beautiful place with so many wonderful friends. I couldn't think of a finer place for this gathering. The rock art here at the Head of Sinbad (or Sin of Headband, as my son used to call it) is some of the most wonderful and mysterious in the world. Not that I need to tell any of you."

He looked around and smiled.

"I'll just take a few minutes to talk about something that is going on, something that I hope some of you can help us figure out. My friend Barbara Haywood here," he gestured toward Barbara, "many of you know her, and Kenny Clements and Tommy Pacheco," Ralph nodded toward his friends, "are here with me trying to figure out why someone is stealing rock art. Somebody has been sawing big panels off of cliff faces in the eastern part of the state. Not amateurish vandals like we've seen all over. Whoever's doing this has been very careful. We think they are getting the pieces off intact. And big pieces. Two by three feet, and two by four feet. That big. And they are not just taking any panel. They are taking the falling man panels. You know the ones I'm talking about, the one in Gooseberry, with the big male anthropomorph pictograph in the rock shelter. Gone. And the one over by Skull Creek—gone. The Lighthouse Canyon Falling Man—gone. We're worried that they'll steal more. These are the only upside down men figures I have seen. We've read about another one, but haven't verified it, so I'm asking you. If you know of any falling man type rock art, or if you have seen where somebody has cut and taken rock art, let me know. This scares me because it seems like it is a professional job targeting a specific kind of art. Who knows, maybe some rich dealer wants a certain kind of art. Maybe it's already out of the area. Who knows, maybe it's in a gallery in Hong Kong or Saudi Arabia or somewhere. Anyway, I'm looking forward to a great symposium and some fantastic field trips. If you have any thoughts about the falling men that are being stolen, talk to one of us. Thanks,"

The reaction to Ralph's announcement was one of general shock. The people at the gathering were some of the most dedicated rock art researchers and aficionados in the world, and the idea of someone stealing art from its original, intended location horrified them. A few people told Ralph about places where someone had tried to chip panels from the rock face, or where they had tried to make a rubber or chemical peel or mold and had failed, ruining the art, but nobody appeared to have information about figures sawn off in their entirety.

After the formal presentations were over, people returned to their camps to eat. Kenny and Tom were putting the final touches on a meal they had started earlier in the afternoon.

"Mmmmm, smells heavenly," exclaimed Barbara as she approached the kitchen area in the center of camp. "What is it boys, another Dutch Oven delight?"

"Yep, and plenty of it," said Tom, as he swept the coals from the top of a large cast iron Dutch Oven and carried it over to the plank they were using as a preparation table. When he removed the lid, revealing the bubbling savory contents, Barbara squealed.

"Oh my, oh my, that is lovely. Heavenly aroma. What is it?" she asked, leaning forward to get a closer look.

"Chicken and rice," said Tom. "Well, beer-bacon Dutch Oven chicken and rice. You've had it before, I make it pretty much every time we camp."

"Yes, I have and I love it," Barbara said, turning toward him. "But there's something different this time, something kind of sweet and exotic. Smells out of this world."

"You amaze me, Barbara," Tom said, smiling. "Can't pull anything over on a chef. I added some curry powder and a little cardamom. And a can of coconut milk toward the end. Just to change it up a little. Hope it's good."

"Oh, it will be divine, Tom. Thank you and Kenny, for making such a fantastic dinner. I'm hungry. Is it ready?'

"Dig in," Tom said. "And for dessert, Kenny made a cake."

"Dutch Oven Blueberry Seven-Up cake," said Kenny. Got the recipe from Julia Child's cookbook *Mastering the Art of Dutch Oven Campfire Cooking for Men and Boys.*"

"Ha!" said Barbara, chuckling. "Bet it's fantastic."

The four friends devoured the sumptuous feast Tom and Kenny had prepared. When they were finishing up, and tossing their paper plates in the fire, Tom rose and lit a propane lantern.

"I know it's a little obnoxious, but I'll just leave it on while we clean up the kitchen."

"Here, let me help," said Ralph, rising from his folding chair. "That was a great meal. You guys take a break."

He started washing the utensils in the warm basin of water Kenny had prepared.

"Did anybody find anything out about the rock art? Anybody know anything?"

"Not much," Kenny replied, as he leaned forward and picked cheat grass seeds out of his socks. "One woman, I think her name is Miller or something like that, said she knows of a falling man petroglyph up around Nine Mile. I told her I'd like to talk with her a little more about it tomorrow. Maybe go take a look if we can."

"Oh, I know her. Elaine Miller. She's from Price. She's good. Really knows the rock art of this area, especially Nine Mile and The Swell. I'd be interested. Wonder if she has pictures? Ooops!"

Ralph exclaimed as he dropped a mug into the dishwater and splashed himself.

After dinner, as dusk descended and the crowd congregated around the central fire, a large pony-tailed man wearing a worn and sweat-stained straw cowboy hat approached Barbara.

"So someone is stealing those upside-down figures," he began. "That one in Gooseberry, and Skull Creek, and now Lighthouse.

Awful, just awful. There are others. I've heard about them, but I can't say where they are. Just rumors mostly. Have you ever seen the sideward panel over by the mouth of the Price River?"

"No, I don't think so," replied Barbara, "but I'm not the expert with rock art. Ralph is the one to ask. He has probably seen it."

"I'm sure he has," the man said, leaning forward and extending his massive hand. "I'm Rick. Rick Rowe."

"Pleased to meet you Rick. I'm Barbara."

"Well, that panel by the Price River wasn't made sideward, it was all made on this big rock—'bout as big as a motorhome—that fell over sometime later. So all the rock art is sideways. Well, not all of it. Some was made later, after it fell. So it isn't like the ones that were stolen."

"No, it doesn't sound like it. The one in Gooseberry is on the side of a huge cliff. It couldn't have turned upside down, unless the entire world flipped!" Barbara laughed.

"No, don't think so," Rick answered. "So how do you think they got the whole panel off? Did they bring concrete sawing gear all the way up there? I mean, that stuff is heavy. I know, I used to work for a concrete outfit, and I did quite a bit of sawing—you know, to put in utilities and things without destroying a street or sidewalk. You have to saw the concrete and pull the chunks out."

"We're not sure. Maybe since you know something about it you could help us out. I don't think we know how they are doing it, other than that they are sawing around the panel and cutting in behind somehow. I don't know. I think Ralph would like to talk with you."

"Well, I'll be glad to talk to him. Glad to," Rick said.

He tipped his hat to Barbara and walked away from the fire.

Later, at their camp, Ralph and Barbara decided to sleep in the open, rather than in their tent, because of the clear, beautiful skies and the bright stars on a moonless night. As they lay in their sleeping bags looking at the stars and seeing rather frequent meteors zip through the sky, listening to the comforting sounds of Tom and Kenny singing and strumming their guitars by the fire, Barbara told Ralph about her conversation with Rick.

"Yeah, I've known him for quite a while, since we were kids, really," Ralph said. "Different sort of a guy. Drives a big four wheel drive Dodge pickup covered with camouflage with 'The Creature' painted on the side of it. That's what people call him—The Creature. Maybe because he's so huge. The truck has a big iron grate on the front like a cow catcher, and a camper on the back. Looks like something from beyond the apocalypse."

"I've seen that truck," said Barbara, rising up on one elbow. "I've seen it a couple of times. In Lost Valley. Like last week. It was parked over by the park. I remember it very well."

Barbara thought for a moment.

"Where does this Rick Rowe live? Nearby?

"No, he lives in the Salt Lake area. Magna maybe," Ralph replied. "Like I said, I've known him for long time. He grew up in Lost Valley, but moved away when we were still kids. He has always been real nice, but he is strange. I didn't know that he worked in concrete. Knows about sawing concrete. Hmmmm."

## Dutch Oven Beer Bacon Chicken

Dice some bacon and sauté in a large cast iron Dutch Oven until starting to get crisp. Add cut up chicken and brown. Stir in diced onion and garlic and let cook until soft. Add one bottle of beer. Season to taste, cover, place coals on top and bottom of Dutch Oven and cook over low heat for at least an hour or two.

You can add potatoes if you like, or some broth or water and rice in the last half hour to make it chicken and rice. A variety of seasonings such as chiles, cumin, oregano, sage, bay leaf, curry powder, cardamom, thyme, or other additions such as cream, coconut milk, and garnishes such as fresh cilantro, tarragon, or basil make nice enhancements.

## Dutch Oven Blueberry Seven-Up Cake

1 box white cake mix
2 twelve ounce packages of frozen blueberries
1 can seven up or any lemon-lime soda

Pour blueberries into a greased Dutch Oven. Sprinkle cake mix over the top. Pour seven up over cake mix. Do not stir. Cook with coals on top and bottom with medium heat for about 45 to 50 minutes. Clean up is easiest if you line the Dutch Oven with foil first. Can substitute any kind of frozen or canned berries.

# Chapter Twenty-one

# Pictures of Pictures of Pictures

Present Day

"We're working on getting our photographs digitized, but it's taking a while," Diane Hackney, the curator at the Castle Valley Museum said as she led Kenny and Ralph to the Special Collections reading room. "You can look through the catalog and let me know which boxes or photos you want and I can pull them for you."

"Thank you, Diane," Ralph said. "I knew about the archaeological and paleontological collections you had, but I didn't realize that you had such an extensive photo collection. Pretty impressive, looking through the online listings. We're here mostly to look at the Rowe Studio photos, as I told you on the phone. Especially the rock art photos."

"They are not filed by subject, unfortunately," Diane said. "They're organized by the number the studio assigned to each negative, and they are assigned consecutively by year. The studio was opened in 1910 or so, and was open through the '60s. The catalog numbers start with the year the photo was taken, and each negative has a single number, starting with one. So, for example, in 1948, the first photo of that year is number 48-1, and so on. So in 1948, there are, let's see, 6, 247 photos. Well, negatives, really. We only have prints for a small percentage of the negatives. The prints are filed by the same number, and it should be marked in pencil on the back—like this, see?"

"We know we want to start looking in the 1938 files, because the pictures we're interested in would have been taken about the same time as the ones that are published in the pamphlet put out by the county historical society in 1939—have you seen it?"

Kenny held up the small, soft covered book.

"Its title is *Indian Writings of the Eastern Utah Canyons*, by Kirk Egnar. Luckily, the pictures in it we are interested in have Rowe's imprint on them down in the corner. We're guessing he took the photographs of Tickup's Cave the year before, in 1938."

"Well, that's easy enough. I'll bring the files and boxes for 1938 and you two can see if you can find what you're looking for. I ask that you use these cotton gloves, and that you not take the negatives from their sleeves. There should be a contact print for all of the negatives, so you can look those over—I suggest using a magnifying glass or a loupe."

"We're all set," said Ralph. "We have everything we need, I think. Will it be okay if we just take a photo of the photos we find? It won't be high quality, but it will be all we need for now."

"No problem," replied Diane. "We just ask that you acknowledge where you got the photo if you publish any of them."

"Sure, of course," said Kenny. "For now, we're just interested in seeing if Rowe ever took pictures of a particular rock art figure we read about. We're really kind of exploring at this point."

After a few moments in the back, Diane brought an archival box to the special collections reading room.

"Here you go," she said. "You can get started on this one. I know there is at least one more from 1938. I'll bring it and see if there are any more."

Kenny took the lid from the box and looked inside.

"Looks like everything's organized in folders. Let's just start from the front and work back. Why don't you take one and I'll take the next, and we'll see where we wind up."

He handed a folder to Ralph, took one himself, pushed the box further back on the table, and opened his file.

"Wow," Ralph said. "This first picture just blows me away. I mean, look at this, Kenny." Ralph held up an 8" x 10" black and white photo. It depicted what appeared to be a Ute family, posed for a family portrait in front of a tipi. Two old men were seated in chairs next to two old women, and around them were what appeared to be their children and grandchildren, several of whom were dressed in fancy fringed outfits. One of the men was wearing a feathered headdress. Ralph looked at the back of the photograph. Here, check this out, it reads 'Julian and White Wing and their Families. Bear Dance. 1938.' They are all decked out for the dance. Look, one young guy has a military uniform on. He's probably home on leave. Jeez, World War II was right around the corner. I wonder if he served in the war. Wonder if he survived..."

"Ralph, remember why we're here. If we spend even five minutes with each picture, we'll be here all week."

"I know, but man, these are some amazing photos. Look at this one of all these Ute girls playing mandolins and guitars. Wow. All it says on the back is Indian School Musical Group. I'd love to hear the story about that group. Wow, a mandolin orchestra."

Kenny looked and smiled. He could have spent days looking at the pictures just in the one box they had open, but felt compelled to keep on track.

"These are really some outstanding photos. No wonder it's taking a long time to get them digitized. The workers probably get distracted, just like we are. But we really do need to make some progress here. I need to be home by six."

The two men patiently looked through two boxes of photographs, taking occasional notes, and showing each other particularly interesting pictures, but they did not find the rock art photos they were looking for. As they were about to wrap up and admit defeat, Diane emerged from the back room.

"Found one more," she announced. "It somehow wound up with the boxes from 1936. I knew there was one more."

She set the box on the table.

"Do you know Rick Rowe," she asked. "The Rowe Studio was started by his grandfather. He was in here just a few weeks ago looking at pictures from this same year—1938. Funny, eh? Anyway, here's the last box."

Kenny and Ralph looked at each other. Ralph shrugged, and they sat back down and dug into the last box of pictures. Immediately they lit up.

"Bingo," Ralph said. "Rock art!"

They worked through the photos, noting the crisp photographic work of the Rowe Studio, and also noting that the photographer had often used chalk to make some of the images a little more visible.

"Wish they hadn't done that," Ralph remarked. "Didn't know better, I guess."

"Now we're getting somewhere," Kenny announced. "Isn't this one of the figures in Tickup's cave? This snake?"

Ralph looked the photo over. He opened his own rock art book and compared it to the photos of rock art in the cave.

"Yep, it's it."

"And these are the rest of them. Here's the large anthropomorph, several shots. And here are the sheep. Oh, hell, here it is! Here's the falling man!"

Ralph stood and came over behind Kenny.

"Whoa," he said. "Look at that, an upside down man, almost exactly like the one in Gooseberry. Actually, more like the one on the shield in your collection, Kenny. And the birds around him are like the ticking around the edge of the shield. Sort of. At least it makes a kind of a border around him. Or a halo."

"Here, check this one out Ralph. It has a hand in it for scale. Amazing, this whole figure and the birds are tiny. And they must be in the cave, since the pictures are in sequence with the other photos of ones in the cave."

He continued to thumb through the photos in the folder.

"Oh wait. It's either in the cave or outside the cave. It's either the last figure he photographed in the cave, or the first outside of it. Well, at least we know it is real. And, it's either in or near Tickup's cave. All right then, we're getting somewhere. Finally. Let's take some pictures of it and we're done for now."

# Chapter Twenty-two

# Rex Jex and Clive Smythe

Turn of the Century—circa 1890 to 1910

Rex Jex was a well-known tough guy. He sometimes worked for the government, sometimes for the railroads, sometimes for cattle barons, and sometimes as an independent troublemaker. He was known in the business as a persuader. A hired gun. A leg-breaker. He acquired his reputation while still in his early twenties, when, having left his family behind in the south, he came upon a robbery in progress outside a bar in Kansas City. He calmly walked up to the armed robber, looked him in the eye, and shot him through the heart with a pistol he had concealed under his long coat. His coolness impressed the victim, who turned out to be Clarice Gapp, a cattle rancher who had just sold 3,000 steers and who was holding a large amount of cash. Gapp hired Jex on the spot to serve as his bodyguard. Jex proved to be a natural in the security business, and quickly expanded his responsibilities to include debt collection, intimidation, contract negotiation, government relations, and risk management. With his expanded role, his fees increased, and Gapp loaned Jex and his services to some of his rancher friends in the Cheyenne area, and soon Jex's name was known and feared from the prairies of Kansas to the deserts of Nevada.

Rex Jex made good money in the contract extortion business, and enjoyed spending it on the finer things in life, especially whiskey, fancy meals, fine hotels, and massages. While spending a few days luxuriating at the Star Hotel in Reno, he made friends with the hotel manager, a beak-nosed, cross-eyed New Yorker named Clive Smythe. He and Smythe became very good friends, and he convinced Smythe to travel with him, as his assistant, his business manager, butler, and traveling companion.

Jex spent his money as fast as he made it, probably owing to the recognition that any day might be his last. He and Smythe traveled throughout the west, and business was brisk. He managed to skirt the reach of the law, as he was very careful to work in the shadows, to work quickly, and to leave witnesses, if alive, terrified to testify against him. The closest he came to being caught by the law was when he was sent to Meeker, Colorado, to convince a man named Wilkins to abandon his homestead and turn it over to one of Gapp's friends who was buying up farm and ranch lands in the area where an irrigation system was being planned. Jex was in a hurry, and could not find Wilkins. He terrorized Wilkins's family for several hours before finally gunning down Wilkins's fourteen year old son Ray in front of his mother and brothers and sisters. When Wilkins returned he reported the crime, but later changed his statement and said his family had no idea who had killed the boy, out of fear that Jex would return and take vengeance on the rest of the family.

Jex and Smythe had come to Lost Valley on several occasions, never saying much about why they were there, and never causing any trouble as far as the residents could tell, but a man with his reputation brings an aura of suspicion wherever he goes, and when he showed up in the remote valley, everyone drew in their breath, looked around, and wondered if he would be visiting someone they knew.

Jex and Smythe stayed at the Lost Valley Inn when they were in the area, and while they were always pleasant and paid their bills, and even tipped, Bill and Maggie Baggs, the proprietors, were uneasy in their presence, and they feared that Jex would one day do something awful, like murder one of their friends. In addition, Jex's sullen arrogance made caring for him and serving him meals unpleasant. Still, they treated him as they did any other customer, with respect and civility.

One September evening Rex Jex and Clive Smythe were dining at the Lost Valley Inn, having arrived unexpectedly late in the afternoon expecting accommodation. Fortunately a room was available. At mealtime Mrs. Baggs rang her triangle, signaling to all that supper was served, and she cheerfully set about seating and serving her guests. Across from Jex and Smythe sat Jesus and Tomas Samaniego, owners of the Cross Arrow Sheep Company, a relatively large lamb and wool operation headquartered higher up in the valley. They were returning from Pleasant Green, having gone there to negotiate a grazing contract for summer pasture. Tickup, a Ute Indian, neighbor and friend of Mr. and Mrs. Baggs, and owner of the Tickup Cattle Company, sat at one end of the table.

As Maggie Baggs brought out the meal—vegetable soup, braised beef, boiled potatoes, fried summer squash, and cornbread—a couple of late-arriving guests entered the room. Isom Dart, a tall, handsome cowboy from Brown's Park, a favorite of all the ladies, rumored to have been the lover of Queen Ann Basset and Etta Place at the same time, was the first to step through the door, followed by his friend, the noted horseman Ned Huddleston. They were two of the very few black men in the territory. Other than Albert "Speck" Williams, who ran the Green River ferry, and the family of Green Flake, one of Brigham Young's employees, black men were uncommon in the territory. Ned closed the door behind them and he hung his hat on the deer antler rack by the door.

"Well, good evening, Isom, Ned," smiled Mrs. Baggs. "You're just in time for supper."

Rex Jex looked up from blowing on his spoonful of steaming soup, and he stopped short. His eyes seemed to burn from beneath his downturned brow. The Samaniego brothers noticed his body language and glanced at each other. Jex shifted in his chair, turned to Mrs. Baggs, and spoke in a quiet voice.

"Ma'am, it's bad enough eatin' with these Mexicans and Indians, but I ain't sharin' my table with no niggers."

The room was silent. Tickup rose slowly to his feet. His and Isom Dart's eyes met. Huddleston stopped and stood by the door, unsure of how to respond or what to do next. Mr. Baggs stood in the kitchen by the stove and moved slowly toward the side door. Maggie Baggs did not hesitate as she continued serving her guests.

"God forgive me," she mouthed, to nobody in particular.

"Well, all right then," she said.

She walked to Jex, served him a wedge of cornbread, the last, from the cast iron skillet in which it had been baked.

"Thank you, Ma'am," Jex said, keeping his eye on Dart as he reached for the bowl of butter to slather on his steaming cornbread.

Mrs. Baggs stepped back, and with a deceptively quick backhand, slammed the bottom of the 10-inch cast iron frying pan flat into the back of Jex's head.

"God forgive me," she mouthed, to nobody in particular.

For years afterwards when Bill Baggs told the story, he compared the sound of the skillet thudding into Jex's skull to that of a watermelon dropped on a rock.

Jex had no idea that the blow was coming, and he slumped forward, stopping only when his forehead smashed the cornbread to crumbs on his plate.

Clive Smythe leapt to his feet. The other men readied themselves for trouble. Jesus Samaniego later related that he had been sitting opposite Smythe, and he thought Smythe might pull his revolver and start shooting at Mrs. Baggs. He said that the only thing that came to his mind was to pick up the steaming bowl of vegetable soup, and to be ready to throw it at Smythe if needed.

"I would have thrown it at him. I would have," Jesus said.

Violence was averted when Bill Baggs reached over his head to his gun rack, took down his shotgun, and held it ready until everyone settled down.

"Take him to his room, Clive Smythe," Mrs. Baggs said. "Clean him up, and I'll be up shortly to tend to him."

# BARBARA'S DESERT CAFE

# Chapter Twenty-three

# The Cast Iron Miracle

Turn of the Century—circa 1890 to 1910

They weren't really sure how to care for Rex Jex, so they just kept him quiet and clean. His head did not appear to be badly broken, just jarred and kind of soft, so they kept him quiet and placed cool cloths on his head and warm compresses on his chest, and after a few days he began to show some signs of life.

When he began talking, it was clear that he was changed. He spoke of the beauty of the fall colors of the aspens and scrub oaks. He complimented Mother Baggs on the flavors of the broths and soups she served him, and on the outfits she wore, however simple and rustic. Despite suffering a significant and traumatic injury, Rex Jex, under the care of his faithful pal, Clive Smythe, and especially with the remarkable attention of Mother Baggs, recovered.

But he was never the same. As he was being nursed back to health, Clive and others gradually became aware that a fundamental change was taking place. Rex Jex no longer seemed consumed by advancement or compensation; he no longer appeared to be willing to do almost anything, no matter how horrific, to obtain money. Indeed, he seemed to be mostly interested in appearance and fashion. While being mostly complimentary, he was often a critic, and wondered why Clive Smythe would wear his brown pants with his blue shirt, and so forth.

"If you're going to wear the blue shirt with those pants you ought to wear your red bandanna about your neck, to complete the color balance," he said.

He began by noticing the clothes people were wearing and cataloging them and commenting on them. He pleaded with Clive to take him to the train station in Woodside, just so he could look at what people were wearing. He sketched outfits for men and women on every piece of paper he could find. He begged Mrs. Baggs to teach him to sew, and she helped him with basic stitches and techniques.

Rex looked forward to Tuesdays, when Eleanora Poultice came to give the children piano lessons. Rex and Clive would listen with rapt attention to her playing. They tried to sing along with her when she sang popular tunes, but she politely asked them not to, and volunteered to give them piano and voice lessons each week when she finished with the Baggs kids. Her lessons became one of Rex's favorite pastimes, and he practiced his singing and piano playing diligently, to his great delight, although not always to the enjoyment of others in the home. Clive seemed to enjoy the music lessons as well, and he and Rex spent many hours at the piano, singing duets and having the time of their lives.

Clive knew that Rex had spoken with some men from Vernal about tracking down Flat Nose Curry, one of the Wild Bunch, and was not sure what Rex had promised them or if money had been exchanged. He knew that Mother Baggs's hospitality would not run out any time soon, but he worried about finances, and especially about creditors.

Things began to look up when the Samaniego Brothers again stayed at the Lost Valley Inn, after having attended a woolgrowers meeting at the Brown Palace in Denver.

"Everybody is getting rich but us," Tomas complained. "These big companies buy our wool for almost nothing, then pay people at a mill slave wages to make it into cloth, then make thousands of dollars selling a suit of clothes or pants for five dollars and even more. It stinks."

"Hmmmmmmm," said Rex Jex. "That's not right. Your wool is wonderful, and you should be rewarded. We should start a business. We could make the clothing ourselves. My friend Reba in Nephi is a weaver. Maybe we can get her to make cloth from your wool. I can work on some clothing designs, and we can find some people in the community sew the clothing. Mother Baggs is a fine seamstress. Clive and I can get in touch with some of our friends in the dry goods business to sell our goods, and, well, my holy heck, I can't see anything to stand in our way."

And so began the very successful run of the Lost Valley Woolen Mills, which provided pants and overcoats, skirts, business suits, scarves, blankets, mittens, and an endless variety of related items to the region for many years to come.

Rex's specialty, and the real key to his success, was his foray into costume design for theatre companies in the region. Rex's designs had caught the eye of a couple of young actors, who wore his creations when going out on the town and to parties. The fashions proved popular within the acting and avant-garde community, and were eventually noticed by Mitt and Orrin Mudd, who were producing the operatic spectacle *Helga of the Meadows*, at the Salt Lake Opera Company. Mitt and Orrin fell in love with Jex's innovative use of color and form, and contracted with him for the entire design and production of the outfits for the show.

"Helga," became the hit of western opera houses, and eventually made its way to the most highly respected theatres of New York and Europe. Rex Jex and Clive Smythe made such a name for themselves that they left behind the site of the miraculous transformation to be closer to the business and cultural centers that were critical to their enterprise. Rex and Clive did, however, return regularly to Lost Valley. They maintained business connections with the Samaniegio Brothers, whose wool remains among the best in the region, and they loved to visit with the Baggses, stay at the Lost Valley Inn, and have a piece or two of their famous skillet cornbread.

## Cast Iron Miracle Skillet Cornbread

1 1⁄2 cup white corn meal

1⁄4 cup flour

1 1⁄2 teaspoon baking powder

1 teaspoon salt

1 tablespoon shortening or vegetable oil

1 tablespoon butter

1 1⁄2 cup buttermilk. Sweet milk will do if buttermilk is not available.

1 egg, beaten

Some people claim a tablespoon of mayonnaise added to the batter adds some magic to the recipe.

Bring oven to 425°F. Place 10 inch cast iron skillet in preheating oven. Combine dry ingredients. Add shortening or oil to preheating skillet. Swirl to coat skillet. Return skillet to oven.

Add milk and egg to dry ingredients. Stir to combine.

Add butter to hot skillet. When melted, stir melted butter and oil into batter. Add batter to skillet. Return skillet to oven and bake 20 to 25 minutes or so.

For variety, add cubed or grated cheese, chopped green onions, chopped chiles, or whatever sounds good to you to the batter. Serve with butter, and honey after dinner.

Do not hit anyone over the head with the skillet. Miracles are very rare, and generally only happen in books and stories about the olden days.

# Chapter Twenty-four

# Lost Valley Clangers



The annual Lost Valley Days Parade and Pageant was an event of great importance for the entire Lost Valley area, partly because it always brought visitors and tourists from all over the region and provided a boost to the economy, but it was also an opportunity to celebrate the valley's unique heritage and have a lot of fun doing it.

This year, Ralph Carter had the honor of portraying Clive Smythe in the parade, who acted as a sort of Grand Marshall, Drill Major, and Provocateur rolled into one. Clive Smythe had been portrayed by a long list of prominent area residents, and it was indeed an honor of sorts to be selected, although many stodgy and conservative residents looked down on the portrayal, and most would be mortified at the thought of dressing and acting in such a manner.

Ralph led the parade, dressed in a ballerina's outfit, styled somewhat conservatively, as it was intended to replicate one worn by the actual Clive Smythe in the one and only Great Parade of Statehood in 1896. Ralph, at six feet seven inches tall, was an impressive figure, much taller than the original, but striking as he strutted, danced, twirled, snarled, and gestured threateningly. He held up a large, round shield, occasionally hid behind it, and then leapt out with crazed look on his face. He aggressively snapped open and closed a pair of old-fashioned sheep shears, as though he was going to use them as a weapon. His frizzy hair stuck out madly in all directions, spilling out from slits in

Ralph led the parade dressed in a ballerina's outfit.

his iron and leather horned battle helmet, a costume element borrowed from the production *Helga of the Meadows*, staged in Salt Lake City by Mitt and Orrin Mudd of the Salt Lake Opera Company, with costume design and production by Rex Jex and Clive Smythe. The curving, pronged horns thrust upward and outward from the helmet, like those of an antelope. Around Ralph's neck hung two large silver forks, one over each pectoral, strung on a silver chain. Ralph (or Clive) was followed by the Lost Valley Marching Band, which consisted of about a dozen musicians dressed in woolen suits with long frock coats and shiny black boots. The instruments they played—banjos, accordions, and bagpipes in about equal numbers—created an unmistakable sound, sometimes eerie, sometimes rollicking, sometimes warlike and frightening. Their repertoire included Garry Owen, The Trembling Bush, Miss Mary's Pig, Up the Creek, and The Floating Island Waltz. It was never thought to be a soothing, or pretty sound, but nobody who had attended a Lost Valley Days parade ever forgot the band or its music.

The band marched backwards down the street as they played, and occasionally paused between songs, or even at prearranged times during songs, to make faces at the crowd—they would scowl, bare their teeth, stick out their tongues, and growl. This particular aspect of their performances, and the peculiar, and to most, unpleasant combination of sounds that constitute their music, is what led to their permanent banishment from both the County Pioneer Days Parade and from the Days of 47 Parade in Salt Lake City. The parade committees cited spooked livestock and frightened children as the official reasons.

Following the marching band came the Cast Iron Miracle Ladies, a group of about twenty women, clad in dresses or overalls and wearing aprons, each one swinging a black cast iron skillet in her hand. Unlike the band, the marching skillet ladies were welcome in any parade, and had marched in parades as far away as Ely, Nevada, Malad, Idaho, and Rangely, Colorado.

The skillet ladies engaged in some intricate maneuvers and highly-choreographed moves, resembling at times baton twirlers, or rhythmic dancers. They would march as a block, then split down the middle, swinging their skillets in great arcs in their outside hands, then weave back together, skillets swinging in what appeared to be dangerously close-together arcs. Skillets twirled, swung, waved, balanced, and flashed in ways that their manufacturers had never imagined. The ladies would sometimes clang their pans together, or smack them on the pavement, but always in a tasteful and well-coordinated artistic way. One of their most thrilling elements was when they arranged themselves in an oval and marched down the street, each woman facing outward, and the oval rotated in one direction while the skillets passed hand-to-hand in the opposite direction. Onlookers often squealed or poked each other in the ribs at seeing such a display. Unlike Clive Smythe and the Marching Band, the skillet ladies smiled, and appeared to be having the time of their lives.

Following the ladies was the outgoing Poet Laureate of Lost Valley, Delbert Bess, sitting in a lawn chair attached somehow to the roof of his Bess Plumbing and Heating Services truck, which was driven by his wife Letty. Boy and Girl Scouts walked along with the truck and handed out small slips of paper bearing Delbert's latest haiku commemorating Lost Valley Days and the Skillet Ladies. Bess's truck pulled a flatbed trailer, on which was set up a DJ with turntables and speakers powered by a small generator. Striding about on the trailer speaking into a microphone was the newly appointed Poet Laureate Baxter Timbimboo (aka MC BigBax), who spoke in rapid rhyme about social injustice, the tragedy of war, partying, and Indian girls' bootys.

The Poet Laureate's vehicle was followed by Mayor Iris Cain riding her Sea-Foam Green Vespa scooter, which sported a flag on a six-foot rod that said in bold letters "Don't Vote For Iris." The Lost Valley Town Council and municipal employees came next, carrying a large banner provided by the Lost Valley tourism council that read "Lose yourself in Lost Valley."

Next came a large float sponsored by the Ute Nation, which featured Miss Uinta-Ouray and her attendants sitting on a raised dais, surrounded by seated members of the tribal business committee, the heads of various tribal departments, and lots of kids, all smiling and doing the "parade wave."

The rodeo queen and her attendants were next, wearing pastel-colored cowboy hats and shiny silk blouses, riding their groomed horses on fancy, sparkly saddles. They were followed by a bunch of people dressed as mountain men, then kids on bicycles, then family groups, church floats, and various businesses promoting themselves.

A Ute drum group called Ouray Hooray filled the back of a pickup, and their pounding rhythm and high pitched calls enlivened the Powwow dancers who followed them—fancy dancers, traditional dancers, little kids, hoop dancers, and marching men and women warriors.

The parade was not a long one, and lasted about a half-hour, and nobody really remembered much of what happened after the skillet ladies, but nobody ever forgot Clive Smythe and the bizarre marching band.

The origins of the tradition of displays of anti-social, antagonistic behavior are said to go back to the time when the Territorial Governor put out a call for entries from all towns to march in a grand parade celebrating the impending admittance of the Territory to statehood. The entire Territory was to participate in a colorful and festive series of events including balls, athletic contests, demonstrations of crafts and arts, livestock and produce shows, beauty contests, artistic and musical performances, and a grand parade the length of State Street in the State Capitol. The Governor had sent letters to all municipalities and counties, requesting their participation, and he emphasized that the Statehood Celebration would be a showcase for the wonderful people of the newest State in the Union, that the Nation and the world would be watching, and that the Prophet himself, along with the Undersecretary of the Army, and the Deputy Administrator of the Department of the Interior, among other dignitaries, would be in attendance.

The citizens of Lost Valley gladly accepted, and made plans to send a delegation of prominent citizens, local beauties, the finest sheep and cattle, cases of the famous Lost Valley Gooseberry Preserves, Lost Valley Clangers, and, of course, the Lost Valley Marching Band, under the direction of Eleanora Poultice.

As preparations were well underway, with band members practicing twice a week, and jam production in high gear, DelMar Cluft returned home from a trip to the capitol to pick up a load of turkey feeders. He brought with him a copy of the New Desert News-Trumpeter, a kind of progressive, racy and often criticized newspaper from Ogden published by Japanese Democrats. Halfway down the second page, under the headline "Governor Praises Citizens," was an article detailing a speech given to the Ladies Voting League about the fine qualities of the local people, including their industriousness, high moral fiber, attendance at church services, physical vigor, regular tithing, and general good looks. What was obviously a rather gushing presentation was documented, although the reporter wrote that after the speech was delivered, in the hallway, in response to a question from a reporter about Lost Valley, the one town that did not seem to fully embody these characteristics, the Governor proclaimed that he "wished that cursed town could be removed from the state, as it was populated by layabouts, loafers, freeloaders, sheep-shearers, and girls of the night, and if he could, he would give Lost Valley to the heathens in Colorado, where it would fit in nicely."

The town leaders gathered to discuss the slanderous remarks, and were saddened and angered by the Governor's statement. They decided to act as though they had not read the article, and pretend that everything was okay. The plan to express their feelings through their parade entry was considered by many to be brilliant, as was the decision to add hot chiles to the gooseberry jam, which, ironically, backfired, as the spicy, sweet jam quickly became the most talked about food product in the region, and it remains popular over a hundred years later.

The parade ends at the city park, where the entrants and parade-watchers descend on the many booths and several stages for more performances by the Skillet Ladies, including a melodramatic reenactment of The Miracle. The Marching Band abandons its face-making and plays a more traditional concert set, although with the instrumentation, its music is nonetheless somewhat unnerving. Other bands perform throughout the day and into the evening, including Dewey and the Unusuals, Blasted Hog, Hammerstone, and Shoshone Joe and the Rockin' Red Men, whose song "My Heroes Have Always Killed Cowboys," while popular on the reservations, has been banned in Lost Valley since causing a near riot several years ago. The Lost

Valley Workers Poetry Stage features poetry recitals all day, and is one of the most well-attended events at the Pageant.

The food booths are very popular, and include roasted lamb from the Samaniego Brothers, beef from the Tickup Cattle Company, barbecued turkey legs marinated in cola and soy sauce from the Broads of Armagh, skillet cornbread, Gooseberry Chile Jam and perhaps the most popular, from a recipe that dates back to Mrs. Baggs, Lost Valley Clangers, a kind of pastry with savory fillings baked into one end, and sweet fillings baked into the other—a complete meal that can be easily eaten at a parade or pageant, or originally, packed in a bag for a worker or cowboy to take along for a meal on the trail or in the field.

## Lost Valley Clangers

The pastry: Make your favorite bread dough, or, use the following.

Place 1/4 teaspoon yeast, 2 cup bread flour, and 1 cup warm water in a bowl. Stir to combine, cover with a damp towel or plastic wrap, and leave for at least two hours, or even overnight. It will pre-ferment and give the bread lots of flavor.

Then: add 4 cup bread flour, 2 tablespoon yeast, 1 tablespoon salt, and 1 cup water to the mixture. Combine. When smooth, knead for 5 - 10 minutes. Place in an oiled bowl, cover with damp towel or plastic wrap, and let rise 45 minutes to an hour. Repeat and let rise again.

Divide dough into baseball-sized pieces. Let them rest for a few minutes, then roll each one into a long torpedo shape, then flatten. Along the center, place the fillings. Make sure the sweet and savory fillings are separated unless you want them to mix. Roll, and close the dough tightly around the fillings. Place seam down, cover and let rise. Brush the Clangers with egg wash (an egg beaten with a splash of water), sprinkle salt on the savory end and sugar on the sweet end, slash several times with a sharp blade, and bake at 420°F for about 30 minutes, until golden brown and cooked through. Let cool for a little bit before eating.

Fillings: The traditional savory fillings are strips of roast beef or ham, with cheese if desired. Other meats, cooked greens, cooked egg, mushrooms, sausage, bell peppers, chiles, and olives are popular.

The most popular sweet filling is diced apples cooked with a little brown sugar and cinnamon—not too juicy or it will leak. Other popular fillings include berries, cooked fruit, and thick jam.

### Gooseberry Chile Jam

Make Gooseberry Jam or any kind of fruit jam of your choice. Add one tablespoonful of crushed red chile flakes to each cup of jam, use more or less, depending on your own taste, and place in jars and process normally.

# Chapter Twenty-five

## *Helga of the Meadows*

Turn of the Century—circa 1890 to 1910

The opening of the grand opera *Helga of the Meadows* was only a few months off, and Rex Jex and Clive Smythe were working feverishly to finish the costumes. They had seamstresses in Lost Valley, Nephi and Grayson working full tilt on outfits for the multitudes of serfs, gods and goddesses, Viking warriors, wenches and the like, while Rex and Clive sketched and cut and sewed and modeled and organized party-like gatherings each Saturday in the Lost Valley Town Hall where they had friends and acquaintances don the various items of clothing and adornment and parade about, as Rex and Clive evaluated their designs. Some proved to be too awkward, heavy, revealing, dull, or ridiculous looking, while others delighted and charmed the reviewers, and met with the approval of the models in terms of comfort and fit.

All the while, as excitement grew for the coming extravaganza, and the producers Mitt and Orrin Mudd gave rave approvals of their work, a deep and vexing concern gnawed at the two designers. They shared a grand and detailed vision of the work as it would be presented; they could see each character down to the finest or most mundane detail. Each shoe, belt, sash, sword, blouse, helmet, and gauntlet was clear and distinct in their minds. All that remained was to realize the vision, to bring the ideas down to earth, and create the real, physical pieces that would convey their essences to the audiences, so the characters would live in vivid detail, giving life to the whole, the grand story of

Helga and the conquest of the Archipelago of Finnesburh, the land of the tyrant King of the Frisians, Finnragnar the Boneless.

The designers had problems. First, they needed to create a look for the Jutish warrior-hero Erik the Brown, also known as Hengist, from the land of Brownwater. He was an average-sized man of great intellect, a military strategist beyond compare. In battle, he was a berserker, fighting madly and without restraint, inspiring and leading his fellow warriors. With Erik leading them, the farmers and sailors avenged the slaughter of the Half-Danes at Finnesburh, drove Finnragnar from their homeland, chased him to his evil archipelago, and shredded his sadistic and oppressive capitalistic Frisian empire. In the triumphant climactic battle, Erik and his men storm Finnragnar's fortress, cleaving unto his wretched legions, culminating in a short but decisive sword battle between Erik and the evil conqueror, ending when Erik severs Finnragnar's vile head with one clean arc of his sword, and hoists it triumphantly for all the world to see.

Costuming difficulties reached their climax, as did the opera, when Erik and his men return to Brownwater, to parades, feasts, and dancing in the streets. In the town square, before a cheering throng, Erik removes his helmet and armor, and reveals to all that he is not Erik the Brown, but is indeed Helga of the Meadows, a beautiful farm girl who inexplicably disappeared during the early days of the revolt. After an initial shock, Helga is borne about on the shoulders of the crowd, and is regaled as a conquering hero/heroine, to the delight of all.

Rex and Clive struggled mightily over how to outfit the Warrior/ Virgin. A feminine warrior would not do, nor would one with no hint of tenderness, femininity or fashion. They wanted someone who would not be noticeably not-masculine, but who would also not be noticeably feminine. Androgyny was not really a consideration, although both Rex and Clive were beginning to understand it somewhat since the cast iron miracle a few years before. They were searching for a distinctive look, to set the Erik/Helga character clearly apart from the rest.

Following one of the costume showings, as a few of the models and a handful of people working with the designers hung around the Town Hall, tidying up and commenting on the designs, Clive lamented their flawed progress.

"The work is coming along nicely. Thank you all for everything you've done. It is truly marvelous. I just wish we were making progress in costuming Erik. We've been perplexed. In a quandary."

He paused and looked around, as though he had not been aware of those listening to him.

"I'm sorry," he said. "Everything's fine. The costumes are wonderful. Rex and I will come up with some designs for Erik. Don't be concerned. Thank you for all your help."

With that he sat down and motioned with a tipping motion of his hand for Rex to hand him his pocket flask.

"I could use a drink," he mouthed to Rex, nodding his head rather vigorously.

Rex and Clive sat quietly as the others tidied up, put the costumes in boxes and bags and carried them out. When everything was nearly all cleaned up, one man lingered for a moment, and approached the two designers.

"Thank you, Julian," Rex said to him. "You can go now. We'll see you on Monday."

Julian nodded. He pulled up a chair and sat down, facing Rex and Clive.

"You know, when my people need help, when we need to solve a problem, or get away from darkness, or even find a new design for a basket or something, we go to church. We sing and pray and we get help. You know, the old ones come and help us. They show us things we couldn't see. We go to church."

He started to get up to leave.

"Well, Clive and I don't go to church, Julian," Rex said. "Thank you, though, for suggesting it.

Julian sat back down.

"Not a church, like the Catholics or Mormons. Not like that at all. No god, nothing like that. No heaven or hell. Not every week, not every month. Just when we need to. We go to a special place and we fast and we take medicine and we dance and sing and pray and when it's over we know what to do. That's all it is. Not many white people know about it, but you can come if you want. My father is the leader.

He will let you in. We're having church next week. On Saturday. Out in Gooseberry."

≈ ≈ ≈

Rex and Clive had only heard rumors about the "church" the Indians had been going to recently. They sounded like revival meetings to Rex, who had heard about them from his mother, who had grown up in Georgia. Neither of the men had ever been particularly religious and they initially dismissed Julian's invitation.

"It is very nice of Julian to ask us to come to the service," Clive remarked, as they relaxed in their room at the Lost Valley Inn.

He poured steaming water from a tea kettle into Rex's cup.

"He is a really talented actor, you know. Just a natural. Never had a lesson and he's one of the best around here."

"He dances, too. At the powwows," Rex added. "He moves around a lot more than the others. I heard he learned it from the Sioux. So his father is the leader of church service. You don't get an invitation like that every day. He's trying to do us a favor. A big favor."

The men sipped their tea in silence. Eventually they looked at each other and both nodded.

"Let's go. What can it hurt? Might be interesting, even if it doesn't help us with Helga."

# Chapter Twenty-six

# Church Meeting

Turn of the Century—circa 1890 to 1910

Rex and Clive prepared for the meeting, following the few directions Julian had given them. They ate only a small breakfast that morning, and had nothing else to eat or drink all day. They bathed and washed their hair, and thought about why they were going to the meeting, which in their case was to get some insight into the character Erik/Helga of the opera so they could come up with appropriate costume designs. Julian had agreed to drive them to the meeting place, and they were waiting on the front porch of the Lost Valley Inn, their buckboard and horses ready, when he walked up.

"Shall we go?" Rex asked.

Julian nodded, and climbed onto the seat. Clive boosted Rex up onto the wagon and slid into the seat next to him. Julian clucked to the horses, urged them on with the reins, and they headed for Gooseberry Creek.

They followed the canyon bottom for quite a while until they reached an area where the canyon widened and a fairly open sage flat had been taken over by a number of Ute families—horses were tethered in the trees at the bottom of the slope, several wagons were arranged in a circle with tents and tarps flung over poles between them forming a sheltered area. Small children ran about making a racket. Dogs lay on the dusty ground under the wagons, enjoying the shade. Smoke drifted from several fires. Just beyond the wagons stood a large tipi, and a dozen or so people were gathered near its entrance, which opened to the east.

"I'll take care of the horses and the wagon in a bit. First, let's go meet my father. He's over there."

Julian gestured, pointing with his lips toward the tipi. Julian got down from the wagon, and whistled to one of the boys who was standing nearby. He handed the reins to the boy, said something to him, and looked up at Rex and Clive. With a tip of his head toward the tipi, he walked toward the small group gathered there. Rex and Clive looked at each other. Rex raised his eyebrows apprehensively, and they followed Julian.

A slender man with his hair hanging over his shoulders in two tight braids was standing with the people in front of the tipi. When Julian approached, he looked up, smiled and reached out to clasp his shoulders. Julian smiled and embraced the older man. When Rex and Clive walked up, they both turned.

"Father, these are Rex Jex and Clive Smythe, the men I have been telling you about. They are making the clothes for the play. I work for them."

"This is my father," he said, turning to face his friends. "His name is Buckskin Charlie. And this is my mother, Emma. They are the Peyote Leaders. This is their meeting."

After exchanging greetings, Buckskin Charlie and Emma entered the tipi. Rex and Clive mingled with the others in the group. They recognized several people, and knew two of them quite well. They were pleased to see Delbert Longhair, a man they knew because he was a foreman for the Samaniego Brothers, from whom they bought most of the wool used in their clothing business. They also made a point to visit with Clifford Lone Bear, the son of their friend Tickup, a healer who many said would be a famous holy man someday. Julian introduced them to his brother, White Wing, who, unlike Julian, was dressed in a traditional buckskin shirt and leggings.

As the sun set in the west and dusk began to spread across the valley, Buckskin Charlie and Emma emerged from the tipi. Everyone was silent as Charlie looked around, nodded, and stepped back into the tipi. Emma followed him, and she was then followed by men

Julian identified to Rex and Clive as participants in the ceremony—
the Chief Drummer, the Cedarman, and the Fire Chief. Everyone else
then entered the tipi, and all were silent.

When their eyes had adjusted to the dim light in the tipi, Rex and
Clive could see a small altar next to a fire. Several items lay on the
altar, including a bowl, an eagle feather fan, a gourd rattle, a bone
whistle, some sage leaves, a cloth pouch and a leather pouch. Next to
the altar, in a small basket lined with a cloth, was a bulb-like piece of
plant material.

"That's the Chief Peyote," Julian whispered.

Buckskin Charlie picked up the Chief Peyote and placed it on the
sagebrush leaves on the small altar and prayed in Ute. He then asked
everyone there to tell why they had come.

"If you have sickness, tell it to us. If you have sadness, if your
husband is mean, if you need money, speak about it, and we can make
prayers to help you. Tell your troubles and we can pray about them.
We can ask Chief Peyote to help you."

"My son has weak legs," a woman said softly. A man repeated
"trouble, trouble, trouble," over and over again. Others spoke of
illness or spiritual difficulties. Rex and Clive felt out of place, and
their quest—to solve their costuming difficulty—seemed so trivial
that they did not speak up. They looked at each other, confused. Rex
had decided to leave, and was just turning, when Julian spoke up.

"My friends need help in their work. They need to dream of other
places and times and learn about the spirit of a warrior woman."

Rex and Clive quietly thanked Julian. He had said it so much
better than they could have, Clive thought. He made something that
seemed silly a few minutes ago sound kind of important. Rex and Clive
looked at each other and nodded. They would stay and participate in
the ceremony.

Buckskin Charlie passed around a pouch of tobacco and everyone
was to make a cigarette and light it with a burning stick from the
leader's fire. Each person took four puffs and blew the smoke toward
the Chief Peyote on the altar. They then placed their cigarettes at the
base of the small altar in the center of the tipi.

"Time to pray," Julian told Rex and Clive.

Everyone was silent for a few minutes, and then Buckskin Charlie passed around sage leaves, which everyone rubbed between their hands, then over their arms and legs, and chest. When they had finished anointing themselves with sage, Emma passed around a bowl filled with bitter tea. Each person drank some, and passed it on. Buckskin Charlie then took out a pouch, took some small dried pieces of plant material into his hand, and passed the pouch.

"Take four," Julian told Rex and Clive. "Eat them. They taste pretty bad, but it will be okay."

They each chewed the bitter tasting buttons of peyote. Some people coughed and gagged; when they were finished, Buckskin Charlie took a wooden staff, the eagle feather fan, and the rattle, and accompanied by the rapid beat of a drum played by the chief drummer, began singing the Opening Song. Clive closed his eyes and was lifted up by the enchanting and powerful music. Some people began to dance a little, or shuffle their feet. Rex swayed back and forth, eyes closed.

The peyote sack was passed around several more times throughout the night, and people sang and prayed and danced. When the Midnight Water Call song was sung more tobacco was brought out and some people offered prayers with four puffs of smoke. Peyote tea and water was passed around. Praying and singing continued nonstop through the night, and when the Morning Water Call song was sung, a shrill whistle was blown four times, and more ceremonies were performed. As morning came, a ceremony with water was performed, the altar cleaned, and some food brought in. When Buckskin Charlie sang the Closing Song, all gathered for more prayers. Then the tipi was cleaned, and all the participants were free to leave. Some followed the Peyote Leader, the Chief Drummer, the Cedarman, and the Fire Chief out of the tipi. Some remained, sitting or lying on the ground, and one man retched and convulsed in the back of the tipi. Outside, a noon meal was ready, and the participants rested, and told of what they had experienced during the ceremony, and of what they had seen.

Exhausted and thoroughly drained, Rex and Clive followed Julian from the tipi and sat down in the first shade they could find, under the arching trunk of a silvery juniper. Neither man talked. They sat quietly, reflecting on what they had experienced, and were still experiencing.

When Julian brought them some roasted corn to eat and a canteen to drink from, Clive spoke.

"I saw things I have never seen before. I saw ghosts. Or spirits. They talked to me but I didn't know what they were saying. They were singing the songs with the singers in the tipi, and they were floating above us. I walked with one of them. I walked right through the tipi and up the hill. I floated up the hill, really. I floated up and up with the spirit. It lifted me, like in a whirlwind, or a tornado. It was red, bright red, and it had forked horns, like antelope horns. It took me up the hill to a cave, and it got something out of the wall of the cave and put it around my neck. A necklace, a necklace with two things hanging down from it. And it held up a big round thing. Like a shield. I didn't feel afraid, I felt like there was something running through me, or filling me up. I thought my heart would explode. I felt big and small and light and heavy all at once. And I felt as though I could see my entire life—my past and my future. I feel like that spirit was me somehow. I, I, I don't know who or what I am. That spirit changed me. It did. Chief Peyote changed me."

Clive covered his face with his hands and lay back in the duff under the juniper.

"Chief Peyote talked with you. You were talking with spirits," Julian said. "Chief Peyote took you to visit spirits. The spirits show you things. They tell you things. They showed you a cave and told you to go there. You will find something important in the cave."

"It is right up there," Clive sat up and looked toward the hill and nodded. "I never saw it before, but that's where the ghost took me. Right up there."

Rex sat on the ground shivering. Drool came from the sides of his mouth. His eyes were tiny slits.

"Rex, talk to me," Clive implored him. "Rex, are you sick? Do you need water?"

Clive held the canteen to his lips. Rex took a sip, and then looked back at Clive. He spoke, barely above a whisper.

"Remember that Wilkins kid? That one over in Meeker?"

Clive nodded.

"I killed him again last night. He cried and begged me not to shoot him and I just shot him and shot him and he didn't die and just kept crying and begging, and I could hear his mother crying and his sisters crying, and I just shot him and shot him again and again, just like I did that night in Meeker. God. Good God!"

He took another swig of the water, closed his eyes, shivered, lay back in the shade, pulled his hat down over his eyes, and wept.

# Chapter Twenty-seven

# High Wind Warning

Present Day

The radio announcer broke into the regularly scheduled noon farm report and bluegrass music hour on Lost Valley and Beyond Radio with an urgent announcement from the National Weather Service.

"A severe wind warning has been issued for parts of Carbon and Emery Counties, Utah. Winds are especially severe in the Nine Mile Canyon, Minnie Maud Canyon, and Range Creek Canyon areas. Residents are advised to take cover in structures when possible, and to avoid driving high profile vehicles."

Ralph slid his chair back from the desk and stood. He walked to the window and looked to the north. Dark clouds clustered over the Tavaputs Plateau and around the Book Cliffs. He could see them roiling and moving, as though they were being turned inside-out. They appeared to be lit from underneath, where the dark black color looked greenish, sometimes yellowish, and electric. He shook his head.

"Damn," he said. "Damn."

Ralph climbed the spiral stairs to the small deck atop his two-story mobile home to get a better look at the clouds. The sky was clear in all directions except directly above the Tavaputs Plateau and Nine Mile Canyon. He decided to call Kenny.

"Have you looked outside?" he asked Kenny, before even saying hello.

"No, what?" Kenny replied.

"It was red, bright red, and it had forked horns, like antelope horns."

"Check out the clouds over the Tavaputs," Ralph said. "Most amazing I've ever seen. They look like the clouds I saw near Denver one time just before a tornado touched down."

"Whoa," said Kenny. "I see them now. Scary."

"Yep," replied Ralph. "They just had a high wind warning come over the radio. For the Nine Mile and Range Creek area. Sounds pretty bad."

There was silence on the line for a few moments. Finally, Kenny spoke.

"Are you thinking what I'm thinking?" he asked.

"Dammit. Dammit dammit dammit," Ralph said. "I can't believe it, but I am. I get jumpy every time I see a cloud these days. I'm falling for it, aren't I? I'm falling for some old legend, some old pile of horse crap about a curse and vengeful antelope gods. Damn, Kenny, what if it is? What if another falling man has been stolen? What now? Should I start believing I'll turn into a homosexual? I mean, this weather thing can't be any more true than the homosexual thing, but here I am calling you because I see some black clouds, and I just have this awful feeling. This awful feeling in the pit of my stomach that we are going to find another falling man has been stolen. I don't even know what to think."

"Well, there's not much we can do about it at this point. Don't stress too much. Let's just wait and see. Maybe it is just regular old weather. You know, the kind that is caused by atmospheric pressure and convection and water vapor. Just regular old weather. Severe weather, just the normal kind."

"I know Kenny, I know," Ralph said. "I'm kind of making myself crazy. Tell you what I am going to do, though. I'm going to call Elaine Miller up in Price, and get her to take me out to the falling man she told me about. I'll feel a lot better if we can make sure it's okay. I'll let you know when we go."

Several days passed before they could get permission to enter Nine Mile Canyon. Two pipeline workers had been injured when the shed they had taken shelter in was torn apart by the high winds. Authorities wanted to search the area for other possible victims. In addition, the windstorm had blown trees across the road that needed to be cleared. When they were able to get permission to enter the canyon, Elaine met Kenny and Ralph at the gas station at the intersection of the main highway and the Nine Mile Canyon road.

"Morning, Elaine," Ralph said, walking up and giving her a big hug. "You remember Kenny," he said, gesturing to his friend.

"Sure do, hi Kenny," Elaine said. "Maybe I can just jump in with you, and we can leave my jeep here. Would that be okay?"

"Sure," Ralph said. "I was going to suggest that, too. We can chat on the way. Anybody need anything from the convenience store? Coffee? Need to pee?"

On their way in to the canyon Ralph and Kenny told Elaine about the strange coincidence of extreme weather and the thefts of rock art. They told her of the legends about Wanzi, the Watchers, and vengeance using storms and lightning. They told her of the stories floating around that there was a curse of homosexuality on Lost Valley that was associated with the Watchers, but which some said came from Brigham Young.

Elaine listened quietly, nodding her head, and occasionally shaking her head and turning to look out the window.

"You know," she said, after Kenny and Ralph had finished. "I've never told anyone about this. Well, other than my husband, who was there. It was just too strange, and we've not really talked about it much since."

She looked ahead down the road, took a breath, and continued.

"My husband Wayne and I were here in Nine Mile one time, years ago, and we were recording a rock art panel just below the Nuttall Ranch, up Mommy Canyon. You may know the panel, it is the one with the headless deer or sheep or whatever they are. There are about five of them, I think. Anyway, when we got there, Wayne noticed two little lines of flat rocks on the ground coming out from the cliff face, kind of outlining a little box. We thought it was a little thing some kids had made, or some new age hiker. We didn't know—still don't. Anyway, Wayne reached down and scuffed the sand away in that little area and found a split twig figurine. You know, like the ones from further south, like from Cowboy Cave? Well, this one was different. It had a horn, a pronged horn. Well, while we were sitting there looking at it and taking some pictures of it, all of a sudden it started to rain. I mean really rain, hard. And we looked down and the wash was filled up with sticks and branches and duff moving down it about three or four feet deep. Then it was just a torrent, and water started pouring off the tops of the cliffs, filling the wash, making a huge flood. We could hear boulders being washed down the canyon. There was no way we could do anything but hunker back against the cliff and wait it out. It took us five hours to get back to our truck, and by the time we got back home our kids thought we must have been killed or something. We left the figurine there. And by the time we got back to the site, maybe a month later, it was gone. The little shrine thing, the stone box, everything. Weird. We still don't know what to think about that whole thing."

Elaine shook her head.

"We still don't."

Kenny and Ralph looked at each other and shook their heads. Ralph reached over and put his hand on Elaine's shoulder. They all sat silently as they drove down the canyon toward the falling man.

≈ ≈ ≈

"Huh," Ralph exclaimed as he looked at the petroglyph Elaine pointed to. "You know, I'm feeling a little weird. Good, and kind of unbalanced, if you know what I mean. Relieved, but a little apprehensive. I guess I really thought it would have been gone. Sawed off like the others."

The three stared at the petroglyph, and Kenny took pictures.

"This one is a little different," Ralph said. "I mean, it is kind of a combination, or hybrid figure. Very interesting. If you look at it a certain way, it looks like someone with two heads and two sets of feet. Like he's both upside-down and right-side-up."

"Or two people somehow melded together. One is one way, one the other. A very interesting panel," Elaine said. "This panel has always intrigued me. And I am very glad to see that it is safe. Very glad."

"Well, maybe that weird storm was just a weird storm. Just a regular old normal weird storm," Ralph said. "I couldn't be happier, really. Still, as I say, a little unsettled, but I'll get used to it."

"Yeah, me, too," added Kenny. "And thank you Elaine. Thank you for bringing us to this very cool site. And for sharing your amazing story. It took guts to tell us that."

"Well, don't go spreading it around. Wouldn't want the word to get out that a scientist was having supernatural relations with a shrine at a rock art panel. Wouldn't want that."

# Chapter Twenty-eight

# Clive's Cavern

Turn of the Century—circa 1890 to 1910.

"It's up there. Right straight up the slope from where the Peyote Tipi was. I floated up there. Chief Peyote took me there. Or the spirit did. Whatever it was. I went there with it and it put a necklace around my neck that looked like a string with a couple of dangly things hanging from it. Right up there."

Clive pointed to the overhang at the top of the talus slope above them, at the foot of the sheer sandstone wall that rose to the mesa top.

"Help me with the horses and we'll head on up there," said Rex.

Two days after the Peyote Ceremony, Rex and Clive had ridden back up Gooseberry Canyon to the place where the ceremony had been held. All they saw was a cleared area where the wagons and fires had been, and a round cleared area with the remains of the fire where the tipi had stood. Clive could not take his eyes from the overhang above them.

"I guess we'll have to start over there and angle up on that deer trail," he said, pointing.

"It's a pretty steep slope. Too bad we can't just float up like you did last time, " said Rex. "You're right. Too steep to just go straight up. Let's go."

The men walked through the piñon and juniper trees at the toe of the slope, and headed away from the overhang until they reached the small trail that angled across the talus toward the foot of the cliff. They walked silently, pausing every now and then to catch their breaths and look around at the scenic canyon and up at the cliffs that rose above them.

"This is it. This is definitely it," Clive announced as they reached the overhang. "The apparition floated over to that wall—Oh, God look!"

Clive stopped talking and pointed to the pictograph on the back wall. He walked up to it and silently examined its every detail.

"I can't believe it. This is the spirit I saw. Just like him, with those forked horns and all. But this one is upside down. It's upside down."

Rex joined Clive in front of the pictograph.

"I've never seen one of these upside down like this. Lots of 'em all over these canyons. Remember the ones in Canyon Pintado? Just like this, but, well, right side up."

"Well, the spirit I saw was floating right about here, right where we're standing. I didn't see the painting, but I was mostly looking at the spirit. And then it floated over this way."

Clive held his hands up in front of him as he turned, indicating where the spirit had gone.

"It floated over there and got the necklace and… Look at that! Look at that Rex! There's the place in the stone wall where he got the necklace. Look—it's blocked off!"

Clive walked over to the back wall of the cavern where what appeared to be a small niche in the sandstone was chinked in by small stones.

"Should we look? Should we see what's behind these stones?" Clive asked, as he walked up to the niche and started pulling at one of the chinking stones.

"Looks like you're already doing it," Rex replied. "Besides, that's the point. The ghost showed you this place, right? I think you are supposed to open that thing up."

Clive carefully pulled the small stones from the wall, revealing an oval-shaped niche, taller than it was wide, in the back wall of the shelter.

"Look Rex. There's some bone in there. A skull I think."

He pulled the remaining stones from the opening, and reached in, pulling out a pronghorn antelope skull.

"Man, that's a big one," Rex said. "About the biggest one I've ever seen. Look at them horns. Goddam big they are."

Clive held the skull in his hands for a long time, looking it over very carefully. He then placed it down on the pile of stones he had taken from the niche and stood up straight and peered into the niche.

Clive gasped.

"It's there, just like I saw it. The necklace. It's the one the spirit put around my neck. Look at it, Rex, isn't it beautiful?"

Clive removed the fine looped cordage from the niche. From it dangled the two long lower legs of a bird, toes splayed at the ends. Clive held it up to his throat and chest, and turned to face Rex.

"It's just as I saw it, just exactly. The spirit put it around my neck. I think I am supposed to have it, don't you?"

He looked at the beautifully-made necklace and began to cry.

"I don't know what to think. How to feel. What is going on?"

He held the necklace to his chest, closed his eyes, and swayed a bit. He hummed a little of the Midnight Water Call song and Rex felt something good sweep over him. He knew that Clive's experience with the spirits had been as good as his own had been bad and he felt that good would come of this.

Clive stood silently, pondering the events of the past few days. Rex tried to not think of the horrible experience he had gone through during the peyote ceremony. Being visited by those he had killed had convinced him that his soul was black and lifeless, and that the demons that visited him could only be quieted by acts of kindness, goodness. That night, with the help of the Peyote Chief, he had vowed to the boy he had killed in Meeker—his name was Ray Wilkins—that he would never kill again, and that he would devote the rest of his life to kindness. He had also promised to himself that he would do something for the kid's family. It would not be enough, nothing would ever be enough to cleanse him of the stain of the dreadful murder he had committed—or any of the many others he had committed—but he promised himself, and had promised the Peyote Chief, that he would do what he could.

Rex was rustled from his reverie by a gust of cold air that seemed to come from nowhere. He looked around, and just beyond the pictograph of the falling man was a crack in the sandstone wall at the back of the shelter. Rex glanced over at Clive, who was still swaying and humming, and walked over to investigate.

The crack in the cliff wall was just wide enough for him to enter, and air was rushing from it. Rex walked to the crack, and seeing light reflecting inside, walked in. The floor was sandy and gently rising, and after twenty feet or so the crack widened, and was filled with boulders. Rex could not go any deeper into the crack, but he could go up, so he scrambled over the boulders, up and up, until finally he emerged through a small opening. He had reached the mesa top. Just above him rose an uplift of sandstone, upon which appeared to be stone rubble topped by a wall. Rex could see a small opening, just big enough to crawl into. Easing himself up through the opening, he found himself on a level floor, surrounded by a stone wall, with several small windows through which he could peer. Far in the distance he heard something. Clive!

Rex slid out through the entrance and leaned over to where he had emerged from below.

"Clive, Clive, can you hear me? Come into the crack and come on up. You have to see this! Come on up, it's pretty easy."

When Clive reached the top they explored the small walled-off promontory, which they agreed must be a fort or lookout of some sort. There were no artifacts on the bare sandstone floor, but the mystery of the structure right above the overhang that Clive had been led to by a spirit made their minds race. After a while they realized that the sun was starting to drop, and having a fairly long hike and ride ahead of them, they crawled back down through the crack to the overhang, and worked their way down.

As they headed down the sloping trail toward their horses, Rex and Clive contemplated what this experience meant for their work. They stopped for a minute to rest, and sat on a large, level stone.

"I think our quest was fulfilled," Clive said. "We wanted to find an answer about Erik and Helga, and I think we found it."

"Uh huh," agreed Rex. "A necklace. He—or she—will wear a necklace like that one."

"Yes, and have a forked horn hat or helmet, like the spirit, and the one in the picture. Like the skull," Clive added. "And a shield. The spirit had a shield. I see it now in my mind. Helga and Erik will be invincible—powerful, both male and female. It will be perfect."

The two friends sat in silence, gazing out over the valley.

"Look!" Rex exclaimed, pointing. "Look."

Below them in the valley, standing in the center of the small cleared spot where the Peyote Tipi had stood, was a large male antelope, and he appeared to be looking straight at them.

# BARBARA'S DESERT CAFE

# Chapter Twenty-nine

# Eleanora Poultice

Turn of the Century—circa 1890 to 1910

When Rex and Clive arrived at Jensen's General Store shortly before closing time, Eleanora Poultice, the town's music teacher and band leader, had just finished placing her purchases—some flour, lard, pinto beans, and hard candies—in a canvas bag to carry home.

"My goodness! My favorite darlings!" she exclaimed, opening her arms wide and approaching Rex and Clive, nearly swallowing the two of them in her ample embrace. "Look at you. Just look at you. Those outfits! You look so nice. Like artists, or musicians. You look so nice!"

Rex and Clive grinned and returned Eleanora's hugs.

"Thank you, Mrs. Poultice," Rex replied. "Thank you. It is so good to see you too."

"I'm so proud of you, working with the opera and all. You make us all so proud! The entire town is excited for you. And everyone is talking about opera! Who would have ever thought a bump on the outskirts of nowhere like this town would have anything to do with the opera!"

"You're so sweet," Rex crowed. "We owe so much to you! I don't think I had any idea what opera was until I met you. Why, you helped me recover from my injury more than anyone, except for Mother Baggs, of course, but your singing and piano music were a godsend for me. I can never repay you for the hours you spent singing to me and helping me to heal."

"Well, I learned from my mother and from her mother before her and back on all the way to the time of Moses that music heals. Yes, it does. Music heals bodies, and it heals souls, too."

Eleanora smiled, releasing her grip on Clive and Rex and clasping her hands in front of her.

"My goodness! My, my goodness!"

Mrs. Poultice beamed.

"We are so happy that our clothing and costumes are attracting some attention and helping people learn a little about music and culture. We owe much of that to you; all of it really," Clive said. "And you taught generations of children to sing and play the piano. Who knows how many lives you've changed," he added, smiling as he looked into Mrs. Poultice's eyes. "You've achieved considerable fame through your students, haven't you? Isn't Mrs. Arnold over at the school—isn't she one of your students?"

"She is, yes, she is," Eleanora replied. "And you know, my best student, the best student I ever had, Bernard Knotts? He's the musical director at the Thurber Academy! Why he sang the National Anthem at the opening of the Tri-State Fertilizer Conference last fall all the way over in Steamboat Springs. That's in Colorado!"

Eleanora Poultice beamed with the well-deserved pride of a teacher.

"Well, I must be getting along. Mr. Jensen told me he was expecting you, that's why I dallied before leaving, so I could get a little visit in with two of my favorite men! It really is so good to see you boys, and I am delighted that things are going well for you."

She opened her arms for a farewell embrace.

"May God bless you boys."

Mrs. Poultice dabbed a tear of love and joy from the corner of her eye, lifted her bag, and as Clive held the door for her, made her way out and down the street.

Ephraim Jensen stepped from the back room of the store, wiping his hands on a dark cloth.

"Rex, Clive," he nodded to his two guests. "Here, let me close the door so we won't be disturbed."

He closed and bolted the door, and turned to face the others.

"Let's go into the back room, he said, leading the way. "I've asked Nephi here to join us," he said, nodding toward his friend, who was standing next to a table in the center of the room.

"Nephi," Rex nodded and reached out to shake hands.

After exchanging greetings, Rex motioned to Clive.

"Go ahead, show them," he said.

Clive stepped forward and set a small leather satchel on the table. He first looked up and made eye contact with the other men, took in a breath, and untied the closure. He reached in, brought out a bundle of flannel cloth, and unrolled it on the table. Ephraim and Nephi drew their breath, glanced at each other, and back at the object in the cloth. Ephraim slowly sank, nearly to his knees, his face ashen. Breathing deeply, he took a few moments to compose himself, and gradually rose again.

"It's the necklace from the cave." He looked at Nephi, then back at Clive. "How long have you had this?"

"Oh, a few years," replied Clive. "We got it just about, well, three years ago, I guess."

He looked at Rex, who nodded.

"What about the skull. The antelope," Nephi asked. "Did you take it, too?"

"No," replied Clive, shaking his head. "I didn't think the, um, ah, well, I didn't think I was supposed to take it. We put it back in the little nook."

"But you took this necklace. Have you had bad luck? Have you seen the antelope in the canyon?" Ephraim asked.

"Yes, yes, we have seen the antelope. A big male. He watches us. But we haven't had anything bad or frightening happen, if that's what you're asking," Rex answered.

"How did you, what did you, um, how did you find this? What were you doing there?" Ephraim stammered, trying to understand the circumstances.

"Let me tell you my story," Clive began. "Then I hope you will tell me yours, because this is the most unbelievable thing that has ever happened to me, to us, and I think there is something remarkable, something significant, going on."

"Yes, yes indeed," Ephraim said, pulling up some chairs.

After putting the necklace back in the satchel, and sitting down around the table, Clive began telling his story about his and Rex's difficulty in coming up with appropriate ideas for a critical design for the opera, about being invited by Julian to the peyote church, about Buckskin Charlie and Chief Peyote.

"I have never seen so clearly as I did that night," Clive told the others. "It was as if I had just been born, and was seeing everything for the first time. In a way, I still feel like that. I am seeing things differently, as though I have never seen them before. And as I was rising, as I was awakening, I was led to the cave and to this necklace by a spirit. I don't know how else to say it. I was led there and shown the necklace, and I knew that I was being told to get it and to do something with it. I don't feel that it is mine, but I do feel that I am supposed to keep it and take care of it. I don't know for what purpose, but that is what I believe I was told."

"I feel that you are telling the truth," Ephraim responded. "I have felt that same spirit, and was told to leave the necklace. I have been given responsibility for some other special and sacred things. Let me show you."

Ephraim and Nephi brought out the shield, the cape, and the feather headdress, and told Rex and Clive of their terrifying experience in the canyon, of the intense feelings of purity and light and beauty they experienced when they handled and wore the items, and of the healing power the objects seemed to possess. They talked about the pronghorn that watched them, and the spirits in the cave. The four men, who until that evening had had almost nothing in common, talked well into the night. They talked about things of great meaning and mystery to them, things that challenged their faith, challenged their entire views of the world, things that frightened and excited them, and which drew them together. The four men felt a bond unlike they had ever felt with other humans, a bond of being chosen for some purpose yet to be revealed. When they departed the store that evening they would never again be all together in one place, and they seemed to know that, yet they felt a common strength and purpose, and left the gathering confidently.

# Chapter Thirty

# Blessing

Present Day

"Hey, Kenny," Ralph said. "Thanks for meeting me here. I ordered coffee for you."

He motioned for Kenny to sit down.

"Sure, no problem," Kenny said. "What's up?"

"You remember Rupert Perank, don't you? Barbara buys pine nuts from him and his wife Betsy. He's a holy man. Descended from Tickup and Clifford Lone Bear, the famous healer."

"Sure, I've met him. That's about all," Kenny said. "He did a blessing at the museum when we opened the new extension where we keep the human remains waiting to be repatriated."

"Yeah, that was him," Ralph said. "Anyway, Barbara was talking with him the other day and told him about all the strange things that have been going on with the rock art being stolen and the floods and winds and all that, and he said he thought we ought to be purified. He told her we had been around some evil, and we should try to protect ourselves. Have the devils pushed out of us. Cleansed. Cleansed of the badness, I guess."

"Jeez, Ralph, if you had all your badness cleansed away there wouldn't be much left."

"Well, that's for sure Kenny," Ralph laughed. "But he's talking about the kind of evil that gets inside you and causes illness, accidents, mental illness, stuff like that. It's all hocus pocus kind of stuff, but

Betsy came forward and lit the sage bundle using a burning brand from the small fire she had kindled.

Barbara really wants me to have him perform his cleansing ceremony. And I figure it won't hurt anything. And if it makes her feel a little better, then I'm all for it."

"You, Ralph, really?" Kenny shook his head. "Why don't you have Father LaPenske perform an exorcism? Or get Bishop Jensen to do a special blessing for you. Maybe he can bless the stupidity right out of you."

"Lighten up, Kenny," Ralph laughed. "You know me a little too well. I think all that supernatural stuff is bunk, sure. But I also think that prayers and rituals and things like that work through the power of suggestion. Like placebos. If you think you are receiving power like from a prayer or a pill, you'll will yourself to be stronger. You can make yourself better thinking you have help from pills or spirits or whatever. That much I do think is true. And, what can it hurt?"

"It might hurt your billfold. How much does something like that cost? Can't be cheap."

"Oh, don't worry about that Kenny. It's not that much. I'll cover it. And it will be worth every penny if it puts Barbara more at ease. All this talk about magic and curses is kind of getting to her. Maybe a blessing will help."

Barbara Haywood, Ralph Carter, and Kenny Clements stood near the entrance of Tickup's cave. They had showered, washed their hair, and worn light, loose-fitting clothes. They had not eaten since noon the day before. Rupert Perank and his wife Betsy were dressed in traditional buckskins. Rupert had a colorful woven sash over his shoulders, a leather pouch hung from his neck, and he carried a bundle of sage and other aromatic leaves and stems in his right hand. Motioning for Barbara to step forward, he nodded to her in greeting, then took her by her shoulders and faced her to the east. Betsy came forward and lit the sage bundle using a burning brand from the small fire she had kindled. Rupert took a small pinch of something from the pouch around his neck. He held his hands out from his body, palms up, and spoke in English.

"We are here to bring balance to these three good people. We are here to help them find strength against evil, to ask for the help and protection of Wanzi. We are here to keep them from being pulled into the darkness, to the place where departed spirits dwell, in the underground passage Na-gun-tu-wip. I will sing and pray for each of you. I will have you face first to the east, then to the north, the west, and to the south. Try to hear the songs I sing and let them move through you. The songs will bring you strength and balance, and the smoke will cover you with its smell and will keep the devils and *Siants* away. Now I will begin."

Rupert sang, and walked around Barbara, bringing the burning smudge bundle close to her, sometimes blowing on it to direct the smoke directly on to her face, her hair, her body. He sprinkled a powder he took from his pouch, spoke in Ute, and sang, turning her to face in the four cardinal directions, and finally finishing by handing her a small pouch, and directing her to go stand by Ralph and Kenny. He sang for a few more minutes, turned in a circle, and motioned for Kenny to come stand by him. He repeated the same ceremony for Kenny and Ralph, and when he finished, went and stood by Betsy. He smudged her, sang another song, handed her the sage bundle and had her smudge him as he sang some more. When he finished singing, he dropped the remaining stub of the sage bundle in the fire, took a breath, and turned to face the others.

"Hope the smoke didn't bother you too much. It can be awful if you breathe too much in, or get it in your eyes."

Rupert smiled.

"I've given you each a little pouch. It has some things to help bring goodness to you. Things the little devils don't like. They should help keep you safe. Safer at least."

He looked at Betsy, smiled, nodded to Ralph and the others, and walked away, back down the hill.

"I'm glad we did that," Barbara said. "It makes me feel a lot better. I know you don't think much of these kinds of beliefs, Ralph, but these storms and things have been hard to ignore. Thanks. Thanks for humoring me."

"You don't need to thank me, Barbara," Ralph said. "You're right. I'm not much for believing in stuff. But this felt right. I'm with you on how weird the storms have been. And how it's hard to keep denying that they've been happening right when something happens to the rock art. So, no, don't thank me. I need to thank you. This felt right. I feel really good right now, so it is worth it. Thank you. We'll get through this. We will. We'll get through this."

# BARBARA'S DESERT CAFE

# Chapter Thirty-one

# Poet Laureate

Present Day

"You seem awfully quiet, Del. And you were kind of squirmy back in the auditorium. Are you okay? Didn't you enjoy the poetry and music?"

Delbert Bess and his wife Letty were driving back to Lost Valley, having attended the Cowboy Poetry festival in Thurber City.

"Oh, I liked it well enough," Del replied, slowing the truck down as they passed through Wellington, a notorious speed trap. "The music was good—I really like that Old Time band. The way they played it was almost like a rock-n-roll show."

"I thought the guitar player was going to hurt himself, the way he kept bobbing his head up and down. If I did that I'd need surgery."

Letty laughed.

"More surgery, I mean."

"Best part of the program," Del added. "That banjo player was something too—she attacked it. Made sounds I never heard before."

He paused, and took a sip from the paper take-out coffee cup, and replaced it in the cup holder.

"That poetry struck me as weird though."

"What do you mean? I thought it was nice. And funny."

"Oh, it was pretty good poetry, and they were entertaining. I just thought it was all kind of a weird fantasy. All these guys dressed up in cowboy boots and hats and drawling poems about riding on the range, chasing cayuses, bucking broncs, chuck wagons, and all that. Their poems are about an imaginary made up world. It's just a fantasy. We gave up horses on our ranch years ago. Hardly anybody ranches the way they did a hundred years ago, but you'd never know it from listening to those fancy dressers. Why don't they write poems about trying to start your motorcycle on a cold morning, or pregnancy testing, or spreadsheets and grazing leases and feedlots and factory farms? They just write about some dreamy world that doesn't really exist anymore. Probably never existed."

"Well, there was that one about driving his dad's old pickup to town on a date. That was kind of modern. And funny."

"Oh, yeah, there were some pretty good poems, I'm not saying that. I liked the one about rescuing the calf on Christmas Eve. But I don't know. It just struck me as silly. Like people at a *Star Wars* convention or something. Some goofy fantasy."

"I kind of liked it, but I know what you mean," Letty replied. "I do get a kick out of some of the outfits people were wearing—I don't think I've ever seen anybody with their pants tucked into their cowboy boots like that. Except maybe in a movie or something. And silk bandannas around their necks! Did you see that man with the gray boots with stars and moons all over them? Bet they cost as much as a new truck."

"You know what it kind of reminded me of?" Del said, turning down the radio. "It kind of reminded me of those Roy Rogers TV shows when we were kids. Did you ever watch them? They had jeeps and cars and things, but they still rode horses and carried six-guns and chased rustlers and bank robbers with posses. It was like they couldn't decide whether it was modern day or olden days, so they pretended that everything was going on at once."

"Well, people do get sentimental about the past. They like to pretend that the good old days were really good and that they still exist. Just a way of making people feel good I guess."

"I'm just thinking that these fancy dancy cowboys have their own festivals so they can write poems about an imaginary world that never existed, but there are lots of other trades that actually still exist and are much more important and interesting. Like plumbing."

Letty looked at Del. A smile spread to her face.

"I can see it now—you wearing your work coveralls standing in front of a big crowd reading a poem about—oh, I don't know—frozen pipes and clogged drains. At least cowboys can write poems about horses and cowboy hats. All you have is wrenches and stinky coveralls."

"At least plumbers and other trades people—all workers, really—at least we have something real and relevant to write about. People need fresh water. And waste disposal. And houses and roads and wiring and cars that work. Stuff people can relate to. I bet of all the people in that audience tonight, every person has had to change a washer or paint a wall or unclog a drain. They can all relate to the work we do. More than they can relate to riding a horse in the snow on Christmas Eve looking to save a calf from a mountain lion. Nobody's ever done that."

≈ ≈ ≈

A leaking toilet
Terrorizes hearth and home
Rescue is my job.

Del stood behind the tall red tool chest that served as the lectern in the empty bay of Tommy Pacheco's Lost Valley Auto Repair shop. About two-dozen people sat on lawn chairs in the garage. Since being named Poet Laureate of Lost Valley several years before, Delbert Bess had organized monthly readings at Tommy's shop. In the early days, Del had written poems in the epic style, with regular rhyme and meter, and people seemed to like them, but he gradually came to prefer haiku, and for the past few years nearly all his contributions were in the form of or similar to haiku. His advertising slogan—proudly painted on the door of his work truck was in haiku:

Your faucet's leaking
And your drain is all clogged up
Del's the one for you

Del liked to try to relate his trade to people's lives through his poetry, and the simplicity of haiku brought him much delight.

Hiding 'neath the ground
Bringing life, taking the waste
Lies the plumber's world

The snake twists and turns
Clearing hair and roots and sludge
So your drain can flow

My hands are cracked, soiled
My tools have cleared your stopped drain
You pay with a groan

As Poet Laureate, Del wrote a special poem each year to be the official poem of Lost Valley Days. A couple of recent ones are:

Lost Valley's water's pure
As the mountain streams above
To bathe our babies

Lost Valley Days are
For parades and bands and fun
Skillet Ladies, too.

The readings proved very popular over the years, and many Lost Valley citizens attended and had even contributed a verse or two over the years. The "Worker Poetry" genre Del Bess had envisioned did not become that popular, although Del and the Lost Valley Worker Poetry Collective that he started won several awards over the years from the Humanities Council and the Ladies Literary Club, and the Collective had even received a grant to publish a collection of favorite poems, which they did, entitled, *Lost Lambs and Lost Souls*, after a poem by Elefar Samaniego.

One year they had the opportunity to host poet Richard Brautigan to do a workshop on Nature Poetry. They invited Brautigan because he had written the book *Trout Fishing in America*, and since Lost Valley's pioneer settlers had survived their first winter by eating trout caught in Salvation Lake, it seemed appropriate. Brautigan proved to be just a touch wacky for the poets of Lost Valley, and while they had an enjoyable and entertaining time at the workshops, they learned more about creativity than they did about poetry on that long weekend that involved a trip to the hospital, a sunken row boat, body painting, tongue-speaking, motionless dancing, and moon-howling.

Lost Valley Worker Poetry Collective readings had become energized in recent years with the inclusion of Hip Hop artists. Young people had transformed the readings, adding beats and musical accompaniment to the relatively staid traditional gatherings. Del and Ralph loved the new rhymers, and it was a revelation to them that poetry was alive and flourishing in the younger crowd, not dead like so many literary know-it-alls had proclaimed it to be.

"These kids are writing better poetry than anybody at the universities. Hip Hoppers are the new Beat Generation. They're the most relevant poets in the world these days," Del proclaimed one evening before introducing the next poet. "Baxter Timbimboo is one of the best poets I have ever heard, and I am proud to be his friend and to introduce him tonight. His rhymes are about hope, kindness, hate, discrimination, love, fear, and beauty. He writes about things that are important, and he makes them real and meaningful. I know it takes some getting used to, just to be able to hear his words, but once you get into the rhythm and hear what he has to say, you will be moved and changed. That is why, tonight, I am announcing that I am resigning my appointment as Poet Laureate of Lost Valley, and will nominate Baxter to be our new Poet. The Board members have already approved the nomination, and we'll need official approval from the Town Council, but I don't think there will be any problem. So, I take great pride in introducing the new Poet Laureate of Lost Valley, a recent graduate of Lost Valley High, my friend, Baxter Timbimboo. He goes by MC BigBax when he performs. Let's give him a hand!"

Baxter's offering "Rapture Plague" brought tears and cheers, and his poem "Beware the Watchers" stunned many in the audience when he referenced the recent thefts of rock art and told of a disaster that would destroy all of Lost Valley because someone was disturbing the ancient ones. He promised to perform it again at the Lost Valley Days Pageant later that summer.

Del thought that the wine and cheese served at cowboy poetry readings revealed the genre's insincerity, and insisted that the snacks served at the Lost Valley Workers Poetry Collective events reflect the kind of foods real workers might have as a snack, so he would bring a package of saltines, a block of Velveeta cheese, and several cans of Vienna sausages, and place them on a table for the guests, along with some cans of soda and beer and a Gott cooler of ice water. The snack became a tradition of the LVWPC, although on occasion kipper snacks, avocado, canned smoked oysters, Spam, Myrlene Webb's garlic bean spread, raw vegetables, salsa, chips, and other items found their way to the snack table.

### Saltines with Velveeta and Vienna Sausages

Open the saltines and pour them into a bowl.

Put the cheese on a board and slice some of it.

Open a few cans of the sausages. Take some sausages out and slice a few of them. Can also use Spam. Top some crackers with a slice of cheese and a sausage round.

Leave a knife so guests can make their own.

### Myrlene Webb's Garlic Bean Spread

One can white beans (or use any cooked dry beans. Pinto or Anasazi Beans work well)

Two tablespoons olive oil

One clove garlic

Crushed red chile flakes

Mash the garlic clove. Drain and rinse, then mash or puree beans. Add the garlic to beans and drizzle in olive oil while stirring. Add chile flakes and salt and pepper to taste. Serve on crackers or small pieces of bread.

# Chapter Thirty-two

# Indian Fort

Turn of the Century—circa 1890 to 1910

Following the successful production of *Helga of the Meadows* in Salt Lake City to rave critical reviews, including near fawning endorsement of the costumes and their designers, the opera was booked for engagements in San Francisco, Denver, Helena, Omaha, Chicago, and New York. Rex Jex and Clive Smythe enjoyed the attention and financial success the fame brought them. Their clothing line, sold in finer stores across the country under the Lost Valley Woolen Mills label, was without rival.

Lost Valley Woolen Mills purchased a considerable amount of wool from the Samaniego Brothers and processed it at their mill in Lost Valley, although their business soon outgrew the local supply of goods and labor. Their purchases of wool, cotton, silk, linen, leather, fur, bone, buttons, wire, paper, packaging, and other raw goods took them around the globe, and they used manufacturing facilities in many places, including England, North Carolina, Georgia, and Argentina.

They maintained a studio in Lost Valley where they employed a few designers and where they sometimes spent time working on special projects, but which they often used as an excuse to come to their rural home for some relaxation. They sometimes stayed in an apartment adjacent to their studio, but for short stays, or when they wanted to be waited on and visit with old friends, they stayed at the Lost Valley Inn.

Rex and Clive loved Lost Valley because it was where they had gotten their start as successful businessmen, but more deeply because of what they called their Two Graces. They realized, and were extremely grateful for, the two events that altered the courses of their lives, two events that were beyond explanation, and which had brought unexpected, and perhaps, as they profoundly realized, undeserved good fortune to two previously wretched characters. They knew had it not been for what they and everyone in Lost Valley called the Cast Iron Miracle, they would have remained in the business of bounty hunting, hired gunning, bone breaking, blackmailing, and out and out murdering until the law or luck or someone's brother caught up with them. As Rex had told Clive on more than one occasion, the miracle was not that it had saved the lives of his future victims, but that it had saved him, saved him from killing and hurting others, thus saving them as well. He considered himself to be the beneficiary of the miracle, and worked to make amends for his past misdeeds.

The second Grace was the visions they, especially Clive, had had during and following the Indian Church ceremony, and the leadership of Chief Peyote. They knew that the inspiration they were granted gave them the creativity to see Helga and Erik and the other characters in the opera in a new, enriched light, and that vision had carried over into all their designs. Their success had come because things outside of themselves had changed them, and knowing it, they were humble, and grateful.

One summer afternoon, following a good day of work at their design studio in Lost Valley, Clive put the finishing touches on some sketches of a new swimwear line they were working on, and remarked to Rex

"This is such a lovely afternoon, and I am so happy with our work, I feel like having a nice dinner at the Inn, getting a good night's sleep, and then going out to Gooseberry just to see the cave and the Indian Fort. Kind of get back in touch with our Two Graces again. We'll be heading for Europe in two weeks, and won't be back in Lost Valley for ages. What do you think Rexy?"

"Perfect. That'll be a perfect way to finish up our stay here. We haven't been out to Gooseberry in ages. Ages."

The following morning they drove their buckboard out of town and up the Gooseberry Creek road. As they neared the turn to Gooseberry Canyon, a large male pronghorn antelope stepped onto the road ahead of them, looked back, and trotted down the road. He turned up Gooseberry Creek, and as they neared the path up to the rock shelter, he veered off into the trees. Rex and Clive looked at each other and nodded.

Not much had changed since they last visited the canyon, and indeed it was nearly the same as when they had come here for the Indian Church meeting. The shrubs and sagebrush had returned to the clearing where the meeting had been held, and no trace of the gathering place was apparent as they stopped the wagon and unhitched the horses.

"That antelope seemed to know right where we were going," said Rex. "Just like last time. And the time before that."

"As beautiful as always," Clive remarked, looking up at the spectacular cliffs rising above them. "I can see just the top of the little rampart. It's almost straight above us," he said, shading his eyes. "If someone was in that fort and wanted to get rid of us, it would be pretty easy, just heave a rock or two at us and if they didn't hit us directly they'd sure scare the heck out of us and we'd be gone and never come back. I bet that's what they did. People would probably think they were being attacked by spirits or monsters of some kind."

"Stop talking like that," Rex said, squinting and looking up. "This place is already a little, um, spooky or something. You know what I mean."

"I'm sorry," Clive responded. "I don't sense anything but positive, spiritual, uplifting feelings here. I just got to thinking about how vulnerable we would be if somebody were up in that fort. That is all."

He looked again up at the cliffs above and at the edge of the walled off promontory.

"Let's head on up!"

Clive reached into a leather pouch he had carried from the wagon and pulled out a string, to which was attached the lower legs and feet of a bird. He straightened the doubled string, held open a large loop, and placed it over his head. He then arranged the feet so they were even and symmetrical, one on each side of his chest.

Rex watched, and nodded as Clive finished adjusting the necklace.

"It sure looks good," he said. "In a way, you look completely different when you're wearing that necklace. I don't know what it is, but it changes you. Makes you seem bigger or something. Stronger maybe. I don't know." He turned and headed up the trail.

As they approached the overhang that sheltered the site and the falling man pictograph, a sharp down gust from a building monsoon thunderhead above blew up a cloud of dust, temporarily stopping the men as they closed their eyes against the blinding, choking dust. As they entered the shelter and their eyes adjusted to the subdued light, Clive gasped.

"Look at that hole. My God, someone has dug this whole place up."

He strode forward to the edge of a large, ragged crater in the floor of the shelter.

"Look at this," he cried, gesturing to Rex. "This is where the burials were. The burials that Ephraim Jensen told us about. Where the headdress and cape and shield came from. Ephraim and Nephi put the bodies back, but someone has come back and destroyed the grave. And look—the nook where the necklace came from—it's been torn open too. And the antelope skull—it's gone! It's just awful! Awful!"

Clive and Rex circled the looters hole, looking in. Shreds of juniper bark protruded from the edges of the roughly dug pit. Clive stooped down and picked up a large, frayed piece of basketry.

"Look, they even destroyed this basket with their wretched digging," he said. "Oh my, oh my!" he exclaimed. "Look Rex, look. A baby's jaw. A little baby's jaw."

Rex squatted beside Clive.

"Yep. And there's more bones too—see there, and there."

He pointed.

"We need to fill this in," Clive said. "This is horrid."

He started pushing back dirt toward the hole with his hands. He then stood and plowed the soft, loose sediments with the side of his foot, raising a cloud of dust. Rex joined him and soon the dust was so thick they could hardly see.

"Hold on a minute, Clive," Rex said, reaching out to take his partner by the shoulders. "You'll make yourself sick. Let's let the dust die down a little."

They walked out of the shelter and into the sunlight. Rex saw something and walked toward the edge of the drop-off.

"Here's a branch we can use to push the dirt back in. You on one end and me on the other. It'll work a lot better than our feet."

When the dust had subsided a bit, the men re-entered the shelter, and using the branch as a plow, smoothed the dirt over the violated gravesite as best they could. Clive walked to the back wall and began replacing the chinking in the nook where he had found the necklace he was wearing. The pronghorn antelope skull that had been in the nook along with the necklace was no longer there.

"I feel violated," Clive said. "And I have no right to feel that way. I took something from this place too. I'm just as bad as whoever dug this big hole and opened the niche. I'm just as bad."

"Now, don't think that," Rex said, coming over and holding out a double handful of chinking stones for Clive to use. "You were led here. You were invited here. You were supposed to take that necklace. Whoever dug the hole and opened this nook was just a thief. You're not a thief. You were supposed to have that necklace."

"I wonder," Clive muttered. "I wonder."

When they finished, a cooling burst of air blasted them from the crack in the rock at the back of the shelter. They could smell the coming storm.

"Just a quick trip up to the fort, then we'll go," Clive said to Rex. "I need to see it. Just for a minute."

He turned and headed for the passageway in the back of the shelter. When they reached the top, the sky had darkened slightly. A single thunderhead blocked the sun; gusty, swirling breezes ruffled their clothing and threatened to take their hats.

"At least it's just a small storm," Rex remarked. "Won't be here for long. Probably won't even bring any rain."

Clive approached the circular entryway to the walled-off promontory. Smiling, he looked back at Rex and squirmed his way into the tower-like structure. Rex watched from below as Clive disappeared through the entry.

"Striking," Clive called out. "Striking, as always! The cliffs are just gorgeous, with the sun hitting them just so. He peered over the stone wall down toward Rex. "Come on up, Rex. It's magnificent!"

Clive gazed straight up, a radiant smile on his face.

≈ ≈ ≈

Rex would later say that the flash was so bright and the thunderclap so powerful that he did not know what had happened for several minutes. He was knocked off his feet and fell hard on the sandstone bedrock upon which he had been standing. When he regained his senses he realized that he had been struck by lightning. He slowly stood, brushed himself off, and called to Clive, telling him that he was not hurt. It was only when he did not hear from his partner that he climbed into the fort and found his friend. The lightning had struck and killed Clive instantly, and it was a horrid scene that lay before his friend. Rex said that it was odd, but the first thing he noticed was that the necklace was no longer around Clive's neck. In fact, it was gone, burned completely up. Rex held his friend's body, the closest and most wonderful friend he ever had or would have, and sat with him through the rest of the storm, leaving only when the moon rose over the plateau to get help and take care of his partner, Clive.

# Chapter Thirty-three

# LGBT Sandwiches

Present Day

"Here it comes! They're starting!" exclaimed Ralph, rising from his chair and leaning out to look up the street.

The droning whine of the vintage fire truck signaled the start of the parade.

"You could knock me over with a feather! Never thought I'd see this, right here in Lost Valley. Never, even five years ago. A Gay Pride Parade! Incredible!"

Ralph and Kenny joined an overflowing crowd of diners packing the patio of Barbara's Desert Café, eating lunch and enjoying the view of the newest cultural event to grace the streets of Lost Valley—The Lost Valley Pride Parade.

"Here comes Iris!" Kenny exclaimed. "Lookin' all Mayor-like!"

Mayor Iris Cain led the parade from her perch atop the fire truck. Dressed in a suit and a tie, most who saw her did not recognize her in the formal, and masculine attire. A banner on the side of the truck read "Lost Valley Pride—no Discrimination!"

"Iris sure is proud of Lost Valley City's new 'Fairness' ordinance," Kenny said. "Quite a feat for a twenty-one year old mayor. She makes us all proud!"

"Wonder why she decided to dress like that?" Ralph pondered. "She's not the least bit manly."

"I think it's kind of a joke," Kenny replied. "It's her brother Joe's suit. I think she's being ironic. Poking at the stereotype. Something like that."

"How's the parade, boys?" Barbara asked, stepping up to the table to check on her customers.

"Barely started," Ralph replied. "The Mayor just passed by, and the City Council float is just about here. Nothing too outrageous yet."

"These sandwiches are great," Kenny said, wiping his mouth with a napkin. "Really, really good. I'd eat them all the time if they were on the menu!"

"Thanks, Kenny," Barbara replied. "I made them up especially for the parade, and I agree with you, they're tasty. Everybody seems to be enjoying them."

She adjusted the angle of the umbrella above Ralph and Kenny's table.

"What's next?" she asked, looking out into the street.

A group of men, eight abreast, in eight rows, marched down the center of the street, all wearing matching chartreuse sweaters and white stocking caps. In advance of them pranced two ponies ridden by young women in sweaters and caps identical to the men's. Hanging from poles they held upright with the ends seated in their inside stirrups was a brightly-colored banner proclaiming the group as the Central Utah Men's Knitting Society.

"Those poles look like giant knitting needles," Kenny shouted over the cheers of the appreciative crowd.

The knitters split into two lines, and began weaving in and out, each marcher waving a bright yellow and orange knit scarf. They moved rhythmically and artistically counting time to the almost tribal beat of congas played by two knitwear-adorned drumming marchers.

On the heels of the marching knitters came a troupe of a dozen unicyclists, all juggling tennis balls, circling around a central rider atop a six-foot tall chain-driven unicycle. Each unicyclist wore a shirt emblazoned "Unisaurs from Dinosaur," referencing a well-known club of off-road unicyclists that had been riding the backroads of northwestern Colorado for nearly fifty years.

"Uh, oh, this looks pretty wild," Ralph said as the next group came into view. "I guess she's supposed to be Clive Smythe, and the rest of them are the skillet ladies! I love it!"

Leading a chaotic group down the center of the street was a woman in outrageously high platform boots, mesh stockings, black leather mini skirt, a leather corset with two prominent shiny metal tridents protruding from above large and substantially-exposed breasts, a shield in one hand and a whip in the other, and wearing a hat that looked like a leather aviator's hat complete with goggles, and, of course, antelope horns. "Clive" danced provocatively, stuck out her very long tongue, cracked the whip, and blew kisses to the crowd.

"Looks just like you, Ralph!" Kenny laughed.

Following immediately behind was a motley horde of leather-clad men and women, mostly wearing bikinis or tight shorts and not much else, each carrying a turkey baster in one hand and a martini glass in the other. They danced in unison, and used the basters to take pretend liquid from the martini glasses and drop it into their or their neighbor's mouth.

"I have no idea what they are supposed to be doing," Ralph said to Kenny. "But they are good at it. Pretty entertaining."

A semi-tractor pulling a flatbed trailer was next, blaring loud dance music. Dancers on the bed humped and thrust to the deafening beat. A banner along the side of the truck read "Little Peter's Halfway Inn Bar and Disco, Thurber City."

Several groups of marchers and assorted floats from supporting groups followed, including a contingent from the Universalist Society, and a fairly large group of Girl and Boy Scouts. A tall, long-haired slender blonde man in minidress and extremely high heels passed out free necklaces with two plastic forks hanging from a piece of twine.

"He calls himself 'Princess Helga,'" Barbara squealed. "Those are necklaces just like the ones on the statue in the park!"

Bringing up the rear of the parade was a float of sorts built on a large utility trailer. In the center of the float was a tall tower. A young man dressed in robes held in his hands what appeared to be two glowing rocks. Signs proclaiming the evils of homosexuality were posted on the sides of the float. Biblical quotes and random proclamations on poster boards carried by a dozen marchers denounced everything from sodomy to same sex marriage. LaVar Jensen stood in the front of the float and spoke into a bullhorn, trying to exhort the audience, but every time he spoke, a loud horn blasted, drowning out his words.

"Holy shit, you won't believe this! Barbara come over here and get a look at this," Ralph exclaimed, running over and taking Barbara's arm to bring her to where she could see. "It's the same Tower of Babel float from the Lost Valley Days parade, turned into a rolling hate-mobile."

Just behind the Tower of Babel float, its large cattle-catcher style bumper nearly touching the trailer, was a huge four-wheel drive pickup truck, painted in a tan and black camouflage pattern. Stenciled on the side of the truck in bold letters was "The Creature." Each time LaVar Jensen tried to speak, the driver of the truck honked his extremely loud horn. His actions clearly upset Jensen and his followers, who turned and yelled at the driver of the truck.

The driver did not seem to mind. He grinned and waved, enjoying every minute of the parade and his role as spoiler. His truck, battered cowboy hat, and general demeanor might have seemed out of place to some, but his actions and attitude made his entry a crowd favorite.

"I can't believe it!" Barbara exclaimed. "It's Rick Rowe—the guy I met at the rock art symposium. What's he doing here?"

"Oh, he's here pretty often these days," said Tommy. "He owns the old Rowe's Studio storefront on Main Street, and a piece of property over near the salt mine. He's been fixing up the old store, and I think he's been getting big stone slabs off his property for some reason. I replaced the transmission in his truck last week. That's some truck, believe me."

"Did he buy the property recently?" asked Ralph.

"I don't think so," replied Tommy. "He said he inherited it from his dad a long time ago. Said his dad was mayor of Lost Valley when Rick was a little kid. Something happened and they moved away.

"That's right, I had nearly forgotten. He's Jack Rowe's kid. Holy cow," Ralph said. "Yep, something happened all right. His dad was accused of being a communist or something and was fired."

Ralph scratched his chin and shook his head.

"Rick Rowe returning to Lost Valley. And he sure isn't making a good impression on Bishop Jensen!"

## LGBT Sandwiches
(Lettuce, Guacamole, Bacon, and Tomato Sandwiches)

Make a bacon, lettuce and tomato sandwich, using guacamole to garnish one slice of toast, and basil mayonnaise (stir finely-chopped basil into mayonnaise) on the other.

# BARBARA'S DESERT CAFE

# Chapter Thirty-four

# Rowe's Studio

Present Day

"Holy shit, Ralph. You won't believe this," Kenny hollered into the phone. "You won't believe it. The Gooseberry Falling Man pictograph. It's right here in town."

"What? Where? Slow down. What?" Ralph yammered. "The stolen pictograph? Where?"

"Meet me at the café," Kenny hollered. "Meet me at Barbara's. I'll be there in ten minutes."

Kenny was sitting on a stool at the counter turning nervously in half-circles when Ralph walked in. Kenny picked up his coffee, gulped down the last of it, and bolted toward Ralph and the still-half open door.

"Come on," he said, grabbing Ralph by the arm. "Come on."

"Where are we going?" Ralph asked, hurrying along with Kenny down the steps to the sidewalk, and up the sidewalk toward the center of town.

"It's here, in town?" Ralph asked.

"You won't believe it," Kenny answered, turning to face Ralph as he hurried down the street. "I about shit. I really did."

The two men hustled down the street past Pacheco's Lost Valley Automotive. Ralph left the sidewalk and hurried toward the door.

"Tommy will want to see. I'm going to get Tommy."

A minute later Tommy and Ralph emerged from the front door

"It's the Gooseberry upside-down man."

of Tommy's shop. Tommy wiped his hands on a red shop cloth, and hurried to keep up with Ralph.

"I guess there's no need to hurry," Kenny said. "It's probably not going anywhere. Come on."

The three men walked to the middle of the next block and Kenny stopped in front of a vacant storefront. He gestured toward the large display window that faced the street. Rowe's Studio had been closed for many years, but recently Rick Rowe, the son of the previous owner, had been working on the place. The men were surprised to see that the window had been cleaned, and the old motors and appliances that had littered the store front had been removed.

"Look in," said Kenny. "Just look right in."

He stepped toward the window and cupped his hands beside his face to cut the glare. Ralph and Tommy did the same.

"See it, right there, leaning up against the wall, next to those boxes? See it?"

"Damn," Ralph muttered. "Jeez, Kenny, what the hell. It is. It's the Gooseberry upside-down man. Man oh man. How did it get here?"

Ralph backed away from the window and looked at the padlocked door. "This place was a photographic studio for years, but closed when I was a kid. Calvin Rubow ran an electrician business out of the building, but he retired from the electrical business. What's that been, five years?" He paced down the sidewalk, looking the building over. "I know that Rick's been cleaning it up. It looks better than it has in years, but jeez."

He let out his breath in an audible huff, put his hands on his hips, and stared into the window.

"Yeah, Rick's been working on the place," Tommy said. "He owns the building and has been fixing it up. You guys know him? The big guy with the 'Creature' truck?"

Ralph and Kenny turned to face Tommy.

"The guy that was in the parade honking at Bishop Jensen? That guy?" asked Kenny. "He's the rock art thief?"

"Looks like it," Ralph muttered. "I can't believe that Rick Rowe's the rock art thief. Barbara kind of suspected him, but, jeez, Rick Rowe? What in the world is he doing?"

"He's been coming down and working on the place for a few months. He's planning to move to Lost Valley and open a business here. I know he's got some property and he's been hauling big slabs of sandstone around in his truck, but I never made the connection to rock art. He brings his vehicles to my shop. I've been working on his truck," Tommy said. "His dad owned this building and now it's his. He used to live here in Lost Valley when he was a kid and now he's moving back."

"This is taking a while to sink in," Ralph said, pacing. "Rick Rowe. Rowe's Studio. Jack Rowe was his father, and he was the Mayor of Lost Valley, too, a long time ago. I've known these people all my life. I never would have suspected Rick. Never."

Ralph paced around in circles on the sidewalk. Kenny and Tommy looked at each other and shook their heads. Kenny walked back up to the window and looked in.

"Looks like there's more rock art in there too. And some baskets. Jesus, the back of this place is full of loot."

He turned to face Tommy and Ralph.

"We need to report this. We need to call the sheriff. And maybe the Feds. This is some serious stuff."

# Chapter Thirty-five

# Search Warrant

Present Day

"I think we ought to call the sheriff right now. What good does talking about it do?" Kenny asked, sliding into a booth at Barbara's.

"I just want to take a minute or two to think about a strategy, that's all," said Ralph as he signaled to Iris to bring coffee. "I mean, you're right, we need to report it, and I want to see the bastard busted, but what do we say to the sheriff? Should we tell the Feds first? Isn't it on Bureau of Land Management land? Shouldn't we tell what's his name?"

"Garth, Garth Smith," Tommy answered. "He's the Area Archaeologist. He'd probably need to call in his law enforcement people."

"What if Rowe found out about the bust and ran? What if he headed for Mexico or someplace?" Ralph asked.

"Who cares?" Kenny replied. "Who gives a flying shit? The cops'll get him, one way or the other. We know that a crime has been committed and we need to report it. I saw the rock art first and I think I should call the sheriff. He can call the BLM if he needs to. I'm calling."

Kenny pulled out his phone and started dialing.

"Don't bother," said Tommy. "Here's Erny. You've got great timing, Kenny. You're about to dial the sheriff and Deputy Taylor walks in."

He slid out of the booth, stood, and walked to the front of the cafe.

"Hey, Erny," he said to the deputy. "Got a minute? We have something we need to talk over with you. Something to report."

"All right then," Deputy Taylor replied. "Iris, I'll be sitting with Tommy and the boys. Could you bring my coffee over to the booth?"

Iris nodded and smiled.

"Thanks," the deputy said, following Tommy.

"You boys look pretty serious this morning," Deputy Taylor said, sliding into the booth next to Ralph. "What can I do for you?"

Iris slid his coffee in front of him. Erny reached for the sugar and emptied two packets into his cup. He stirred his coffee with a spoon and looked up at Kenny, then at Tommy.

"Well?"

Ralph turned to face the deputy.

"Remember when I reported the that some Indian rock art had been sawn off a panel over in Gooseberry? Last Spring?"

Deputy Taylor nodded.

"And then another one too, right? One in Skull Creek?"

"Yep, those, and one more from up in Lighthouse Canyon, up on the Forest. Three of them now. Well, we've spotted at least one of the stolen paintings. Kenny saw the Gooseberry one, along with some other artifacts and things. They're just about a block away. In the old Rowe building."

"You mean the one that guy's been fixing up, that 'Creature' guy?"

"That's the one. Looks like the piece that got cut off the panel is there in the rear part of the storefront. And some other things too—some baskets, maybe some pots, and more rock art. Looks like a lot of loot."

"Okay then, we'll want to go over and take a look. If you'll let me finish my coffee, we can go over and you can show me what you saw. Is anybody there? Is the building open?"

"Don't think so," Ralph said. "We didn't see anyone."

"Rick, the guy who owns it, lives up in Salt Lake, and he only comes down on weekends," said Tommy. "Sometimes on Fridays, but mostly weekends. He just left Monday—yesterday. He stopped in for gas yesterday morning. Said he was heading to Salt Lake. I think he said he'd be back next weekend."

"How did you guys see the stuff—is it right there in plain sight?" Erny asked.

"Well, kinda. It's towards the back of the store," Kenny replied. "I was looking in the big front window just to see what was going on in there. It's been vacant for so long, I was just curious."

"Well, he's not that smart of a criminal if he leaves his loot out in the open," Erny said, scooting out of the booth. "Let's just head over there and you can show me what you saw."

The men paid their bills and headed for the door.

"Did I hear right?" Iris asked Ralph. "You might have found the stolen rock art?"

"Looks like it," Ralph said. "Just down the street."

He raised his eyebrows, shrugged a little, and headed out the door after the others.

Erny pulled his patrol car in front of Rowe's Studio just as the others walked up. He stood next to Kenny and gazed through the plate glass window.

"See that thing leaning against the wall, over there to the left?" Kenny asked. "The tall thing? See the drawing on it? It's a slab of sandstone with the upside down rock art man on it. He sawed it right off the cliff face. I bet he's trying to sell it to some rich art collector or something."

"I see it," Deputy Taylor said. "And a bunch of other stuff too. Boxes and things, but there are other stone slabs with drawings on them, and some bowls, and maybe some baskets too. You think all that stuff is stolen too?"

"No way to know without getting a closer look," Ralph said. "But if a guy's stolen one rock art figure, I'd bet he's done it more than once. And dug some graves to find pots and baskets too."

"I'll need to get a warrant," Erny said. "Why don't you guys come with me down to the courthouse and we can get this all taken care of, and we'll come back and take a look at what's all in there."

He took out a notebook, wrote few things down, and got into his car.

"Pile in," he said.

Ralph and Kenny slid into the back door, but Tommy stayed on the sidewalk.

"I need to head back to the shop. Ralph and Kenny are the experts. You don't need me. I'll see you all later."

He pushed the door closed and headed back down the street toward his garage.

≈ ≈ ≈

"Okay then," Deputy Taylor said. "Looks like the easiest thing will be to cut this lock off the back garage door and enter that way. What do you think?"

The others nodded their heads in agreement. Taylor stepped forward, bent over, opened the handles of the bolt cutters he was carrying, put the jaws on the lock, and cut it off. He removed the lock from the door, opened the hasp, and raised the door. Deputy Taylor, Ralph, and Kenny stared into the open space in front of them, waiting for their eyes to adjust. Deputy Taylor stepped in and flipped on the light.

"Holy crap, there's a lot of stuff here," Kenny said. "Look at all the rock art. And these bowls—they're perfect!"

Ralph walked in and glanced around at the dozens of ceramic bowls, baskets, and stone slabs. He went to the large slab that was leaning against the wall and began examining it. He turned it to get better light and asked Deputy Taylor if he would shine his flashlight on the figure.

"That's it," Kenny said. "That's the one that we could see from the front. "It's the falling man. The falling man from Gooseberry Creek."

"Hmmmm," Ralph said, bending close to examine the sandstone slab.

He took the heavy stone piece in his hands and turned it, looking at the sides and back. He shook his head and looked up at Kenny and Erny.

"Jeez," he said.

He looked down at the slab he was holding.

"See this paint? See how fresh it is? See how I can rub it off with my finger? Man, have we screwed up. Shit."

"What," Kenny asked. "What?"

Ralph looked up at Kenny, then over to Deputy Taylor.

"It's the Gooseberry Creek Falling Man, all right. But it's not real. It's not stolen. It's a reproduction. I'll bet these are all reproductions. We've just broken into a legitimate business. Jesus."

Ralph sat down in a folding chair in the center of the garage and ran his fingers through his hair.

"This makes me feel better and worse at the same time. Creature is not a criminal. That's a relief. But we were ready to accuse him of being one. And we reported him to the cops and broke into his business. Shit."

# BARBARA'S DESERT CAFE

# Chapter Thirty-six

# Zucchini Casserole

Present Day

"That's funny," LaVar Jensen said to his wife Janell as he tried the door to his car after their usual Wednesday evening dinner at the cafe. "It's locked. I don't think I locked it. Did you lock it?"

"I don't think so," Janell replied. "I only lock the car when I go to Provo, or Salt Lake. And even then I forget half the time."

"Well, I guess one of us must have bumped the lock button when we got out," LaVar said, unlocking the car.

"What's that smell?" LaVar said as he eased into his seat, sniffing. "What is that?"

"Zucchini," Janell answered, leaning over and looking into the back seat. "Somebody left us a whole grocery bag of zucchini."

"Well, that's one reason to lock your car around here. It's a good thing we didn't plant any this year. You didn't tell anybody, did you? That we didn't plant any in our garden this year. That's a sure way to get zucchini bombed. I'm just glad nobody left a banjo in with the zucchini."

LaVar chuckled at his joke.

"No, that's not the sort of information I'd spread around," Janell said. "It'll be okay. We can always do something with extra zucchini. It won't go to waste. I'll make a zucchini casserole. I'll make two and take one over to Mrs. Bigelow. She'd appreciate it."

"I love your zucchini casseroles, Janell. They are one of my favorite summer food groups, along with tomato sandwiches and fresh sweet corn. We sure do eat well in the summer. I don't know what I'd do if I couldn't grow a vegetable garden. I guess it's in my blood. Our blood."

Jensen looked over at his wife and smiled as he put the car in gear.

"It sure is different these days, with just the two of us for most meals," Janell said. "And in less than a month, Alma will be in a dorm up at BYU and we'll be all alone. Empty nesters. Used to be, when all the kids were at home, I could have used that whole sack of zucchini plus a pile of tomatoes and onions for just one meal. Now I'll have to be pretty creative just to use that much zucchini. We'll be having broiled zucchini, baked zucchini, zucchini bread, zucchini brownies, zucchini omelets...."

"Zucchini scampi, zucchini gumbo, fried zucchini, zucchini burgers," continued LaVar, doing his best Forrest Gump impression.

They both laughed as LaVar turned the car down Main Street toward their home.

"I hope Alma does better at college than he did in high school," LaVar said.

"What do you mean," asked Janell. "He did just fine in school. What do you mean, LaVar?"

"Well, socially, I guess. The other kids always had dates and friends and sports and things like that. Alma just has a few weird friends. What about that one kid who wears black all the time. Weird. I just hope he meets some better kids at BYU, that's all."

"LaVar, you must know why Alma is different, don't you?" asked Janell. "I know you probably don't want to think about it or deal with it, but you know. You know why Alma is different."

"I know what you are getting at and I disagree," LaVar said, turning the car down their street. "If you are saying that he is homosexual, I don't believe you. I think he is just shy. And confused. He just needs to meet a nice girl. A girl who will pay some attention to him. Then he'll come out of his shell. Then he'll be okay."

"It's not a shell he needs to come out of," said Janell. "He knows who he is. He's known for a long time, since at least eighth grade. And so have I. He is gay, LaVar, and there is nothing wrong with him. He is a wonderful boy, just as wonderful as our other children. I love him and I know you do too, and we just need to accept him as he is."

Janell opened her car door and stepped out of the car.

"I disagree. You know how I feel about homosexuality. It is a disease. A disease caused by Satan. Satan gets in people and makes them do things that are sinful and evil, and they lure others in, draw them in. It is a curse on the earth, and especially on this valley. I think even my own great grandfather, Ephraim Jensen, may have been affected. And he was a very strong and spiritual man. It is a disease—a spiritual disease, but people can be cured of the sickness. If Alma thinks he is a homosexual, there are people who can help him. I know there is a clinic in St. George where they cure homosexuals. Turn them into normal people. We could send Alma there. I think we should."

"We are not sending Alma to some scam of a clinic. I have been reading a lot about homosexuality, LaVar, and it is not a disease, it is part of who he is. He can't be turned into a heterosexual by therapy any more than you could be turned into a homosexual. It just doesn't work. It's in the wiring. It's in the genes. Love him just the way he is, LaVar. He's your son. He is a wonderful son. Don't treat him like there's something wrong with him –there's not. He is a fine kid."

Janell closed the door and walked up the sidewalk toward the front door. As LaVar got out of the car, she turned to face him.

"You've already hurt him by being so cold toward him. You've treated him differently since he was a young kid. You've hated his tender side, and you've hurt him LaVar. You've hurt him deeply. If he needs therapy it is because of you. It's time you started being his father instead of his bishop. I mean it."

Janell turned and went into the house.

LaVar looked around to see if any of the neighbors had been listening. He opened the back door of the car, got the grocery sack of zucchini, and followed his wife into their home.

## Zucchini Casserole

In a buttered casserole dish, alternate layers of sliced zucchini, tomato and onion. Salt and pepper each layer, sprinkle with grated cheese, and repeat until casserole dish is full. Some people like to put a few spoonfuls of canned cream of mushroom soup on each layer. Bake at 350°F covered for about an hour, then remove the cover and bake for another 15 – 30 minutes, until the top is brown. Let cool slightly before serving.

# Chapter Thirty-seven

# The Statue

Present Day

"The statue has to come down. It is a monument to perversion. It is a disgrace to our community. It has to come down!"

Bishop LaVar Jensen's voice rose with a passion he rarely achieved.

"I know that Clive Smythe was an important figure in Lost Valley's early days. He and Rex Jex did a lot for our town. I know that. But they were homosexuals! They were stricken by the curse of this valley. The ancient curse put Satan into their souls and turned them into homosexuals. And that statue—with his tongue sticking out, and that costume—the tutu, the horns on his hat, the forks hanging on his chest—it's just not how I want our town to be known. And it's, it's, it's just…weird is what it is, weird. And perverted. That statute represents how people think of our town—weird. And homosexual. I think it should come down. We should melt it down and make a more appropriate statue—a big cast iron skillet maybe—that would be good."

The members of the town council were a bit irritated and amused, but not surprised by this proposal, made during the normally quiet "Other Business" portion of their agenda. Bishop Jensen approached them at least once a year about tearing down the statue.

The statue of Clive Smythe had been in the town park since before the World War I artillery piece across from it was installed. Everyone in town knew the story of how Rex Jex erected the statue to honor his friend and assistant Clive Smythe. The famous San Francisco artist Everett Nicholas had crafted the eight foot bronze statue using descriptions and photographs provided by Rex Jex. Smythe was depicted as he appeared in the grand Statehood Day Parade in Salt Lake City when the Lost Valley entry had mocked the self-congratulatory pomposity of the parade in retaliation for derogatory remarks made by the Governor and others regarding the town of Lost Valley and its citizens. Clive Smythe had led the Lost Valley group, dressed as a caricature of Helga of the Meadows/Erik of Brownwater, the hero in the grand operatic production of *Helga of the Meadows*, staged by Mitt and Orrin Mudd, with costumes by Rex Jex and Clive Smythe. Every Lost Valley Days parade since has been led by Clive Smythe, or following his death, someone portraying him.

"So now you're saying that because the statue is weird, we should take it down?" Mayor Iris Cain asked Jensen. "Of course it is weird. He was trying to be weird. He was trying to irritate the jerks in Salt Lake who hated Lost Valley. And he did a good job of it. Everybody did. It's the coolest thing about this town. We're weird and we're proud."

Several members of the audience clapped.

"Well, I know you won't understand this, Mayor," LaVar began. "But, well, it seems to me that we are glorifying homosexuality. We've got a big statue of a homosexual in our town, and it's like telling our kids 'It's okay to be a homosexual. Homosexuals are our heroes.'"

He paused and folded his arms across his chest.

"Heavenly Father would not approve. And I don't approve. I think we should tear the perverted thing down."

"Will you ever let up on this, LaVar?" Mayor Iris asked, her eyes flashing. "We are well aware of your crusade against homosexuality. Your ranting about how gays and lesbians are ruining the world is getting old. Especially here. You know that I'm a lesbian. You know that we have gay and lesbian people here in town, yet you still insist on attacking us, and even attacking the town's most important symbol. We're not going to tear down the statue, Bishop Jensen. And if anything happens to it, you are going straight to jail, no questions asked."

"Well, Mayor, I'll just say one more thing and then I'll let you all go. Thanks for allowing me to address the Council."

LaVar Jensen looked around the room.

"You're right. There are some homosexuals in this town. Some of them are my good friends, members of my ward. Even you, Iris. I like you. I think you're a good mayor. But my studies lead me to believe that the curse on this town was not placed on it by Porter Rockwell, or even by Brigham Young, as many have speculated. I think it started a lot earlier, back before the pioneers got here, back when the cliff dwellers lived here. And Clive Smythe, and maybe even my own great, great grandfather Ephraim Jensen—they unleashed something awful. They disturbed something ancient and powerful and it has cursed our town ever since. And it is a curse of homosexuality. That curse turned Smythe and Jex into homosexuals. And many others, too. That's why so many otherwise good people have been afflicted with it. That includes you, too, Mayor. And I'm sorry if it bothers people, but I will work to lift this terrible curse, if it's the last thing I do. Thank you."

With that, LaVar Jensen turned, and walked back to his seat near the back of the room.

"Just so you know, Bishop Jensen," the Mayor said. "Lost Valley doesn't have a corner on homosexuality. We're all over. Even in Provo."

She looked around to the other members of the council.

"Any comments? Other business? Anyone else like to address the council? I will entertain a motion to adjourn."

With the meeting adjourned, all in attendance mingled at the rear of the council chambers, and snacked on cookies and iced tea punch.

### Evelyn's Iced Tea Punch

Mix together in approximately equal proportions:
Iced tea
Orange juice
Lemonade
Pour over ice. A very refreshing drink on a hot day.

# BARBARA'S DESERT CAFE

# Chapter Thirty-eight

# Aspen Camp

Present Day

The road to Aspen Camp wasn't really a road. On the USGS Quadrangle Map it was designated a cattle trail. In ascending the 950 vertical feet between Lost Valley and the camp at the edge of the Pariette Plateau, the "road" switched back on itself twenty two times. At each of those switchbacks, Ralph had to pull as far around the turn as he could, back up, try again, back up, try again, sometimes having to back nearly to the edge and ease forward four or five times before he could negotiate the tight curve. Although the distance the road covered was only four miles, it took nearly an hour, and it seemed as if they had come a long way.

"Jeez," Kenny exclaimed, as they stopped partway up to open a gate. "Why would there be a gate here? If you couldn't get through, you'd have to back all the way down. That would be a nightmare, if it is even possible."

"That's why you don't head up roads like this unless you know where you're going, and you have permission," Tommy responded, opening his door to go open the gate. "Roads like this aren't made for big trucks like Ralph's. A jeep can get through these corners in one try."

Ralph eased the truck through and Tommy closed the wire gate behind them.

"This is actually my favorite road. This part here and the side

211

trail off the lower part that goes up over Beaver Ridge. I make lots of money off these roads."

"What do you mean," Kenny asked. "You make money from these roads? How?"

"Did you see the sign at the bottom—Rough Road, Travel at Your Own Risk?" Tommy asked.

"Sure, couldn't miss it," answered Kenny.

"Well, did you see the little coffee can hanging from the post next to it?" asked Tommy.

"Yeah, sort of," said Kenny.

"If you had come up this road and gotten stuck, or broke your axle, or tore your tires to shreds and walked down looking for help, you'd see it. It has these cards in it."

Tommy handed one to Kenny.

Kenny took the card and looked it over.

Pacheco's Lost Valley Automotive, it said. Stuck? Broken down in the back country? No Problem. Call Tommy Pacheco at 1-435-857-5309.

"Turns out there's pretty good cell reception from right near the sign. I get lots of calls all summer. Triple A calls, too. I hire one guy—Clifton Longhair did it for me this summer—just to rescue four wheelers who get stuck and broken down."

"So a lot of people get in trouble out here?" asked Kenny.

"It's hardly ever locals, or people who know what they're doing," Tommy said. "It's these people who have a new fancy SUV. The TV ads make it seem like these SUVs with leather seats and silly wheels can go straight up mountains and over glaciers and through rivers and even get on top of red rock spires and cliffs. The ads make it seem like if you have four wheel drive you can go anywhere. And the Travel Center helps, too—they encourage people to 'Adventure Offroad' and things like that. So, people do, they break their very expensive vehicles—I'm talking Cadillacs, Lexuses, things like that. Best thing that ever happened for my business—the whole SUV thing. And the funny thing is, they really do have an adventure. And we rescue them. Works out pretty well, all the way around."

The truck suddenly crested the final grade, reaching the top of the plateau, going from shade to full, direct sunlight. Ralph stopped the truck to allow his eyes to adjust to the dramatic change. The three men blinked and squinted and reached for sunglasses. The top of the plateau opened before them—morning mist rising from sage and grass-covered meadows, spruce and fir forests that covered the slopes gave way to scattered groves of aspens and more evergreens along the drainages. From their vantage spot the top of plateau sloped gradually to the east where it was dissected by Damnation Canyon. Beyond, the land rose again, forming ridges and plateaus that extended to the horizon.

"Man, you can see forever," Kenny exclaimed, rubbing his eyes.

"At least fifty miles," Ralph added. "Well, even more. "That white plume way over there—that's the Dragon power plant. It's at least forty miles. And we can see way past it."

After taking in the spectacular vista, their eyes having adjusted sufficiently to the light, they continued on. A few miles along the bumpy but well-maintained road brought them to a spring and a corrugated steel stock pond, around which a few white-faced cattle lingered. Ralph steered onto a small two track that led into a copse of quaking aspens. A half mile in, the trees opened up, revealing a small meadow that contained a water trough, a pole corral, and a fairly large stone-ringed fire pit, surrounded by stumps and logs for sitting.

A male antelope stood near the center of the meadow and watched as they drove toward the camp. As they approached, it turned and walked into the trees.

"That's strange," said Ralph. "I've never seen an antelope up here. They usually stay at lower elevations. That sure was a big one."

"Yep," said Tommy. "Really big."

"Well, here we are," announced Ralph, killing the engine and opening the door.

He took a deep breath and smiled.

"Aspen Camp!"

Ralph's family and friends had been coming to this same spot for the deer hunt for years, since his grandfather first came as a young man in the 1920s. Some of Ralph's fondest memories originated here, and he loved Aspen Camp as no other. In Aspen Camp he had learned to set up tents and kitchens, to cook and clean up, to endure the cold, the wet, the freezing conditions without whimpering, to tell jokes, to play poker, to sing songs around a campfire, to drink whiskey, kill, clean, and hang a deer, and how to properly poop in the woods. In Aspen Camp, Ralph had learned to be a man, as had his father before him. Ralph passed that knowledge down to his own son, and had shared many trips here with his good friend Tommy. Now they had invited their young and enthusiastic friend Kenny to join them on their annual stay at Aspen Camp.

Saturday morning was the start of the hunt and they had nearly all day Friday to get settled into camp. They set up tents, arranged the kitchen gear, hauled water from the spring, set out their sun showers to warm in the sun, and went over their rifles and other gear.

"This is about the smallest group I can remember," said Tommy, poking at the fire burning under the large water kettle. "Good thing we brought Kenny, or you and I would probably be like Felix and Oscar here in camp, grumbling at each other—me smoking cigars and you running around in a little apron dusting off the rocks."

He chuckled at the image of Ralph in an apron with a feather duster.

"How come Barbara and Janice didn't come? Don't they like camping?" Kenny asked.

"Oh, they like it. And Barbara has come up for the hunt a time or two," Ralph answered. "It's mostly been a thing for the guys though, going way back to Grandpap's time. Back then, all the women and kids would go up and stay at the lodge at Pine Lake. They'd eat fancy dinners and have tea and read books and have a grand time. When I was a kid I sort of wanted to keep going with the women, but when I was around twelve I started coming with the men. All in all, I think the women had a better time. At least they never did get frostbit. Or food poisoning."

Ralph looked up at Tommy and they both nodded, recalling a shared calamity.

≈ ≈ ≈

Ralph woke first and made coffee and oatmeal. He poured coffee for the two other men and took a steaming cup to each and left it by

214

their tent doors.

"Time to rise, time to pee, time to hunt you lazy runts," he sung softly, repeating a morning Aspen Camp ritual that went back longer than Ralph had been coming there.

After eating and dressing for the crisp but not exceedingly cold weather, the men packed their knapsacks with some food and water and other necessities, donned their blaze orange caps and jackets, shouldered their rifles, and left camp. After walking for about twenty minutes, Ralph slowed, gave a hands-down "quiet" signal to the others, and softly approached the edge of the forested area they had been walking in. The sun was just approaching the horizon in the east, and the frost-covered leaves appeared gray and fuzzy in the first light. Ralph entered a small open area, surrounded on three sides with pioneering aspen saplings that afforded an unobstructed view of the large, gently sloping meadow ahead. He stopped, looked around for a bit, and sat down on a large tree stump. Tom took a seat on a nearby log, and motioned to Kenny to join him.

In front of them, a grand tableau appeared. The first rays of the rising sun lit the tops of the trees on the far side of the meadow, and the clear light gradually illuminated the entire mountainside. In the far distance they could see the top of the mountains to the west appearing in the first light. The vista appeared to be awakening after being frozen in time, as the frosted limbs and needles sparkled with the advancing light. The three witnesses to the splendor that was repeated daily in this spot were mesmerized by the scene in front of them.

Seven buck deer, cautiously making their way up the drainage, emerging from the cover of the trees to forage in the more open grassy fields, entered the meadow. Kenny spotted their movements, and started to rise. Ralph and Tom, who had been here many times and who had experienced the very same sequence of events, both reached out to let him know to have patience.

The bucks cautiously but with certainty left the forest and began traversing the meadow. A large four point led the way, stopping occasionally to look about or to check the scents in the morning air. When they reached a grassy knob just a hundred yards in front of the men, Ralph and Tom signaled to Kenny to begin hunting.

Taking his time, he measured his breaths, chose his shot and took it.

"Go ahead," Ralph mouthed, nodding.

Kenny slid from the log to one knee. He undid the covers and adjusted a knob on his rifle scope, slid his arm through the leather sling, worked the bolt, and brought the rifle to his shoulder. Taking his time, he measured his breaths, chose his shot, and took it. The four-point leapt forward, landed, and its legs collapsed. It twitched twice, and was still. The other six bounded for cover. Ralph and Tom patted Kenny on the shoulders.

"Very good. Great shot Ken."

When they reached the buck, all life had left him. Kenny's shot had pierced his heart. As Kenny leaned his rifle against a bush and prepared to get out his gear, Ralph took him by the arm.

"Wait," he implored his friend.

Ralph and Tom stood facing the buck, and motioned to Kenny to join them. The three men stood in a circle around the deer and joined hands

"A valuable life has been taken this morning," Ralph said. "A beautiful animal has given his life, so that we may eat. We thank him for allowing himself to be taken. Let us be thankful for this bounty, and give honor to the deer family for providing our children with nourishment. We honor you, beautiful friend, and offer our gratitude."

He patted Kenny on the back, removed his rifle from his shoulder, set his pack on the ground, and prepared to assist in processing the buck.

The next morning, the scene was repeated, and the next, but no more deer were taken. On the second day they saw three bucks in the same spot. Ralph had shouldered his rifle, his grandfather's well-worn Winchester Model 94 30-30, but he kept the muzzle low, and did not raise it up to aim. Tommy did not even load his rifle. Kenny thought it odd, and finally, as they sat around the campfire sipping George Dickel and frying deer liver and onions, asked them about it.

"Are you guys not really hunting?" he asked. "You've both had chances to take deer. Even easier shots than the one I took. What's up with that?"

"I don't really need the meat," said Ralph. "When I hunt it is because I need the meat. I shot plenty of deer and elk when I was providing for my family, but I never liked killing. Never liked it at all. I shot a young buck once—just crippled it—and when I got up to him he screamed and cried like a kid. He didn't want to die and I had to look him in the eye and kill him. That was a long time ago, but I still remember it like it was this morning. I think everyone who eats meat should know what it is to kill for food. I don't really eat much meat at all these days, and I don't enjoy killing, but I do love hunting. Love everything about it, so I come up here and hunt. And it makes me feel good to not kill an animal that I could have killed. Guess I got that from my dad and grandpap. They were both big hunters who fed their families for years hunting, but gave it up when they got older. Tender-hearted is what Grandpap called it. He was just tender-hearted."

"Same with me," added Tom. "I drew an elk permit for later this fall up on the White Rocks, so I don't need a deer this year, but I still love coming up here. Been coming with Ralph and his family to this very spot for –what is it now—twenty years?"

"So you guys probably think I'm a jerk for shooting this deer," Kenny said, checking the sizzling liver. "Bring me hunting and don't tell me that you're not really hunting. What kind of a joke is that? Shit."

"No, Kenny, we're not messing with you. We like you and know that you have to eat. You have nieces and nephews and others who rely on you. I'm happy to hunt with you and bring you to one of the best hunting spots in the state. I wouldn't have invited you if I didn't want to help you get a deer. Don't feel bad. I'm not against hunting. My family has always hunted. Humans are hunters, going back millions of years. I just figure that when we no longer need to kill to eat, that's our own choice."

The men sat in silence for a few minutes. Ralph took a swig on the Dickel and passed the bottle to Ken.

"The ones I do despise are those so-called hunters who kill for fun. They call themselves 'sportsmen.' They don't need the meat. They don't even always eat it. They kill coyotes and prairie dogs and cougars and bears and anything they can shoot. The rich ones pay guides to take them to the biggest deer or elk or moose so they can kill it and take their picture with it and hang its head on a wall. My

Grandpap hated that kind of crap. He said that men like that were going to the lowest part of hell, where everyone else's shit would fall on them. He said God put the animals on this earth to be respected and used when needed for sustenance, not killed for fun. The idea of killing something just to make yourself seem like a big man was something Grandpap hated. And I do too. Have you ever looked at those 'sportsmen' magazines, with pictures of people posing with all the animals they killed? Porn. That's what it is— porn. I'd probably just as soon shoot one of those assholes as shoot a deer. I would. I really would."

## Deer Liver and Onions

Clean and slice the liver. Soak it in milk or buttermilk for at least 30 minutes. Sauté sliced onions in butter until starting to brown. Remove liver from the milk, drain, season with salt and pepper, and dredge in flour. Add more butter to the pan, and fry the liver until just cooked.

# BARBARA'S DESERT CAFE

# Chapter Thirty-nine

# Huevos Pendejos

Present Day

"How many times have we been out here now?" Ralph pondered as he placed tortillas on the griddle. "This makes three, doesn't it?

"Three," said Kenny. "Twice with just the two of us, and now with a whole search and rescue squad. I'm starting to think that last little falling man must have washed away since old Mr. Rowe took those pictures. We've looked all over this dang cave and the cliffs around it. I've personally double-checked every rock art figure in your book, in Rowe's photos, and in the files at the State, and have found them all. I know you have, too. Just not the little one. Not the main one. The most important Wanzi of them all."

Kenny chopped onions and jalapenos as he helped Ralph fix breakfast at their camp at the bottom of the canyon below Tickup's Cave. Barbara, Iris, and Ruby sat quietly in low camping chairs and sipped coffee from steaming enameled mugs. They had spent all day Saturday scouring the cliffs and cave walls searching for the one rock art figure that eluded them. They knew about it from journals and historic photographs, and they knew that it must be somewhere in or near Tickup's cave, but they had not been able to find it.

"I think you're right, Kenny," Ralph said. "That's the only explanation that makes any sense. It must have faded or washed away in the what, 75-80 some years since Rowe photographed it? Lots of things can happen in 80 years. We can't find it because it doesn't exist

221

anymore. Faded, just like most of the rock art that was ever painted on these cliff walls. Lasts for a while, then it's gradually erased by nature. Erosion. Rain. Sunlight. Eventually, they're just gone. Like all things. Exist for a while, then they're gone."

Ralph spread refried beans on the tortillas, motioned for Kenny to add some jalapenos, and started frying the eggs.

"Maybe it's the best you could hope for, really," Iris said, standing and walking over toward the camp stove. "I mean, if it's gone, then the thief can't steal it. There's nothing to steal. Crime spree's over."

She reached into the bowl of grated cheese and took a pinch.

"No loot, no crime."

"That's kind of what we're thinking, Iris," Ralph said. "Maybe the whole thing is over. Maybe the thief has run out of falling men to steal."

"Does that mean the curse is over too?" asked Barbara. "If there's no Wanzi left on the rock, there are no angry Antelope Watchers. No more deadly weather. That'd be nice."

"Sure would be," Kenny added. "My biggest worry has been that, well, even though I don't really believe in curses and that kind of nonsense, well, my biggest worry has been that there might be a huge rainstorm, or even worse, an earthquake, that would bring Salvation Lake over its banks. You know what that would do, don't you? Wash the whole town away. Lost Valley would be Gone Valley."

"Aren't you being a little paranoid for a non-believer Kenny?" Iris asked. "Sounds like you've been working overtime on worse-case-curse scenarios. Floods and earthquakes that will wash the town away. Isn't that a little overboard?"

Ralph placed fried eggs on the top of the bean-covered tortillas, spooned on some salsa, added a sprinkle of grated cheese, turned down the heat, and placed a tent of foil over the griddle.

"Breakfast in one minute," he announced.

Ruby squeezed lime juice over sliced Green River cantaloupe and honeydew melons, and sprinkled them with crushed red chile flakes.

"Let's eat," she declared.

The friends ate quietly.

"Great huevos, Pendejo," Kenny said to Ralph.

"Thanks, Kendejo," Ralph said. "Learned to make these from my Uncle Mick. Said he got them from a guy he used to herd sheep with."

As they were finishing up their breakfast, Kenny rose, got the coffee pot from the stove, and filled everyone's cup. He remained standing, took a sip of his coffee, and gestured toward the far side of the valley.

"Everybody has heard about the Tabyako fault, haven't you?" Kenny asked. "Runs right up the side of the valley. It's why there is a valley. The valley bottom has dropped every few thousand years when the fault slips. Causes a pretty big earthquake. Some of them have been enough to liquefy the sediments in the valley bottom. You know, shake the ground so much that it acts like a liquid. Kind of like Jell-O, maybe. Rocks and trees and houses just sink into it. No fun. Seismologists from the Geological Survey have been doing some studies around here—maybe you've seen the trenches they've dug over by the old Samaniego shearing barn. Anyway, they say that we're due for a quake. They can't predict it with any precision, but they say a quake could come any time in the next few hundred years or so, and they say it could cause liquefaction. That would mean, besides everything sinking and moving all around, the lake would overflow its banks and wash the town away. It's happened in the past. Well, before there was a town, but if there had been a town it would have washed away. And another thing—the lake is very high. And with all the recent rain, there's some worry about a possible breach. I'm not saying any of this stuff will happen, but with all the weird weather and stuff that's been happening, I just don't know. I mean, you know, I get to wondering...."

"That's not wondering, Kenny," Barbara said. "That's worrying. That's the kind of thinking that we've all been trying to avoid since all this crazy stuff started happening. Worrying. Doesn't get us anywhere, doesn't bring us anything but insomnia."

"Maybe it's all over, like we were saying before. Maybe we can stop worrying. Maybe it's all over," Iris said, setting her coffee cup on the table. "That's what I think. Yep, that's what I think. And I'm sticking with that story, too."

## Huevos Pendejos

Fry two or three tortillas per serving in a little olive oil until softened and starting to get crisp. Reduce heat to low. Place so they overlap a little, and spoon on some warm refried beans. Fry a couple of eggs. Place the cooked eggs on top of the refried beans. Top with chopped green onion, fresh jalapenos, and cilantro. Finish with salsa, grated cheese, sour cream, or whatever you find pleasing. Serve. It's best to eat some of the eggs and beans with a fork, and then pick up the tortillas, fold over the remaining beans and eggs, and eat like a taco, using the tortillas to sop up the juicy drippings on the plate.

# Chapter Forty

# Mole Negro

Present Day

"Hey, turn that up," Kenny shouted from the back seat of Ralph's crew cab pickup truck. "It's Pussy Riot. I love Pussy Riot"

"I'm sure you do, Kenny," Barbara remarked, turning to face him, raising her eyebrows and giving him a crazed look.

"No, it's a band. A political Punk band from Russia. They pissed off Putin and he threw them in jail," Kenny retorted. "And I like saying their name. Pussy Riot. Pussy Riot. It's a memorable name don't you think?"

"Yep," replied Ralph, looking up in the rear view mirror. "No question about that. Very memorable. I remember a band called Harry Peters and the Rhythm Method. Can't remember a thing about the band, but I'll never forget the name."

He chuckled to himself.

"Is Pussy Riot's music any good?"

"Well, it's, um, well, just sort of average modern Russian Punk. You kind of have to be in the mood for it. It's more about their political statements than their music. They're real heroes to lots of people."

Pussy Riot's anthem Prayer filled the cab of the truck as the trio of friends made their way up the freeway toward Salt Lake City.

"Only Community Radio would play a song like this. Best station in the entire region," Kenny said, mostly to himself.

Ralph finished drinking his kombucha, and after checking the rear view mirror, let down his window and heaved the bottle with a big left-handed hook shot over the cab and off into the weeds at the edge of the freeway.

"What the hell?" Kenny yelled. "What are you doing? I can't believe it. Why did you do that? There's a trash bag right here. I saw you put your sandwich wrapper in there, why not the bottle? Jeez, I can't believe it."

"I'm not really a litterer," Ralph replied. "I'm a saboteur."

"Who are you sabotaging, the American people?" Kenny asked.

"No, just Bob. Bob Knoll. The owner of Bob's Stop and Gas. Did you see the sign we just passed? 'This stretch of highway adopted by Bob's Stop and Gas.' I'm just giving them something to pick up. I used to gather up a whole bag of trash every time I came this way and throw it all out. Just for shits and grins. Bob's a dick. It's just my way of saying 'Bob's a dick.'"

Kenny nodded. Most of the people he knew despised Bob Knoll. His Stop and Gas took most of the fuel and snack business away from the town of Lost Valley, and he was always trying to expand. His motel along the freeway got most of the overnight business, and he was widely known as a ruthless businessman. People wouldn't have minded it so much, except that Bob was a jerk to everyone. His only supporters were people he bought or beat into submission. He was the area's representative to the legislature, and to hear him talk his constituents were all solidly opposed to taxing the wealthy, in favor of carrying guns everywhere, loved hunting for majestic animals and mounting their heads on walls, killing coyotes, bears, mountain lions and wolves, hated welfare, did not want or need medical insurance, despised the United Nations, were ready to take up arms against the U.S. Government, wanted to hang environmentalists, loved all-terrain vehicles and wanted unrestricted access for them across the entire state, hated Mexicans, loved coal mining, oil wells, nuclear power plants, and thought all government regulations were the work of the devil. Bob worshipped money and seemed to be able to convince quite a few people that worship of money was an honorable, sacred American right.

"Yep, he's a dick alright."

The three friends were on their way to Salt Lake City to see what they could do about the disappearing rock art. They were headed to the State Historic Office to check the computerized database for similar rock art, and to see if other panels had been sawn off and taken. They also had an appointment with the head archaeologist to see what the state could do to help stop the loss and to track down the perpetrators.

Liz Obra, the historic database manager welcomed them to her office. Neat three ring notebooks with labels and tabbed pages sat on her cherrywood desk. Matching shelves and credenza held books on management, Geographic Information Systems, and photos of smiling children.

"You're here to search our database? I understand that you had some trouble getting into the system," she said, motioning to the three of them to sit down.

"Well, I have access, and all the necessary permissions," Kenny began. "I'm Kenny Clements from Salvation Lake State Park."

Kenny stood and shook Liz's hand.

"We've met a time or two. I'm the curator of collections there. And I have a state archaeology permit, so I'm familiar with the system."

"Well, what kind of problem are you having," asked Liz. "Is the system not working?"

"No, that's not it," Kenny answered. "I just want to see if it can search for an unusual combination of variables. You see, some rock art is being stolen, sawn off the cliff walls, and we would like to find out where they might strike again. We thought maybe the database would have some information that would help."

"Like what," Liz asked, tilting her head a little.

"Well, first off, we know that the rock art portion of the database is limited. What we were hoping was if we could combine variables, such as first find all the anthropomorphs of the Fremont Culture in the Lost Valley area, then query that set about whether there has been vandalism. And also see if there's some way to tell if the anthropomorphs might be upside down."

"What do you mean, upside down?" Liz asked.

"The figures that are being stolen are painted upside down on the rock. We know of three of them," Kenny looked over at Ralph, who nodded, "and all three have been stolen. We're wondering if there are others that we don't know about. Maybe others have been stolen too."

"First off, I don't know of any way to query the database about upside-down figures. There's no way to code that. And I don't think we would get any updated forms about vandalized or stolen rock art. So, I guess I'm saying that there's not much we can do. Maybe you could ask people at the Rock Art Society."

Ralph, Barbara, and Kenny looked at each other and shook their heads.

"It was worth a try, anyway," Kenny said, rising. "Thank you Liz."

He shook her hand and turned as he headed out the door.

"Which office is Manson's?" he asked. "The head archaeologist."

"Oh, he's just down the hall," Liz replied. "First right past the bathrooms."

Head archaeologist Max Manson didn't look much like an archaeologist. Wearing a rumpled black suit with white shirt and a red tie, he reminded Ralph of Alfred E. Newman of Mad Magazine with his insincere-seeming gap-toothed-smile greeting. His small hands, bright red complexion, and greasy hair gave them all a creepy feeling.

"Come right in," he said, gesturing them toward a round table behind the door. "There's room for everyone. What can I do for you today?"

After a round of introductions, Kenny told him about the missing rock art. Manson sat back in his chair listening, his hands together in front of his face, his fingers making and unmaking little steeples. He nodded every once in a while. When Kenny and Ralph had finished explaining the situation, Manson spoke.

"You know, I have visited thousands of rock art sites, all over the region," he began. "And many more in Europe and Australia. I am close personal friends with Jean Clottes, and Grahame Walsh and Polly Schaafsma. Did you know that I worked with Doug Snow, and many other artists? I probably know as much about art and rock art as anyone. Of course, I don't need any recognition or credit, but when it comes to rock art, well, I understand it, as an artist and scientist."

Manson rocked back in his chair, almost grinning.

"Upside down figures are nearly universal. They generally represent a person of great power who has died, or who is telling of the death of another. We, and I mean, we, as in rock art experts, generally call the upside-down figures 'Shaman' figures. Some think they represent homosexuals as well, which may well be, as homosexuals were often thought to be holy, or at least different, and many were shamans."

He looked directly at Barbara and said, "Very few women were shamans. They are helpers to shamans. I have worked with many shamans, and usually their women helpers are nude. It is just a part of my research."

Ralph glanced over at Kenny and Barbara with a look of amused incredulity.

"Yeah, yeah, we're sure you are an expert, but what we want to know is if you can do anything about these thefts. Can you start an investigation? Can you see if the stolen pieces are showing up in art sales or in galleries? What can you do to help stop this plunder?"

"Well, now you're talking to the wrong person. I'm a scholar. My degree is the same as a Ph.D., really. My master's degree is the equivalent of, or even better than a Ph.D. from most American schools. I am a scholar. I can tell you how to preserve an eroding rock art figure. I'm one of the world's best. I advise many agencies about how to care for their sites."

Manson paused, and fiddled with a small glass pyramid in the center of the table.

"I am a scholar, not a pot cop. If you want to chase down thieves, talk to the BLM Rangers or the County Sheriff. I'm not a pot cop."

≈ ≈ ≈

"Well, that was a wasted day," Ralph muttered as they neared the exit to Lost Valley in the dimming orange light of the setting sun. "That Manson is a trip. I thought he was going to pull a muscle, patting himself on the back."

"He's as creepy as they get," added Barbara. "What was that about nude women? Did you see the way he was looking at me? Ick. That's all I have to say. Ick."

"Sorry guys," said Kenny. "I thought they might be able to help. Guess not. Those people are fools. They think archaeological sites

229

are just another thing to be managed, like so many potholes or rental properties. They think it is a game to be played. Their database is more or less worthless for anything except telling the legislature what a big database they have. Most consultants have their own databases. And nobody keeps very good track of rock art. Lots of people like it—love it—but they are mostly secretive, like the people in the rock art society, and they keep the best places to themselves. They don't want people messing up important sites."

"We sort of met on a rock art site, didn't we, Ralph?" Barbara said, looking over toward Ralph with a smile.

"We sure did," Ralph replied, turning toward Barbara and returning her smile. "Over at Rochester Creek, on one of Doc Diamond's jeep tours. I remember seeing this beautiful blonde girl with shorts and a tie-dyed tank top. Couldn't take my eyes off of her. Still can't."

He looked again at Barbara, grinning.

"And I thought the tour leaders were the coolest guys I ever met. Doc Diamond was as cute and twinkly-eyed a man as I have ever met. And that tall guy with him reminded me of a giant Mark Twain. Still does."

Ralph and Barbara looked at each other for a second, then turned to look out the front windshield as the truck headed up Main Street, passing Pacheco's garage before making a U-turn to pull up in front of Barbara's Desert Café.

"Thank you both," Ralph said to Barbara and Kenny. "We'll figure out what's going on. Don't let those doofuses at the state get you down. I had a good day. Can't beat lunch at the Iguana. Thanks. We'll figure this out."


**Mole Negro**

For the finest mole north of Mexico, go to the Red Iguana Restaurant in Salt Lake City.

# Chapter Forty-one

# Head Hunter

Present Day

"I just got off the phone with Elaine Miller in Price," Ralph said as he walked up to the table, pulled out a chair, and sat down with the others. "She went out to Nine Mile this morning to check out a place where some hikers reported a rock art panel had been vandalized. She checked with Sally Manning and Sally showed her some old pictures of the panel, and you guessed it. It was an upside down man—a head hunter! So, she confirms that another upside down figure has been sawn off. Probably right about the time of that big wind storm. We just didn't know where to look. She says it's the only head hunter Sally knows of south of the Uinta Basin. It's from a site the locals call Battle Ridge. It's got about a dozen rock art panels, all with battle scenes. This is the only head hunter though."

Iris, who had been filling water glasses as Ralph arrived, waited as he sat down to pour his water.

"What do you mean 'head hunter?' Is it a painting of somebody cutting off a head?"

"Pretty much," Ralph replied. "There are a number of rock art panels in the Uinta Basin that look like they show people holding a severed head in their hand or on a pole or something. Some are very realistic, even showing tears coming from the eyes of the severed head. A head hunter depiction has been cut off in Nine Mile. A Falling Man Head Hunter. Jesus. This one's not painted though, it's pecked."

"I've got them plotted out on a map, and it's pretty interesting," Kenny said, moving the napkin holder out of the way and unrolling a large paper map on the table. He used the salt and pepper shakers to hold down the upper corners.

"Look," he said, pointing. "Here's Lost Valley, and here's Gooseberry, where the first figure was cut off. Now look at where the other stolen figures are—the Skull Creek falling man is over here, to the west. Lighthouse—where the other falling man was stolen, it's over here, to the south. The head hunter is, where Ralph?—here to the North?"

"Yep, right there," Ralph pointed. "Right there, on the south side of Nine Mile Canyon."

Kenny marked the spot on his map.

"Holy Crap!" he exclaimed. Look at this!"

He pointed at the map with his pencil.

"See the little diamond around Lost Valley—Head Hunter on the north, Gooseberry on the east, Skull Creek on the west, Lighthouse to the south, and guess what's right in the center."

He pointed to a spot and looked up at the others.

"Aw, man," moaned Ralph. "It's the cave. Tickup's Cave. That's exactly where the cave is. It's a perfect diamond with Lost Valley and Tickup's Cave in the middle. Let me look at that again. Is this just random, or is it intentional?"

"Looks intentional to me," said Kenny. "It's an almost perfect diamond with the head hunter at the top and Lost Valley City in the center."

"How crazy is this?" Kenny continued. "This isn't random. It looks to me like these were placed in this arrangement intentionally. Amazing."

"Well, what's freaking me out about this is whoever is stealing these figures knows about this arrangement too," Ralph said. "This isn't a run-of-the-mill thief. This is planned and calculated and strange. This is starting to freak me out a little."

"Or a lot," said Barbara.

"This is weird. Too weird," Tommy nodded.

"What do we do now?" Ralph pondered, shaking his head. "What the hell do we do now?"

"Well, you *could* order," Iris said, order pad and pen ready in her hands. "You need to tell Sheriff Taylor, so he can start investigating. But first, would anybody like to order some food? Drinks?"

"Sorry, Iris. I didn't mean to ignore you," Ralph said. "And you're right: we do need to tell the sheriff. The Headhunter panel is on Bureau of Land Management land—the federal government. I think Pam has already reported the theft. Lighthouse is on Forest Service land, and Elmer and their rangers are investigating. I think all the landowners know of the vandalism. What I worry about is what's next."

He looked at Kenny. They both shook their heads. While the others ordered, Ralph leaned forward and looked at the map.

"You're right, Kenny," Ralph said. "You're exactly right. This isn't a coincidence—these panels were created where they are because of their locations relative to Lost Valley. I wonder if our suspicions of someone selling the panels to sheiks and art gallery owners were all wrong. This is something of a different sort altogether. I mean, we can all understand greed—someone stealing for profit. Or even vandalism. At least we've all seen enough of it to not be perplexed by it. But this… What the hell is going on?"

"Well, like Iris said," Tommy answered, setting his coffee cup back in its saucer. "Like she said, we need to start by reporting this to Sheriff Taylor. As weird as it all seems, they need to know what's been going on."

"But what do we tell them?" Kenny asked. "That we think there's a pattern and we think we know where somebody is going to strike next? Do we tell them that we think there's another rock art figure that might be stolen, except that we can't find it, and that it may not even exist? Do we really want to sound that crazy? And what about the thief? Do we just wait for them to strike again, or is there some way to start figuring out who it is?"

"And, the sheriff might not be anxious to listen to us. He is still taking a lot of flak for busting into Rowe's Studio. Rick Rowe is still pretty angry about that whole thing," Ralph said.

"The police would probably have ideas," Barbara said. "That's what they do, isn't it—track down criminals. They know more about catching bad guys than we do."

"I just wish we knew where the little tiny Wanzi figure is. If it even exists. Maybe we could save it by going public. Maybe somebody knows where it is," Tommy said.

"You know what adds another weird twist to this whole thing," Kenny said, looking at pictures of the head hunter panel that Elaine had sent to Ralph. "This head hunter dude, the way he's holding this head in his hand, and a stick or a sword in the other. He looks like the guy in the opera."

"What are you talking about," asked Tommy.

"The opera, *Helga of the Meadows*," Kenny said. "I just watched a video of the opera with my niece. She had to watch it for her history class. In the big climactic scene, the hero—Erik, who is also Helga, cuts off the head of the bad guy—Finnragnar the Boneless—with his sword and holds it up for everyone to see. Looks like this rock art is a scene from the opera."

"What worries me is that there is some creepy weirdo out there cutting rock art down and causing all of us to go crazy," Barbara said. "It's probably somebody from this community, don't you think? Somebody we know. And what else is he doing? What other kinds of twisted thoughts does he have? Freaks me out."

"Think it could be Rick Rowe?" Kenny asked. "He's got some beef with Lost Valley, right? His father got run out of Lost Valley City. Maybe he holds a grudge. And I just don't trust the guy, I just don't."

"If that's the case, then I'm the one who should be worried," said Iris as she refilled the coffee cups, "since I'm the Mayor. But I know Rick, and I don't think he's that type. He's a nice guy. Odd, but nice. And did you see how he bombed LaVar Jensen's Hate Float in the Pride Parade? He got my vote for biggest balls that day. Just thinking of it makes me smile."

"Still, he might have something against the town," Tommy said. "Of course, who doesn't, really? Anybody who's lived here for long is sure to have some complaint. Only who would act on it, that's the question. Who?"

"Oh, he's pissed," Ralph said. "He's still pissed at the town for what it did to his father. And he's not happy that we set the cops after him and his store. He's pissed all right. And he has the tools and know-how to saw the stone and take the rock art. I just don't know whether he'd do something like this. I really don't think he would, but we can't just rule him out. Not by any means."

Ralph ate the last of his pie and finished his coffee. He sat up straight and looked around the table at his friends.

"Here's what I think we need to do. Kenny's right, our theory is too wacky to be telling the Sheriff just yet. I think we should keep looking for that little Falling Man figure. If we can find it, we can tell the Sheriff, and he can help us watch it to see if the thief strikes again. If it hasn't been stolen already, that is. If it even exists. We can keep an eye the area, and maybe monitor the road and traffic. Seems like 'too little, too late' but I don't know what else to do."

He pursed his lips and looked around at his friends. He scooted his chair out and stood to leave.

"Thanks guys. Thanks for all you've been doing to help figure this out. We'll get this sorted out. We will. Yes, we will."

# BARBARA'S DESERT CAFE

# Chapter Forty-two

# Ancient Treasures

Present Day

"Did you see the sign?" Kenny yelled to Ralph from across the parking lot. "Did you see it?"

"What? What are you talking about?" Ralph answered back, hurrying toward Kenny's vehicle.

"The sign at Rowe's Studio. The new sign."

"I saw that some work was going on. What's the sign? What's it say?"

"Ancient Treasures. Ancient Treasures. Can you believe it? Jeez. Just as blatant as can be."

"You know he is only selling reproductions. It's a legitimate business. Nothing wrong with that," said Ralph.

"I just don't believe him," Kenny replied. "I think he's going to all these pains to make exact reproductions because he is also selling the real deal. I bet he tells these big collectors: 'Here's a nearly exact reproduction. But, for the right price, I can get you the real thing.' You know how collectors only want the authentic item. They couldn't care less about reproductions."

He paused for a moment.

"And even more than that, even worse. He could be trying to bring Lost Valley down. Bring on an earthquake or something. I really don't trust him. I don't."

"Well, we don't have any reason to suspect that he is breaking the law, so let's just be neighborly. You can keep your eyes open, but I'm terribly embarrassed about breaking into his business, so I think we should just give him the benefit of the doubt. And his reproductions are amazing. Really amazing."

Ralph waited for Kenny to join him and they walked together into the town hall for the Lost Valley Days planning committee meeting. Inside, they greeted the other members of the committee, and as they were sitting down around the conference table to begin, they were surprised to see Rick Rowe enter the room.

"Oh, hi Rick, welcome," Mayor Iris Cain greeted the new arrival. "Everybody, this is Rick Rowe. He is originally from Lost Valley and is moving back here this summer. He's been remodeling his father's photographic studio, you know, Rowe's Studio, just down the street. He's opening a business here and told me he'd like to be part of the Lost Valley Days planning group, so here he is."

Rick tipped his hat to the committee and Iris introduced the members.

"Don't let me interrupt your group," Rick said, taking his seat. "I just told the Mayor I'd like to be involved, and maybe throw out a few ideas, now that I'll be moving back to town and opening a business on Main Street."

"Well, welcome Rick." Iris began. "For those of you who don't know, Rick's father, Jack Rowe, was Mayor of Lost Valley back in the, what, Rick, the early 60s?"

"Yes, that's right," Rick said. "Sixty-two to sixty-seven. Five years, about."

"I think he was the last elected Mayor, before we started selecting Mayors by random drawings, isn't that right?" Iris said.

"I wouldn't know about that," said Rick. "He, um, he well, he left office suddenly, and well, we had to move away. It wasn't really a very friendly end to our stay in Lost Valley. He never really got over it. Never did."

"I knew that something strange had happened," Ralph said, "The way your family left in the middle of the school year. What was it, if you don't mind me asking?"

"Hi, Ralph," Rick said, nodding. "Well, not to take too much time away from the meeting, but we did, we left in a hurry."

He looked around at the faces around at the table.

"Most of you are too young to remember, but back in those days things were tense, with the Cold War and everything, and, well, even here in Lost Valley, there were some ugly politics. Anyway, the rumor started that my dad was a communist. There was a man, Cleon Shumway, he was a leader with the John Birchers, and he had it out for my dad. Said all these bad things about him. Said he was a spy for Russia, that he worked for the United Nations, things like that. Got so bad that the town council voted him out. Well, he lost his job and nobody would hire him to take pictures or do portraits. Even the school wouldn't hire him for class pictures any more. So we moved. I was in the eighth grade. That's when we left. I wish it could have been different, but that's just how it was."

Bishop Jensen, who until now had occupied himself by looking at his fingers as if contemplating getting a manicure or nail extensions, coughed, and looked at Mayor Cain.

"There might be a little more to the story than that," he said. "And being a communist back then was no small matter. Maybe even a bigger matter than being a communist or socialist today. We still don't need them, either here or in the White House."

"Now just hold on a minute," Rick said. "What do you know about it? Do you think you know more about what happened to my father that I do? And what difference would it make if he had been a communist, which he wasn't. It's not against the law. Never has been."

"No, but there are plenty of other things that are against the law. Now and back in the sixties," Bishop Jensen said.

"What are you saying?" Rowe said, rising tall in his chair. "Are you accusing my family of breaking the law? After all these years. What the hell are you saying?"

"Okay, okay then, everyone please calm down," Mayor Cain said, raising her voice. "I had no idea. I had no idea we would be at each other's throats in less than five minutes. Let's stop this right now. We are here to discuss the parade and pageant. We are here to discuss who is going to be Clive Smythe this year, and that's why I invited Rick to the meeting. Are you still interested in leading the parade, Rick? In being Clive Smythe?"

"More than ever," Rick said, looking straight at Jensen. "More than ever."

# Chapter Forty-three

# Bacon Jam



Present Day

"Come on back, Rick," Ralph said, motioning toward the rear of the cafe. "We can sit in one of the back booths where we can chat."

"Just as long as there's room for me to squeeze in," Rick replied. "Sometimes booths aren't made for someone my size."

"Oh, this one is plenty big," Ralph replied. "I have the same problem—can't even fit my legs in a lot of booths, but this one is spacious—Barbara had it expanded just for me!"

The two large men slid into the booth on the well-worn Naugahyde seat cushions.

"Well, I'm sorry things got crosswise back there at the meeting. I don't know what LaVar—Bishop Jensen—I don't know what he was getting at, but I apologize. Sometimes I don't know what drives him, I really don't."

Ralph sipped his coffee.

"Oh, I do. I know exactly what he was talking about," replied Rick. "It's like time has stood still for all these years. I guess I was just dreaming that I could move back here. First the sheriff breaks into my store thinking I'm a thief and violating the Antiquities Act, and now Jensen bringing up crap from fifty years ago. I think this town just has it out for me and my family. Don't know why I ever thought about coming back. Claudia—my wife, you may have met her at some rock art meetings—she told me. She told me this town would come after me just like it did my dad, but I told her things would be different. I love this country, this valley and the canyons, you know, I really do. But the town...."

He shook his head.

"I don't know. I really just don't know."

"Well, I have to apologize for the Sheriff and the search and all," Ralph said. "It's just that we've been kind of obsessed with the rock art disappearing, and when somebody saw what looked just like one of the stolen panels, well, I guess we just jumped to conclusions. The wrong conclusions. I'm sorry about it. I really am. I feel like a real ass."

Rick stared at his coffee cup and rocked it back and forth a little, watching the coffee reach to the edges and nearly spill over. He clenched his jaw and shook his head.

"I can't believe you didn't just call me. You know I'm in the rock art society. We've known each other since we were kids. Why didn't you just call me? I would have told you what I had in the shop, that it was just reproductions. It pisses me off, is what it does. It just pisses me off."

"I don't know, Rick. We just got carried away. I don't know. We were jerks. I know that. All I can do is say I'm sorry. And I am. I am truly sorry."

"Well, maybe you can answer me one thing. How did you know the big one—the "falling man" was fake? How did you know that it wasn't the actual stolen pictograph?"

Ralph thought for a minute.

"I didn't at first. The way the edges of the rock were sawn and kind of broken—rough—that looked like the real thing. The size was right, and the painting was perfect. That's what I noticed. It was a little too perfect. The paint seemed a little too bright. And I could see one spot where the paint was a little thick—the actual rock art looked more like a stain after all these years. More of a stain than a painting. I knew when I saw it that it was a reproduction. A really good one. A really great one, but just a little too fresh looking."

Rick pondered what Ralph had said. Finally, he looked at Ralph and nodded.

"Good. That's good to know. I still have room for improvement."

"If you're trying to make it look exactly like you sawed it off the cliff face, then you've done a very good job. I doubt if very many people in the world would have known it was a fake. Not very many at all."

"That's what I'm shooting for. Well, I mean, not so much to make it look like a stolen figure, but to make it look authentic. I have buyers who want these things for their homes, offices, that sort of thing, and they're willing to pay for high quality reproductions. That's why I have been studying the rock art so much lately. To see the techniques, to see the details of how they were made, and how they have weathered, so I can reproduce them. I'm not trying to sell them as authentic—I engrave my name and date on the back—I'm selling them as very good reproductions. Museum quality. So, in a way, I'm flattered that you mistook them for stolen rock art. Maybe I can use that in my marketing. I can tell people that I fooled the experts enough that they reported me to the cops!"

Rick chuckled and sipped his coffee.

"Good reproductions can bring positive attention to the rock art, without endangering it, if it is done in the spirit of conservation. But, some people are driven to own the authentic piece. They're not satisfied unless they own the original. I'm sure you know that, Rick, and I am glad that you are not catering to it."

Ralph signaled to Barbara and asked her to bring them a couple orders of toast with bacon jam.

"Well, what with the raid, even if I can put a positive spin on it, and now that Jensen fellow bringing up all that crap about my father, it just makes me think about all that old talk about a curse. Maybe this place is cursed. My dad thought so, and so did Uncle Pete. They were sure of it. And now maybe I think they were right. This whole damn place is cursed."

Ralph smeared some bacon jam on his toast.

"Here, have some Rick. It's sinfully good. I got a double order so we can share."

He pushed the plate toward the middle of the table between them and took a bite of his toast, followed by some coffee.

"I've heard about this curse thing since I was a kid," Ralph said, "but until recently I never thought much about it. I thought it was just something people said about Clive Smythe and Rex Jex, something from the olden days."

"Oh, there's more to it than just stories about Clive Smythe. Goes back a lot farther—back to the ancient times. You know, my mother's Ute. Full blood. Her family name is Chuponas. She's the granddaughter of Weeche. She says the curse, well, they don't say curse, but they do say that the rock art and the animals have spirits, and the spirits can have great power—power to do good. And, sometimes, power to do bad things. Cause a flood, or a blizzard. Sometimes, they say, little devils can get in people and cause disease. Or even make people crazy. Things like that. You know, Mom still thinks that Dad got run out of Lost Valley because of those pictures—the ones of the Watchers. She thinks a lot of people here in Lost Valley have those little devils working in them. People like Cleon Shumway. And this Bishop Jensen. Man, there's a guy full of little devils. You know the real story, don't you? You know it wasn't really about being a communist. That was just a convenient lie to tell in public."

"I don't know if the things that happen here are because of a curse, because of little devils and Spirit Watchers and Long Lookers, or just because we have a lot of dumbasses around here. Seems like this state is full of people who can't stay out of other people's business. They are so convinced of their own righteousness, they can't accept someone who's the least bit different."

Rick paused, and spread some of the bacon jam on a slice of toast.

"I think in some ways it is just an old story or legend people like Jensen have used to hurt others here in Lost Valley. You see, my father was accused of being a communist, and that's what they said in meetings and that's what they used to get the city to vote him out, but that's not what was really going on. No, sir."

Rick bit into his toast, and rolled his eyes back in feigned euphoria.

"Holy crap, you are right. That's too much. I could gain a hundred pounds having this—what is it—bacon jelly—around. Mmmmmmm."

He finished the piece of toast, washed it down with coffee, and continued, "My grandfather and my dad, they took lots of pictures of the Utes. And of rock art, too. They loved the rock art. That's where I got my interest. And grandpa, especially, he was really intrigued by the falling men. The upside-down figures—the ones being stolen. My mother told Dad to stay away from them. She said they would bring bad luck. She said he would get sick or cause a flood or something if he kept taking pictures of them. She made him get rid of them. He gave all of his rock art pictures to the museum up in Price. They have them. All of them. And, since Dad passed, they have all the pictures, not just the rock art, all of them—we donated them—pictures, negatives, everything. All their notes and stuff too. All at the museum."

Rick continued, "No, being a communist was not all they said. You know, my Uncle Pete, he never married. He, um, well, he never came out and said that he was homosexual. People just didn't do that in those days, but other people talked. They talked behind Pete's back. You know he and Dad were business partners. They both owned Rowe's Studio, even though Dad was the primary photographer. Well, people talked. They said he had the same curse as Clive Smythe and that it would affect my Dad, too. They said Pete was Dad's sidekick. That's what they called him, his sidekick. They meant his, well, his boyfriend. His lover. They said my dad and his brother were queers. And it was that Cleon Shumway doing it. He was behind it, and it ruined my Dad's business, and they got him kicked out of office. It almost killed him. We had to move away and start over. It was awful. And I still hate this place for what it did to him, to us. I still fume over how mean some of these people are. And it seems like this LaVar is going to carry on with it. Jesus."

Rick looked at Ralph. Ralph felt the intensity of his emotions. They sat quietly for a few moments.

"I have a question, Rick. It's kind of related," Ralph said. "Your father or grandfather took some photos of a tiny pictograph somewhere around Tickup's Cave. A tiny, upside-down man. Do you know anything about it? Like where it is? We've been looking, but can't seem to find it."

Rick thought for a moment, and shook his head.

"No, I, well, I can't say. Dad may have shown it to me once. But it was one Mom said to stay away from. She said it was the Main

Watcher. The most powerful Wanzi. She said she was told that if it was disturbed it would destroy the entire valley. She made my Dad promise to never go there again—ever. And he didn't. No, he never did go back. It's not something to mess with. No, sir."

## Bacon Jam

For each serving, take one slice (or two, depending on the size and thickness) of freshly-cooked, good-quality bacon. Chop finely, and mix with two tablespoons of your favorite jam. Add a dash or two of crushed red chile flakes for extra zest, if you like. Serve on toast or biscuits.

# Chapter Forty-four

# Voodoo

Present Day

"Do you think this curse business could be real, Ralph," Barbara asked. "I mean, it seems like between the old stories, and the floods and fires and things, something pretty weird is going on. Maybe the old Utes and even Bishop Jensen are on to something. Maybe, I don't know, maybe there's something to it. Do you think?"

Ralph leaned back and looked up at the ceiling for a moment. He took a deep breath, and turned to Barbara.

"No. Well, if you had asked me that a year ago I would have said no. Absolutely not. I mean, how could it be? How could something that I do not even believe exists—a spirit or something—influence storm clouds? No, it can't be. No way."

He rubbed some dirt from his thumbnail.

"I've always thought that witches, you know, like Navajo witches, they could only hurt people who believed they could hurt them. Same thing with voodoo and other kinds of spell-throwing. If you believed somebody had special power, and that they were using that power against you, then you might actually help it happen by being all stressed out, not sleeping, being accident prone, paranoid. Kind of how a placebo works. It works because a person thinks it will work. I always thought that was how spells and witching worked. You had to believe, and it might actually work. No real power, no spirits, just the power of suggestion."

Ralph cocked his head, raised his eyebrows, and shrugged.

Barbara leaned forward on the couch and put her hand on Ralph's knee.

"I think you're right. I do. I just don't know how to think about the storms. I mean, even if we believed that devils were sending the storms, it seems crazy that they're hitting just at the right time. Right when somebody harms the falling men."

"And maybe it is crazy. Maybe we're just being crazy. Really, now, if we hadn't heard of that curse, would we even make the connection between bad weather and the rock art disappearing? I mean, shit, there's bad weather all the time. And people desecrate rock art all the time. I think we are enabling this curse to come true. We are matching two unrelated things up in our minds—the rock art and the weather—when there is absolutely no connection. We heard of a curse and we are imagining that it is true. That's all. That's all it is."

"Maybe so," said Barbara. "I think that really applies to Bishop Jensen. He sees homosexuality all over and blames it on the curse, when really there's no connection, no curse. There's homosexuality and he doesn't like it so he blames it on a curse, and makes himself believe it. Since he has something to blame, he has something to rail against, something to get people whipped up about. I think you're right, Ralph. We're making connections between things, when they are really completely unrelated. I feel better now. I can probably get some sleep tonight without worrying. No, probably not. Well, maybe a little better."

Ralph stretched and faked a yawn.

"All this talk of curses and witches and storms is making me sleepy. I'm so tired I could sleep all night."

"Shut up, you dick," Barbara said. "We can tell ourselves all kinds of things to make ourselves feel better, but you and I both know that this rock art-weather thing is kind of freaking us out. Voodoo or not, it is freaky."

Ralph nodded, and reached to embrace Barbara. They sat on the couch and hugged each other tight.

# Chapter Forty-five

# Salvation Lake Museum

Present Day

"Come on back into the lab, Mr. Jensen," Kenny said, motioning for Bishop Jensen to follow him. "I have already pulled some of the artifacts you asked to see."

The two men walked down the hall past several offices and storage areas in the administration section of Salvation Lake State Park and Museum. At the end of the hall was a door marked 'Museum Curation—Staff Only.' Kenny unlocked the door, turned on the lights, and gestured for Jensen to follow him.

Rows of shelves lined with identical cardboard boxes filled most of the room. Massive moveable shelves on railroad-like tracks saved space and gave the room an industrial feel. Several vault-like cabinets housed particularly sensitive or fragile artifacts. Occasionally a shelf contained a large object wrapped in paper or plastic. Some held a stone, a ceramic vessel, or a piece of a log, or a rolled up blanket. LaVar Jensen looked around at the stored items as they entered the room.

"I had no idea there was so much back here," he said. "What is all this stuff?"

"We have a pretty large collection," Kenny answered him, stopping to point out a side room full of similar shelves. "Most of these artifacts are from the state parks in this part of the state, plus some from Federal lands. We're a designated repository for archaeological collections. It all started because of the artifacts your ancestor Ephraim Jensen had, and also some they found in the big cave up above the lake—Tickup's Cave. When the state took the property for a park, they needed a place to put the artifacts, so they built a little museum. And your great-grandfather's collections are a big part of the collection. It's bigger now, but still, it's more of a little visitor's center than a museum. The main role is as a repository, not so much for displays."

"May I ask you a personal question, Kenny," Bishop Jensen asked as they passed through a large heavy fire door.

"Sure, whatever," Kenny replied. "What would you like to know?"

"Well, I'm not sure how to ask this, but you know when Janell and I ran into you leaving the café the other night? We were going in and you were leaving. With Iris."

"Sure. You reminded me of our appointment this afternoon."

"Yes. Yes, I did. Well, you kind of had your arm around Iris, or so it seemed. I just was wondering, I mean, well, you know, the Mayor, she's, well, I thought she, um. What I mean is, are you, or is she, um, kind of, well, you know…"

Kenny laughed.

"What are you asking, LaVar? I did have my arm around Iris. We're good friends. We hang out together. What are you asking?"

"Well, I thought she was a, um, well, she told me that she was a, um, a uh, a lesbian. That's what she told me. And well, I just wondered, that's all."

"It's really not any of your business, Bishop. Not at all. But I'll tell you this—Iris and I are good friends. We like each other and hang out together. You can take that however you like, but it's really none of your business. You don't just snoop around and ask about people's sex lives. Her sex life and orientation isn't any more of your business than your sex life is her business. Or my business. What if I asked you if you and Janell did it that night? What if I asked Janell? Is that okay? Come on, Mr. Jensen, I know what you are getting at, and it is inappropriate for you to ask or even think about. It is something private. Very private. Everyone's sexuality is their own business, and they decide what to tell others. Just respect Iris, and she, and I, will respect you. Okay?"

Kenny turned and continued walking.

They walked past a last row of shelves and the room opened up. Kenny switched on some more lights, and before them was a large table covered with white paper, upon which were several large objects, carefully laid out.

"Oh, my," said Bishop Jensen. "Oh, my. I haven't seen them in years. Oh, my."

He took a deep breath and stepped around to the front of the table, taking in the artifacts laid out before him.

"Just look at that. Look at those feathers. Like it was made yesterday."

Jensen leaned forward and reached out to touch the feathered hat.

"Wait, wait, please, LaVar," Kenny rushed over and took Jensen's arm. "Put these gloves on before you touch anything. We don't want any oil or dirt from your fingers to get on the artifacts. Here, just put these cotton gloves on."

Jensen stood up straight and smiled.

"Certainly," he said, reaching to take the gloves from Kenny.

"You can touch the artifacts," Kenny said. "Just be careful."

Jensen smiled and nodded.

"Oh, I will. You know I will. These mean more to me than you can ever know."

He leaned forward and inspected each of the artifacts on the table—the flicker feather headdress, the hide shield, the basket and the ceramic pot that fit in it, and the cape. Jensen paused when he noticed a particular object.

"What is this?" He asked. "This stick figure. What is it, and where did it come from?"

"Oh, it's a split-twig figurine. It's very interesting, because it is clearly a pronghorn—see the forked horn? There are a number of these from mostly further south—in the Canyonlands area and the Grand Canyon. But this is the only one I've ever seen that is clearly a pronghorn. None of the others have horns."

"Where did this come from?" Jensen asked. "My grandfather's notes mention an object like this, but it was lost."

"Let's see," Kenny said, scrolling through rows of catalog

information on the computer screen. "It was from the Simpson collection. We got it at the same time as the human remains. Maybe they dug it up when they dug up the burials. The notes aren't clear."

"Interesting, very interesting," Jensen said.

Bishop Jensen looked for a long time at each object, examining each one, not as a scientist might have looked, but more as a child looking at beautiful gift. He seemed to glow as he moved about, always looking to Kenny for permission when he wanted to lift a corner of the headdress, or hold and examine a string tie on the cape. He moved his fingers gingerly and smoothly over the objects, pausing occasionally to gently touch or even softly tap the edge of the shield or basket with his fingertips. Bishop Jensen spent nearly an hour looking the artifacts over carefully, lovingly. Kenny waited patiently, thumbing through the bound copies of Ephraim Jensen's journals that described the discovery and condition of the objects, and contained sketches and detailed descriptions of each.

"My great grandfather took very good care of these garments and things," Bishop Jensen said. "He knew how important and powerful they were. He respected them and cared for them as one would care for anything of great value. He did not want the family to part with them, but I think, in the end, the family had no choice. The government was going to take them, so they—my grandfather Hyrum Jensen—made the decision. He thought that donating them would be the best way for them to be cared for properly.

"Do you think we're doing a bad job?" Kenny asked. "Should we be doing something different?"

"Well, no," Jensen answered. "You seem to be taking care of them physically. They seem to be in good shape. But remember, the donation papers stipulated that my family would be allowed to visit with them, to bring them to life each year. It has been a long time since that has happened. You're the first one at the museum to even let me look at them and touch them."

"I'm sorry if the other curators were inconsiderate. We have legal responsibilities for the collections, and sometimes we forget that they have meaning beyond their scientific value. And that doesn't only apply to you. What about the Indians—lots of the objects we have are important to them, and we've mostly just ignored their wishes. We're trying to improve. That's why we are going through the claim process with these artifacts. That's why we are here today."

"Well, you know my concern," said Bishop Jensen. "Some tribe will claim them and take them away and the family will never see them again. That's what I'm afraid of."

"That could very well happen," Kenny replied. "But if it does, it will be because the tribe demonstrated that the items really do belong to them. They should be cared for by their rightful owners, shouldn't they?"

"They were in my family for a very long time. My great grandfather found them more than a hundred years ago. Doesn't that count for something?"

"It may," Kenny replied. "We'll have to see. You know that these objects were found with human remains—three people were buried with them. That's why we are asking the tribes if they want to claim the artifacts—they are funeral objects that should be returned to the descendants of those who were buried there."

"I know. My great grandfather excavated the artifacts. I read his journals. But he left the burials. It was a little family—Dad, Mom, and a child, all in a circle. He thought they should stay together. He left them there."

"Yes, that's true, but somebody else dug them up. I think it was the Simpsons. The bodies—they're partial mummies, you know— were on display at the trading post for years. They got turned in to us in the 80s. And you know, even though people have called them 'The Family' or 'The Indian Family' for years, they weren't exactly that."

"What do you mean?" asked Jensen.

"When we had the remains examined by physical anthropologists, they identified the remains as two males and a child. There was no mom, just two men. Maybe a dad and an uncle or something, but no mom."

Bishop Jensen furrowed his brow and rubbed his chin. He shook his head.

"I had never heard that," he said. "Never heard that. Hmmm."

Jensen resumed looking at the objects. He circled the table several

Finally he turned and faced Kenny. "May I put them on?"

times, sometimes humming a little. Finally, he turned and faced Kenny.

"May I put them on?"

"Um, put them on—like the hat and cape?" Kenny asked.

"Yes, I would like to. I believe my great grandfather put them on. My grandfather wrote about seeing him wearing the garments when he prayed over some hurt and sick babies. It was his wish that someone in the family bring them to life each year. You have read his journals and the statement he made when he donated the artifacts. It might be the last time I will ever get a chance to put them on. I have never had the opportunity. Please. This is something I feel I need to do."

Kenny looked at Bishop Jensen. He rubbed his chin. He could feel Jensen's sincerity. He could see the hope in Jensen's eyes. He knew that it was against museum policy. He knew better. He really did.

"Okay," he said. "But, you have to put something on your head so the headdress doesn't touch your hair. I'll get you a little bonnet for your head. And I will handle them and put them on you. And you can never tell anyone that I let you do this. Not anyone."

Jensen nodded. He placed the museum's bonnet over his head. He put the cotton gloves back on and turned his back to Kenny, and he waited.

≈ ≈ ≈

LaVar Jensen felt light, as if he would float through the ceiling. He saw almost nothing, as a perfectly smooth white light seemed to envelop him. He felt as if he was radiating light, and he lifted his head and raised his arms. He had never felt anything like it before. He could feel the presence of his father and his grandfather and his great grandfather, and of many, many grandfathers and grandmothers before them. He felt peace. He felt love. He felt clean and strong and he knew that there was good in the world.

≈ ≈ ≈

Kenny laid the cape in a tissue-lined box, smoothed the fabric out, and folded the tissue over. When he put the lid on the box and closed it, the last of the artifacts was gone from sight. As he pushed down the lid on the cardboard box, LaVar Jensen heard not the smooth rustling of paper, but the loud jarring of a door slamming. He felt a darkness come over him. A chilling, cold feeling ran through his core. He knew that he would never again see those items that were so meaningful to him and to his forbears. He thanked Kenny for allowing him to see and commune with the sacred objects, and as he crossed the parking lot to his car he cried.

# Chapter Forty-six

# The Cove

Present Day

"I'm worried about the dogs," Ralph said, pausing. "The cliff's just past where Zac is now and I'd hate to see one of them go off it."

"I'll call them," Barbara said. She put two fingers in her mouth and whistled loudly. "Zac, come! Puppies come!" she called.

Zac stopped, turned, and ran quickly to Barbara's side. The Chihuahuas, all thirty of them, followed the big red Doberman.

"Never ceases to amaze me," Ralph said. "As long as I have known you and your dogs, it never ceases to amaze me. I've never known anyone with a dog as well-trained as yours, and you have thirty of them!"

"Thirty-one," Barbara corrected him. "I wouldn't say that they are trained. We just communicate well. We're like a pack and I am the leader. Well, Zac and Cookie are the co-leaders, I guess. Zac is like the General in charge and the little guys all like that. They like being part of the pack, the gang. They're like 'we're with him,' and it makes them strong, stronger than any one of them could be. Makes them less afraid. More like dogs."

"I guess I never thought of it that way. Most Chihuahuas, I don't think of as dogs. They're more like dolls, or guinea pigs. At least the way people treat them—put ribbons in their hair, paint their nails, carry them around. Yours are real dogs. Tough dogs. Just little."

Barbara reached down and stroked Zac's head and scratched his ears.

"Heel, Zac. Stay close pups," she said to the little ones, as she followed Ralph toward the canyon rim.

"What a beautiful place," Ralph said, stopping short of where the mesa dropped off into Piñon Creek. The piñon and juniper forest gave way to an exposure of sandstone just before the abrupt cliff that formed the canyon wall.

"Look across—see the granary up on the other side? In that little overhang by that dark crack. See it?"

He handed his binoculars to Barbara.

"Ummmm, near that dark stain?" Barbara asked, scanning the cliff opposite them.

"Yeah, just to the left of it."

"I see it. Wow, there are poles to the side of it, and one in the crack. It's like a platform. Amazing!"

"Yep. Whoever built that put a lot of work into it. Just think of how much work it would be to just climb up on that cliff face, let alone to haul poles, and stones, and mud for mortar up there. And that's a big one—about three feet in diameter and four feet tall. It would hold a lot of corn."

"They must have been really worried about thieves, to have gone to that much work. And risk. Climbing up there, man. I don't know how someone could do it, even with modern climbing gear."

"It's not easy. Jim Ballantine and the Search and Rescue squad climbed to a few of them as part of their training a few years back. They had nothing but awe for whoever built them. Said the Indians must have had stone balls."

"I'm sure of that," Barbara replied. "I'm sure of that."

"We're going to walk along the cliff here for about another quarter mile," Ralph told her, pointing downstream along the abrupt edge. "That's where The Cove is, around the corner and down a bit. It's a big box canyon. The cave—Tickup's Cave is back over that way—only a half mile or so over that way."

"I can't wait," Barbara said, petting Zac's head. "I've heard about The Cove. That's where the settlers kept their livestock, right?"

Ralph nodded. He and Barbara, along with their canine entourage, made their way along the rim, mostly staying a bit back in the trees to avoid having to navigate through the jagged cracks and boulders that marked the edge of the drop-off.

"Just about there," Ralph said as they skirted around a small drainage and turned back toward the cliff.

As they approached the cliff, they could see where a narrow trail wound down along the edge of the cliff, leading down toward the box canyon. Ralph walked ahead then turned to Barbara.

"Come on, it's just steep for another hundred yards or so."

He pointed to what looked like a large blocky boulder at the bottom of the trail.

"It opens up just past that rock."

Barbara and the dogs followed Ralph down the narrow path, which, by the time they had gone about halfway, was less than a few feet across.

"I think I'll leash Zac up," said Barbara. "Just to be sure. Help me keep an eye on the little guys and keep them away from the edge."

"No problem," Ralph said. "I'll take it easy.

As they neared the bottom of the steep, narrow trail, Ralph pointed to the top of the cliff.

"See all those rocks up there? That's a wall. That whole end of the ridge is walled off. It's like a fort. Like the one out in Gooseberry where Clive Smythe got struck by lightning and killed. I think his buddy Jex was squirming up through the hole when the lightning struck. Jeez, what a way to go. It's like one instant you're looking around, the next instant you're gone."

"Like a bug getting smashed," Barbara said, swatting at a gnat on her arm. "Just like that."

"Nobody really knows what these forts or lookouts were used for. Kind of fun to speculate though."

"There are lots of mysterious places and things around here, aren't there," Barbara asked, looking around.

"Yep," Ralph answered. "Quite a place. Must have been something when these places were occupied. Hard to imagine what was going on, what with these forts and granaries and mysterious artwork. Really gets you to thinking."

"This whole area is where they used to keep livestock," Ralph said. "There's a seep back in there for water, and with just a little bit of a fence, this whole place is like a great big corral with no way for the animals to get out. Pretty cool, eh?"

They took a few pictures, found a shady, level spot for lunch, and shared a tasty snack of crackers with jalapeño cheese spread and avocado slices, apples, and tomato juice. They lingered in the peaceful spot, taking in the sounds of the breeze through the trees, the calls of the piñon jays, and watching the cliff swallows race about overhead.

"Better be getting back," Barbara said, tidying up their picnic utensils. "I need to get back to the café by five. Have a big group coming in tonight—the Moab football team—on their way back from a game in Nephi."

Ralph hoisted his daypack over one shoulder, and gave Barbara a hand up.

"We'll just loop through The Cove. You'll see why it is such a great place for livestock. Then we'll head down through the wash. It's an easier walk than back out the way we came."

They skirted around an outcrop of boulders and headed through the open, grassy meadow that was surrounded by vertical sandstone cliffs. Zac raced ahead and the Chihuahuas followed. Barbara looked up and high above them saw two crows chasing a red-tailed hawk. As she walked with eyes skyward she jolted as she bumped into Ralph, who had stopped abruptly.

"What the…" Ralph exclaimed.

Ralph walked rapidly along edge of the small drainage.

"Shit."

"What?" Barbara asked, following him.

Then she saw what had upset Ralph: ATV tracks.

"Crap."

"They came right out here into The Cove," Ralph called out. "Right up the wash. This is a Wilderness Study Area. You're not supposed to ride ATVs out here."

Ralph strode about, cursing and muttering.

"And what is this—some sort of a corral?" Barbara asked, walking into a small cluster of piñon trees. "Jesus!" she called out, refastening

Zac's leash and backing away. "Ralph, come here! My God, it looks like a shrine!"

"What?" Ralph rushed to her side. "What? What the…."

Ralph stood by Barbara, near the center of what looked like a corral built out of juniper logs. On closer inspection, it consisted of four pairs of upright posts set at the compass points of a twenty-foot diameter stone circle, each pair topped with a crosspiece. In the center of the circle was a platform made of more juniper posts, with a single upright rising from the center. An antelope skull was impaled on the upright. From the horns of the skull hung a bird carcass. Blood stains ran down the upright post. Leaning on each of the four surrounding uprights was a sandstone slab, each containing a single rock art figure.

"It's the Falling Men, and they're all upright," Ralph spoke, his voice quavering. "The Falling Men are all here, all right side up! This is the one from Gooseberry. That's the one from Skull Creek. Jesus! And Lighthouse. And the Head Hunter! Look at that one. It's the Head Hunter from Nine Mile. This is awful. This is just awful!"

Ralph strode about, taking it all in.

"This is too much," Barbara said. "Look at Zac. He is freaking out. He knows something's wrong."

"I can't believe it," Ralph said, muttering to himself. "I can't believe it. Look, here in the center—there's a little platform. A place made ready for one more figure. For the tiny upside down man I bet. That's gotta be it—it's for the Chief Watcher. The final Wanzi. Somebody has turned four of the upside down figures upright and they're ready for the fifth, the last."

He paced around in the circle, Chihuahuas moving away from him in small waves.

"Shit," Ralph muttered, and stopped walking."

"What now," cried Barbara.

"This is a crime scene and we're messing it all up!"

## Jalapeño Cheese Spread

Add enough mayonnaise to grated cheese to make it spreadable. Stir in finely chopped fresh Jalapeño chiles (no seeds) and green onions. Use however much or little suits you. Add a shake or two of garlic powder. Delicious on crackers or in sandwiches. Add chopped cilantro if you like.

A cracker topped with jalapeño cheese spread and a slice of avocado is a delightful snack.

# Chapter Forty-seven

# Repatriation

Present Day

"He knew it was wrong. He knew it. He wrote about it in his journal."

Bishop Jensen's voice quavered with emotion as he addressed the committee.

"Those items had been entrusted to him by the Lamanites. They were placed there for him to find. He was directed to that place because of the great power for good that those garments brought. They healed people, you know. They cured him of his cough. They cured J.D. Jennings of his arthritis. He knew they belonged in his care, but when he got older, people were telling him that they belonged in a museum. He knew it would be a mistake. And now his prophecy is coming true. The government is going to throw them away. They'll be lost forever. I beg you to do the right thing. They belong in my family. They belong in this community. Do the right thing, please. Please."

Bishop Jensen turned to return to his seat.

"Now you say it was your grandfather that dug them things, them artifacts up?" Wallace Hazel, a member of the Native American Remains Committee, a representative of the Shoshone Tribe, asked Lavar Jensen.

"Yes, my great, grandfather," Jensen replied, returning to the podium. "Yes. He and his friend Nephi Madsen. They found them and dug them up."

"Weren't there three dead people with these things? Didn't they dig up three burials to get these things?"

"Well, yes," Jensen answered. "But they didn't take the bodies, they reburied them. Somebody came by later and took the bodies. Grandfather Jensen told us and wrote in his journals about how sad that made him."

"Then he was nothin' more than a grave robber. He robbed the grave of some Indians that lived hundreds of years ago, and now you're saying that stuff is yours? Stuff your grave-digging grandpa pulled out of a sacred burial site? Suppose I went over to the Lost Valley cemetery and dug up your grandma's grave. Should I get to keep the stuff I found because I didn't take her body? Should I take her dress and put it on and act like I'm a white woman and say I'm gonna cure diseases? Hell no. That's wrong. That's just plain wrong."

Wallace paused, and addressed the committee.

"Mr. Jensen feels like this hat and robe and shield belong in his family because his Grandpa dug them up out of a grave and liked to put them on and act like he was some kind of an Indian Healer or Shaman or something. Well, I know how I'm going to vote. These things should go to the Ute tribe, so they can give them a real burial and return them to the earth where they belong. Where they would be except for Bishop Jensen's pot hunting, grave robbing grandpa? I hope everyone votes with me."

The committee chair, Rena Perry, nodded toward Kenny Clements, who was representing Salvation Lake State Park. Kenny rose and approached the podium.

"Thank you, Bishop Jensen," he began. "These things are not easy. I think everyone in this room understands how you feel, and how your grandfather and all of his family felt. Those artifacts had a profound effect on them. I've read some of his journals, and I understand your argument that these artifacts are sacred to your family. But as Wallace pointed out, somebody else placed them where your grandfather found them. They were obviously meaningful to them, too. I know you think that it is wrong to return them to the Ute Tribe, and you think that returning them to the earth is a sacrilege, but those things should go to their rightful claimant. I believe we at Salvation Lake

State Park have done our duty in caring for these very special artifacts over the years. And now we know that the right thing to do with them is to return them to the people to whom they are sacred, the people who have made a strong and compelling case for them, the Ute Tribe. That is the determination of the State Park, and I recommend that the Native American Remains Committee concur with that determination and return the sacred objects to their rightful owners and caretakers, the Ute Tribe."

"But the Utes were a thousand miles away when those things were buried!" Bishop Jensen blurted out. "They aren't remotely related to those people. The Utes probably killed off the last of the Ancient Ones, the Fremont, or whatever you call them. Maybe Hopi or Zuni have a claim, but the Utes? No! And don't forget about the curse. Don't forget that."

"Please sit down, Mr. Jensen, please sit down," Ms. Perry politely asked. "You have had your chance to speak. Please sit down."

She gave Jensen a stern look, and waited until he was seated and appeared to calm down. She then turned to the committee.

"Are there any more questions? You have the information in your notebooks, and have listened to the presentations. Are you ready to vote? Please mark the slip of paper that Anna is passing out. Please vote yes or no on whether the artifacts should be repatriated to the Ute Tribe."

The room was silent as the ballots were passed out, marked, and returned to the chair.

"The vote is unanimous," Ms. Perry reported. Seven ayes, no nays. The objects are to be returned to the Ute Tribe."

≈ ≈ ≈

"Man, that was wild," Richard, Kenny's co-worker at Salvation Lake State Park, said to Kenny as they drove back to the Visitor Center. I thought Jensen was going to flip out or something. Man, that guy's something else. And what's that about a curse? Who does he think we are, a bunch of Junior High kids?"

Kenny silently reflected on the committee meeting, which was the culmination of several years' work trying to determine the proper thing to do with the robe, the headdress, the shield, the basket and ceramic jar—artifacts that were among the most popular and important ones in the collection at the small State Park museum—indeed they were the reason there was a museum—it was built at least in part to house Ephraim Jensen's artifact collection. Kenny also knew that no matter who kept the items, others would be unhappy and certain that the wrong decision had been made. He recognized that there were problems from a scientific perspective with the Ute claim. Jensen was right—it was highly unlikely that Utes were even in the region when the artifacts had been made and buried. But the Utes had made a good case for ownership and showed how shields and hats and capes like the ones found had been used by Ute holy men and healers. The Utes claimed that the tradition had continued, even if the earlier people had been of a different culture, that the traditions and practices had continued through time and had been honored by the Utes. Kenny realized that, although most people thought it absurd, Bishop Jensen's claim was not that different. His grandfather had clearly been affected by the artifacts, and they had fit in with his own belief system.

"You've heard about the curse, haven't you," Kenny asked Richard. "Supposedly Brigham Young or somebody put a curse on the valley because he thought the people here were a bunch of cudwhacks."

"Sure, but Jensen was talking about something different, wasn't he?"

"Well, kinda," Kenny replied. "Jensen thinks the curse came a lot earlier. He doesn't think Brigham Young cursed Lost Valley. He thinks it's a lot older. Like back to the time of the Anasazi or Fremont. Maybe he thinks the Lamanites or Nephites cursed this place. I don't know. I do know that he thinks it had something to do with the bad luck that so many people around here seemed to have, including that Clive Smythe guy who got struck by lightning. You know, the one in the statue? And somehow he thinks it causes homosexuality. Lightning and floods and natural disasters are part of it, too. Well, Jensen thinks the artifacts kept the curse away. Now the shit is really going to hit the fan, he says, if the Utes bury those things. He thinks something really big and really bad is going to happen."

"Like what?" Richard asked. "Like BYU having a losing football season? Or maybe an ice cream shortage?"

"I don't know." Kenny shook his head. "I do know that he is really sincere. He's frightened of what might happen. Terrified. Really terrified."

# BARBARA'S DESERT CAFE

# Chapter Forty-eight

# Chiranhas

Present Day

The first thing Barbara and Ralph noticed was the smell. Zac noticed it, too. He held his nose high in the air and trotted back and forth testing the air. He looked at Barbara for a second, then ran off with the other dogs. The Chihuahuas were busily scouring the underfoot landscape for anything of interest, and nearly everything at their minuscule scale attracted their interest.

They thought they might have caught a whiff of diesel fuel, but they were a long way from the road, and couldn't think of any source of that odor. After a few seconds they no longer noticed it, and kept walking with Barbara's "chiranhas," or "land piranhas," as Ralph had dubbed them.

Ralph, Barbara and her pups were hiking to Tickup's Cave, which they and their friends had been thinking was in the vicinity of the remaining Falling Man pictograph. Since discovering the shrine, they were convinced that the next rock art panel to be taken would be the one in or near the cave. Although there had been no apparent activity in the area in months, they still checked on the site regularly, and they both enjoyed the hike and beautiful scenery. The dogs had become very familiar with the area and knew where each burrow, nest, and trail along the way was located, and they checked them out with great interest and intensity.

There were no fresh tire prints in the area where they usually

269

parked, and no footprints on the trail, so they were pretty confident that nobody would be in the area and that the pictograph, if it existed, would be safe. Ralph and Barbara and her pups could enjoy a nice walk on a beautiful spring day. The piñon trees looked strong and healthy, and were forming lots of small cones. Barbara made a mental note to tell Rupert Perank, as things looked promising for a good piñon nut crop in this area in the coming fall.

Barbara stopped for a minute to examine some footprints—large boot prints. She called to Ralph, and they looked closely at the prints.

"He's been here," Barbara said. "Rick Rowe's been here recently. Or somebody else with great big feet."

Some of the prints were wind-blown and indistinct, but others were more clear and crisp, so they were not able to tell how recently they had been made. Barbara made note of them in the notebook she carried, and Ralph took some pictures, and they continued.

Zac roamed ahead of the meandering Chihuahuas, looking out ahead, sniffing the air and the ground, investigating anything interesting he encountered, and checking back with Barbara every minute or so. Sometimes he would run all the way up to her, give her a look and a sniff, just to be sure she was okay, before racing back to the front of the group. Sometimes he would just glance back, to make certain he knew where she was. Barbara appreciated Zac's attentiveness, and she enjoyed knowing his whereabouts as well.

As they rounded the toeslope of the broad ridge just below the outcrop that contained the cave, Barbara noticed Zac's intensity level rise. She nudged Ralph and nodded toward Zac. He pricked up his ears alertly, and scanned back and forth, sniffing, looking. Barbara headed for him, hoping he hadn't caught a whiff of a bear or a mountain lion, or even a porcupine, anything that might cause chaos and perhaps harm to the pack. She clucked her cheeks to quietly summon her pups as she headed for Zac. As she rounded a spreading juniper, she paused to look about. Zac came to her, and the smaller dogs followed. Barbara noticed as Zac cocked his head, listening. She could hear it, too: The low humming of a motor.

"Ralph, Ralph, come here," she called in a loud whisper. "Do you hear that?"

Ralph came to her, cupped his hand over one ear, listened, and nodded.

"Stay close pups," she told her dogs, and most of them did.

They headed up toward the cave. Zac led, staying a short way ahead of the rest. Just as they came within sight of the cave mouth, Barbara gasped.

"Zac, come," she called, trying to keep her voice low. "Zac come!"

Just ahead, alongside the entrance to the cave, stood a man, standing by a large green all-terrain vehicle. He was facing away from them, toward the cliff face, and he walked quickly away, behind some trees.

"It's Rick!" Barbara cried. "Ralph, it's Rick Rowe! He's the one!

"Zac, come," she called again, backing away, trying to gather her pack with her as she headed for the cover of nearby trees.

"Stay here, stay behind these trees," Ralph said, taking her arm. "I'm going to try to get a little closer and see what's going on. Maybe get a picture."

Ralph held her arm and led her back behind a tall piñon tree.

"Be careful, Ralph," Barbara said, pulling him close and giving him a kiss. "I don't want you to get hurt."

"Don't worry. I'm pretty sneaky," Ralph said, easing out from behind the tree before trotting across the open space in front of them toward the cover of another bunch of trees closer to the cliff face.

Barbara held Zac's collar and knelt under the branches of the tree. Her Chihuahuas sat or lay quietly around her. She found an opening in the branches that afforded her a good view of the spot where they had seen Rick, and she waited and watched. The low droning of the motor continued, and sometimes the RPMs increased markedly, and then decreased again. Barbara could hear a whining sound. She concluded that she was hearing a generator and some kind of a saw. Rick was cutting the panel from the cliff face.

Suddenly the motor stopped. Barbara watched the open spot near the cliff. She heard some loud voices, and then Rick appeared from behind some bushes much closer to her than before. He was holding something in his hand—a gun?— and motioning with his other hand toward the trees. Suddenly he began running and Barbara saw Ralph jump from behind a bush and begin running downhill toward her, just ahead of Rick. She could hear yelling, and she tried to duck behind the trunk of the tree, but Zac lurched forward, tearing his collar from her hand. The Doberman sprinted toward the men, who had now turned and were heading toward some large shrubs beside a steep-sided arroyo. Barbara peeked around the tree trunk and saw Ralph running toward the arroyo, followed by Rick only about twenty feet behind him.

Bawhoom! Barbara heard the sound of gunfire. Bawhoom! She heard it again. Barbara screamed for Ralph and for her dogs. She peered around the tree, but could no longer see Ralph, or anyone. Then she saw Zac, near the cliff, charging at top speed toward where she had last seen the men.

"Zac, come!" she screamed.

Bawhoom! The blast came again, the report seemed louder, and it brought a chill to Barbara's soul. She later said that she thought she could feel the bullet as it pierced Zac's chest and took his life with it.

Barbara could not see Zac or Ralph or Rick. The rest of her pups ran in a frenzy up the hill.

"No pups, no," Barbara cried, stumbling after them. "No."

Barbara ran toward where she had last seen the dogs and Ralph, and she heard incredibly chaotic sounds—shrieking, growling, screams, groans, thrashing. She ran toward her man, toward her pups, her darlings, her true loves, and her instincts were those of a mother and a lover, not a pet owner. As she ran toward the sounds, she ran around the all-terrain vehicle, and saw a rifle on the ground beside it. She picked it up and looked frantically around. Ahead she could see her pups, all thirty of them, covering and savagely attacking a writhing figure on the ground. The man was face-down and he was moving uncontrollably, reacting to the savage attack that covered every inch of his body. And there, on the man's back, teeth bared, growling and holding him to the ground, was Zac!

Barbara opened the bolt of the rifle and made certain that a round was in the chamber.

"Out, pups," she cried, "Out! Out!"

Some of the dogs obeyed immediately, others continued attacking.

"Out puppies, out!"

Finally, the frenzied assault abated.

"Come, pups. Come."

The small dogs assembled at Barbara's side. Zac remained on the prostrate man's back, teeth bared. Each time the man moved as much as a muscle, Zac warned him with a fierce, fearsome growl.

"Out Zac. Good boy. Out," Barbara called to him. "Come."

Zac stood, and still facing the man on the ground, backed to Barbara, stopping when his thigh touched her leg. He maintained contact with her as he watched the man.

"And don't you move, Rick, or I'll set the dogs on you again. And I'll shoot you," Barbara asserted.

The man groaned. His clothes were shredded, and he was bleeding in several places.

"Keep your hands out in front of you," Barbara ordered.

The lying man slowly rolled over and pulled himself up on one elbow. His hat fell to the ground, revealing his bleeding scalp and ear.

"Oh my god!" Barbara gasped. "Oh my god!"

The man shook his head and averted his eyes, looking down at the ground.

"Bishop Jensen?"

# Chapter Forty-nine

# A Girl's Best Friend

Present Day

"When I saw who it was, at first I thought it must be a mistake. I thought 'What is he doing here?' and I felt a little sorry for him. I mean, I never thought Bishop Jensen would be the one stealing the rock art. I thought I'd see Rick Rowe lying there."

Barbara paused and took a sip of water. When she resumed talking, she again placed her hands in Ralph's at the center of the table between them.

"Then he starts saying things like 'Why did you sic your dogs on me?' and 'Don't point the gun at me, I didn't do anything wrong.'"

"At this point I got really confused. I thought maybe he just happened to be there like we were, looking at the rock art or something, and maybe he hadn't done anything wrong."

"I started looking around, like maybe Rick would walk up and shoot us both. We'd seen him from down below, and I saw him running after you, chasing you, and it looked like he had a gun in his hand, so I was very confused. And then when I saw Rick walking toward me, it startled me, and I almost shot him. I really did. I turned so I could keep the gun ready, in case either he or Jensen made a move. I was frightened and confused."

Barbara took a deep breath and reached over to pet Zac's head and scratch his ears. She smiled at the big dog.

"You saved our lives, buddy. You really did. I love you, Zac."

"Well, luckily, the first thing Rick did was hold out his hands and show them to me—they were empty. Then he said 'Don't shoot. Ralph is okay, but he needs help.' That's when I saw you crawling up the hill. All you said was 'Don't hurt Rick. Don't hurt Rick. He saved me. He saved me.' I thought you had been shot, until you and Rick told me what had happened."

"Rick said he'd take Jensen's ATV and go to where he could get cell coverage and call in the sheriff and medical help. I didn't trust him, so I held the gun on him and made him stand by Jensen while I checked you out. I didn't know what else to do, but you kept saying that you were okay and that Rick had saved you. I felt so much better. I just told him to hurry. Turned out just fine. He was on our side all the time."

"Zac bit LaVar pretty good. Got him on the thigh, the arm, the shoulder, and on his right cheek. The rest of the pack kind of shredded him all over. I mean all over. His clothes were just rags and he's covered with bites. Lots of little bites, but some pretty nasty big ones, too. In all the chaos, a couple of the little ones got dinged—Jesse hurt his leg, Maybelle got kicked in the ribs, and Doc lost a tooth. They'll be okay. Sooner than LaVar will. Sooner than you will."

"Oh, I'll be okay. Not the first time I've broken a leg. I'm too old to be running and jumping like that. It's a good thing Rick was there, too. I think Jensen was about to shoot me, and Rick threw a rock at him and hit him and distracted him just long enough for us both to run. By the way, that was a camera in Rick's hand, not a gun. He had been there for a while photographing Jensen from the bushes when we showed up and Jensen saw me. We really kind of blew it, blundering up the hill like that. We could have gotten us all killed, Rick included."

Ralph reached down and scratched his leg near the top of his cast.

"Then Zac appeared out of nowhere and saved the day," Ralph smiled. "You are the hero, Zac, no doubt about it. You all are," he said, smiling at the Chihuahuas. "You all are."

"Jeez, what a day!" Barbara exclaimed, shaking her head. "Unbelievable! Bishop Jensen's been stealing the rock art. And all this time we thought it was Rick Rowe. I feel like an idiot."

"Well, you shouldn't. If you hadn't been there with your pups, I don't know how it would have turned out. I am very proud of you, running up there, picking up the rifle and taking charge. You were in danger. We all were. And you were unbelievably courageous and brave. You did everything right. You and your pups saved us and caught the thief."

"But Bishop Jensen. I still can't believe it," Barbara said. "What I really can't believe is that he had a rifle there and was ready to use it. He must really be delusional or something. Something."

"Well, he wasn't talking too much last night, but this morning I talked with Sheriff Taylor and he told me that Jensen's wife, Janell, came in as soon as they called her, and she said LaVar had been obsessed for quite a while with the rock art, and he blamed it for the curse. He thought if he could turn it all right side up, the curse would go away, and the curse of homosexuality would be lifted. I guess their son Alma is gay, and that's at least part of what has had LaVar freaked. I've known Alma for years. He's a good kid. It must be awful for your father to react so strangely. Poor kid."

"You know, it's really too bad. LaVar isn't that terrible of a guy, really. But I can see now that his issues go a little deeper than I ever imagined. I hope he can get some help."

"What gets me is Jensen knew where the tiny Wanzi was all this time. And so did Rick—it was way back in the cave, on a low part of the ceiling facing the rear. Who would have ever thought to look up there? I never did. And it was dark back there. I must have walked right under it a dozen times.

"I did, too," Barbara said. "I remember being there and warning you to watch your head. Funny how we were so close to it and never even knew it was there."

"Well, we caught LaVar before he was able to do any real damage. He had just started sawing—made one cut along the side. It'll be okay."

"I'm just happy to see a bright, sunny, beautiful day today," Barbara said. "I think this whole curse thing is over. It's behind us. I couldn't be happier."

# Acknowledgments

Thank you to Barbara Evert for supporting me throughout the entire process of writing and editing this book. To Nick Jones for his advice, support and encouragement. To Steve Trimble, Dorothee Kocks, Amie Tullius, Brenda Cowley, Melissa Bond, Kurt Proctor, and Dave Jones for reading various drafts and providing me with invaluable comments. To my friends the late Clifford Duncan, Forrest Cuch, Larry Cesspooch, and Rick Chapoose for sharing with me their vast knowledge of modern and traditional Ute culture. To Bill D'Aubin and his chihuahua Cookie for showing me how incredible the tiny pups can be. To Barbara Evert and her doberman Zac for demonstrating how a powerful dog can be a caring, protecting friend. To the late Jimmy Olsen, chef, cook, camp manager, wonderful man, for his inspiration in the kitchen, for his delightful way of treating people , and for showing me how to make frugality and limited range of ingredients into satisfying and memorable meals.

And for all those who read various drafts, or who sat politely around a campfire or living room while I read random chapters to them, including Jeannine Willett, Andy Yentsch, Joel Boomgarden, Mick Krusow, Amber Koski, Rick Chapoose, Dennis Willis, Jim Sayers, Ron Rood, David Madsen, Bill Davis, Steve Simms, and others, thank you.

To Brad Wolverton for his phenomenal cover art, and the award-winning Carel Brest van Kempen for the incredible illustrations that enrich and enhance the story. To Darlene Cypser for taking a chance and publishing this book, and to everyone else who played a part in inspiring and advancing the stories that wound up here.

And for those who provided or inspired me with recipes:

The late Mae Timbimboo Parry, her mother Amy, sister Hazel Zundel and Hazel's husband Wallace, members of the Northwestern Band of the Shoshone for teaching and showing me how to harvest, roast, hull, and winnow piñon nuts, and for making and sharing their wonderful piñon gravy with me.

My late mother Evelyn Jones, a wonderful cook, for inspiration in how to put love in the food she prepared, and for her zucchini casserole, dill pickle cole slaw and her iced tea punch.

Mick Krusow for his "Eggs Bendejo."

Jamie Jones for his spicy jerky.

The Aché people of Chupa Pou Paraguay for their corn and chicken chowder.

Steven D. Creasman for his skillet cornbread.

Finally, to all writers, artists, cooks, singers, songwriters, and poets out there, thank you. Keep making art, keep making the world a better place, keep keeping us human. I love you all!

## About the Author

Kevin T. Jones is an anthropologist, archaeologist, musician, and writer. He served as state archaeologist of Utah for seventeen years. He played mandolin and guitar and sang in the award-winning bluegrass band The Lab Dogs and in the rock band Hammerstone for over 20 years. He has written many scientific publications including peer reviewed papers, monographs, book chapters, and popular articles. He lives off grid with his wife, Barbara Evert, in southwestern Colorado.

### Books by Kevin T. Jones

***THE SHRINKING JUNGLE***. An anthropological novel set among the Aché, hunter-gatherers of eastern Paraguay among whom Kevin lived and studied as part of his dissertation research. The novel follows a band of Aché during their last year in the deep forest.

***STANDING ON THE WALLS OF TIME; ANCIENT ART OF UTAH'S CLIFFS AND CANYONS***, with photographs by Layne Miller. Essays about and inspired by the incredible art of the aboriginal people of the Colorado Plateau.

***A QUICK TRIP TO MOAB; INSURRECTION IN THE WILDERNESS***. An environmental thriller. Passersby are chased through the San Rafael Swell of eastern Utah by anti-wilderness protestors gone awry. Finalist, Colorado Book Award for general fiction in 2023.